PENGUIN BOOKS

HOLDING UP
THE UNIVERSE

HOLDING UP

THE UNIVERSE

Jennifer Niven

PENGUIN BOOKS

PENGUIN BOOKS

UK | USA | Canada | Ireland | Australia
India | New Zealand | South Africa

Penguin Books is part of the Penguin Random House group of companies
whose addresses can be found at global.penguinrandomhouse.com.

www.penguin.co.uk
www.puffin.co.uk
www.ladybird.co.uk

First published in the USA by Alfred A. Knopf, an imprint of Random
House Children's Books, and in Great Britain by Penguin Books 2016

017

Grateful acknowledgment is made to Jack Robinson for permission to
reprint lines from "I Love to Love (But My Baby Just Loves to Dance)",
words by Jack Robinson, music by James Bolden. Used by permission of
Robin Song Music SARL and ROBA Music Publishing.

The moral right of the author has been asserted

Printed in Great Britain by Clays Ltd, St Ives plc

A CIP catalogue record for this book is available from the British Library

ISBN: 978-0-141-35705-8

All correspondence to:
Penguin Books,
Penguin Random House Children's
80 Strand, London WC2R 0RL

MIX
Paper from
responsible sources
FSC® C018179
www.fsc.org

Penguin Random House is committed to a
sustainable future for our business, our readers
and our planet. This book is made from Forest
Stewardship Council® certified paper.

for Kerry,
Louis,
Angelo
& Ed,
who help hold up my universe

and for all my readers everywhere,
who are the world to me

"Atticus, he was real nice. . . ."

"Most people are, Scout, when you finally see them."

—*To Kill a Mockingbird,* Harper Lee

. . .

I'm not a shitty person, but I'm about to do a shitty thing. And you will hate me, and some other people will hate me, but I'm going to do it anyway to protect you and also myself.

This will sound like an excuse, but I have something called prosopagnosia, which means I can't recognize faces, not even the faces of the people I love. Not even my mom. Not even myself.

Imagine walking into a room full of strangers, people who don't mean anything to you because you don't know their names or histories. Then imagine going to school or work or, worse, your own home, where you should know everyone, only the people there look like strangers too.

That's what it's like for me: I walk into a room and I don't know anyone. That's every room, everywhere. I get by on how a person walks. By gestures. By voice. By hair. I learn people by identifiers. I tell myself, *Dusty has ears that stick out and a red-brown Afro,* and then I memorize this fact so it helps me find my little brother, but I can't actually call up an image of him and his big ears and his Afro unless he's in front of me. Remembering people is like this superpower everyone seems to have but me.

Have I been officially diagnosed? No. And not just because I'm guessing this is beyond the pay grade of Dr. Blume, town pediatrician. Not just because for the past few years my parents have had more than their share of shit to deal with. Not just because it's better *not* to be the freak. But because there's a part of me that hopes it isn't true. That maybe it will clear up and go away on its own. For now, this is how I get by:

Nod/smile at everyone.

Be charming.

Be "on."

Be goddamn hilarious.

Be the life of the party, but don't drink. Don't risk losing control (that happens enough when sober).

Pay attention.

Do whatever it takes. Be lord of the douche. Anything to keep from being the prey. Always better to hunt than be hunted.

I'm not telling you all this as an excuse for what I'm about to do. But maybe you can keep it in mind. This is the only way to stop my friends from doing something worse, and it's the only way to stop this stupid game. Just know that I don't want to hurt anyone. *That's not why.* Even though that's the thing that's going to happen.

Sincerely yours,

Jack

PS. You're the only person who knows what's wrong with me.

* * *

Prosopagnosia (pro-suh-pag-NO-zhuh) *noun:* 1. an inability to recognize the faces of familiar people, typically as a result of damage to the brain. 2. when everyone is a stranger.

18 HOURS EARLIER

LIBBY

If a genie popped out of my bedside lamp, I would wish for these three things: my mom to be alive, nothing bad or sad to ever happen again, and to be a member of the Martin Van Buren High School Damsels, the best drill team in the tristate area.

But what if the Damsels don't want you?

It is 3:38 a.m., and the time of night when my mind starts running around all wild and out of control, like my cat, George, when he was a kitten. All of a sudden, there goes my brain, climbing the curtains. There it is, swinging from the bookshelf. There it is, with its paw in the fish tank and its head underwater.

I lie on my bed, staring up into the dark, and my mind bounces across the room.

What if you get trapped again? What if they have to knock down the cafeteria door or the bathroom wall to get you out? What if your dad gets married and then he dies and you're left with the new wife and stepsiblings? What if you die? What if there is no heaven and you never see your mom again?

I tell myself to sleep.

I close my eyes and lie very still.

Very still.

For minutes.

I make my mind lie there with me and tell it, *Sleep, sleep, sleep.*

What if you get to school and realize that things are different and kids are different, and no matter how much you try, you will never be able to catch up to them?

I open my eyes.

My name is Libby Strout. You've probably heard of me. You've probably watched the video of me being rescued from my own house. At last count, 6,345,981 people have watched it, so there's a good chance you're one of them. Three years ago, I was America's Fattest Teen. I weighed 653 pounds at my heaviest, which means I was approximately 500 pounds overweight. I haven't always been fat. The short version of the story is that my mom died and I got fat, but somehow I'm still here. This is in no way my father's fault.

Two months after I was rescued, we moved to a different neighborhood on the other side of town. These days I can leave the house on my own. I've lost 302 pounds. The size of two entire people. I have around 190 left to go, and I'm fine with that. I like who I am. For one thing, I can run now. And ride in the car. And buy clothes at the mall instead of special-ordering them. And I can twirl. Aside from no longer being afraid of organ failure, that may be the best thing about now versus then.

Tomorrow is my first day of school since fifth grade. My new title will be high school junior, which, let's face it, sounds a lot better than America's Fattest Teen. But it's hard to be anything but TERRIFIED OUT OF MY SKULL.

I wait for the panic attack to come.

Caroline Lushamp calls before my alarm goes off, but I let her go to voice mail. I know whatever it is, it's not going to be good and it will be my fault.

She calls three times but only leaves one message. I almost delete it without listening, but what if her car broke down and she's in trouble? This is, after all, the girl I've dated off and on for the past four years. (We're *that* couple. That on-again, off-again everyone-assumes-we'll-end-up-together-forever couple.)

Jack, it's me. I know we're taking a break or whatever but she's my cousin. My COUSIN. I mean, MY COUSIN, JACK! If you wanted to get back at me for breaking up with you, then congratulations, jerkwad, you've done it. If you see me in class today or in the hallways or in the cafeteria or ANYWHERE ELSE ON EARTH, do not talk to me. Actually, just do me a favor and go to hell.

Three minutes later, the cousin calls, and at first I think she's crying, but then you can hear Caroline in the background, and the cousin starts yelling and Caroline starts yelling. I delete the message.

Two minutes later, Dave Kaminski sends a text to warn me that Reed Young wants to kick my face in for making out with his girlfriend. I text, *I owe you.* And I mean it. If I'm keeping score, Kam's helped me out more times than I've helped him.

All this fuss over a girl who, if we're being honest, looked so much like Caroline Lushamp that—at least at first—I thought it *was* her, which means in some weird way Caroline should be flattered. It's like admitting to the world that I want to get back together with her even though she dumped me the first week of summer so that she could go out with Zach Higgins.

I think of texting this to her, but instead I turn off my phone and close my eyes and see if I can't transport myself right back into July. The only thing I had to worry about then was going to work, scavenging the local scrap yard, building (mind-blowing) projects in my (kick-ass) workshop, and hanging out with my brothers. Life would be so much easier if it was just Jack + scrap yard + kick-ass workshop + mind-blowing projects.

You should never have gone to the party. You should never have had a drink. You know you can't be trusted. Avoid alcohol. Avoid crowds. Avoid people. You only end up pissing them off.

LIBBY

It's 6:33 a.m. and I am out of bed and standing in front of the mirror. There was a time, a little over two years ago, when I couldn't, wouldn't look at myself. All I saw was the bunched-up face of Moses Hunt, yelling at me across the playground: *No one will ever love you because you're fat!* And the faces of all the other fifth graders as they started to laugh. *You're so big you block the moon. Go home, Flabby Stout, go home to your room. . . .*

Today, for the most part, I only see me—adorable navy dress, sneakers, medium-longish brown hair that my sweet but slightly demented grandmother once described as "the exact color of Highland cattle." And the reflection of my giant dirty cotton ball of a cat. George stares at me with wise gold eyes, and I try to imagine what he might say to me. Four years ago, he was diagnosed with heart failure and given six months to live. But I know him well enough to know that only George will decide when it's time for George to go. He blinks at me.

Right now, I think he would tell me to breathe.

So I breathe.

I've gotten really good at breathing.

I look down at my hands and they're steady, even if the fingernails are bitten to the quick, and, weirdly, I feel pretty calm, considering. I realize: the panic attack never came. This is something to celebrate, so I throw on one of my mom's old albums and dance.

Dancing is what I love most and dancing is what I plan to do with my life. I haven't taken lessons since I was ten, but *the dance is in me,* and no lack of training can make that go away.

I tell myself, *Maybe this year you can try out for the Damsels.*

My brain goes zooming up the wall, where it hangs, shaking. *What if it never happens? What if you die before anything good or wonderful or amazing ever happens to you?* For the past two and a half years, the only thing I've had to worry about has been my survival. The focus of every single person in my life, including me, has been: *We just need to get you better.* And now I'm better. *So what if I let them down after all the time and energy they've invested in me?*

I dance harder to push the thoughts out until my dad thumps on the door. His head appears. "You know I love a good Pat Benatar song first thing in the morning, but the question is: how do the neighbors feel?"

I turn it down a little but keep on moving. When the song is over, I find a marker and decorate one shoe. **As long as you live, there's always something waiting; and even if it's bad, and you know it's bad, what can you do? You can't stop living. (Truman Capote, *In Cold Blood*)** Then I reach for the lipstick my grandmother gave me for my birthday, lean into the mirror, and paint my lips red.

JACK

I hear the shower running and voices downstairs. I pull the pillow over my face, but it's too late—I'm awake.

I turn on my phone and text first Caroline, then Kam, then Reed Young. The thing I say to all of them is that I was very drunk (an exaggeration) and it was very dark (it was) and I don't remember anything that happened because I was not only drunk, I was upset. *There's just this shit happening at home that I can't talk about right now, so if you can bear with me and find it in your heart to forgive me, I'll be forever in your debt.* The shit happening at home part is completely true.

For Caroline, I throw in some compliments and ask her to please apologize to her cousin for me. I say I don't want to contact her directly because I've already made a mess of things and I don't want to do anything else to make things worse between Caroline and me. Even though *Caroline* was the one who broke up with *me,* and even though we're currently in an off-again phase, and even though I haven't seen her *since June,* I basically eat crow and then throw it up all over my phone. This is the price I pay for trying to keep everyone happy.

I drag myself down the hall to the bathroom. The thing I need most in this world is a long, hot shower, but what I get instead is a trickle of warm water followed by a blast of Icelandic cold. Sixty seconds later—because that's all I can bear—I get out, dry off, and stand in front of the mirror.

So this is me.

I think this every time I see my reflection. Not in a *Damn, that's me* way, but more like *Huh. Okay. What have we got here?* I lean in, trying to put the pieces of my face together.

The guy in the mirror isn't bad-looking—high cheekbones, strong jaw, a mouth that's hitched up at one corner like he just got done telling a joke. Somewhere in the neighborhood of pretty. The way he tilts his head back and gazes out through half-open eyelids makes it seem like he's used to looking down on everyone, like he's smart and he knows he's smart, and then it hits me that what he really looks like is an asshole. Except for the eyes themselves. They're too serious and there are circles under them, like he hasn't slept. He's wearing the same Superman shirt I've been wearing all summer.

What does this mouth (Mom's) mean with this nose (also Mom's) and these eyes (a combination of Mom's and Dad's)? My eyebrows are darker than my hair but they aren't as dark as Dad's. My skin is a kind of middle brown color, not dark like Mom's, and not light like Dad's.

The other thing that doesn't match up here is the hair. It's this enormous lion's mane Afro that looks like it's allowed to do whatever the fuck it wants. If he's anything like me, the guy in the mirror calculates everything. Even though this hair *cannot be contained,* he's grown it for a reason. So he can find himself.

Something about the way these features add up is how people find each other in the world. Something about the combination makes them go, *There's Jack Masselin.*

"What's your identifier?" I say to my reflection, and I mean the real identifier, not this giant lion fro. I'm having a right serious moment, but then I hear a distinct snicker, and a tall, skinny blur goes breezing by. That would be my brother Marcus.

"My name's Jack and I'm so pretty," he sings all the way down the stairs.

Top 5 Most Embarrassing Moments of My Life
by Jack Masselin

• • •

1. That time my mom picked me up from kindergarten (after getting her hair cut), and in front of my teacher, the other kids, the other parents, and the principal, I accused her of trying to kidnap me.
2. That time I joined the pickup (uniform-free) soccer game at Reynolds Park and passed every ball to the opposite team, setting the all-time park record for Most Disastrous and Humiliating Debut Ever.
3. That time I'd been working with our high school sports therapist because of a shoulder injury, and, in the middle of Walmart, told the man I thought was my baseball coach, *I could use another massage,* only to discover it was actually Mr. Temple, Mom's boss.
4. That time I hit on Jesselle Villegas, and it turned out to be Miss Arbulata, substitute teacher.
5. That time I made out with Caroline Lushamp and it was actually her cousin.

LIBBY

I don't have my license, so Dad drives me. One of the many, many things I get to look forward to this school year is driver's ed. I wait for my father to offer me sage words of advice or a stirring pep talk, but the most he comes up with is "You got this, Libbs. I'll be here to pick you up when it's over." And the way he says it sounds ominous, like we're in the opening scene of a horror movie. Then he gives me a smile, which is the kind of smile they would teach you in a parenting video. It's a nervous smile taped up at the corners. I smile back.

What if I get stuck behind a desk? What if I have to eat lunch alone and no one talks to me for the rest of the school year?

My dad is a big, handsome guy. Salt of the earth. Smart (he does IT security for a big-name computer company). Smushy heart. After they freed me from the house, he had a hard time of it. As awful as it was for me, I think it was worse for him, especially the accusations of neglect and abuse. The press couldn't imagine how else I would have been allowed to get so big. They didn't know about the doctors he took me to and the diets we tried, even as he was mourning the loss of his wife. They didn't see the food I hid from him under my bed and deep in the shadows of my closet. They couldn't know that once I make up my mind about something, I'm going to do it. And I'd made up my mind to eat.

At first, I refused to talk to reporters, but at some point I needed to show the world that I'm okay and that my dad isn't the villain they made him out to be, stuffing me with candy and cake in an effort to keep me there and dependent on him like those girls from *The Virgin Suicides*. So against my dad's wishes I did one interview with a news station out of Chicago, and that interview traveled all the way to Europe and Asia and back again.

You see, my whole world changed when I was ten. My mom died, which was traumatic enough, but then the bullying started. It didn't help that I developed early and that all at once my body felt too big for me. I'm not saying I blame my classmates. After all, we were kids. But I just want to make it clear that there were multiple factors at work—the bullying coupled with the loss of my most important person, followed by the panic attacks whenever I had to leave my house. Through it all, my dad was the one who stood by me.

I say to my dad now, "Did you know that Pauline Potter, the World's Heaviest Woman, lost ninety-eight pounds having marathon sex?"

"No sex of any kind for you until you're thirty."

I think, *We'll see.* After all, miracles happen every day. Which means maybe those kids who were so hateful to me on the playground have grown up and realized the error of their ways. Maybe they've actually turned out to be nice. Or maybe they're even meaner. Every book I read and movie I watch seems to give out the same message: high school is the worst experience you can ever have.

What if I accidentally tell someone off so that I become the Sassy Fat Girl? What if some well-meaning skinny girls adopt me as their own and I become the Fat Best Friend? What if it's clear to everyone that my homeschooling has really only equipped me for eighth grade, not eleventh, because I'm too stupid to understand any of my classwork?

My dad says, "All you have to do is today, Libbs. If it completely and totally sucks, we can go back to homeschooling. Just give me one day. Actually, don't give it to me. Give yourself one day."

I tell myself: *Today.* I tell myself: *This is what you dreamed of when you were too scared to leave the house. This is what you dreamed of when you were lying in your bed for six months. This is what you wanted—to be out in the world like everyone else.* I tell myself: *It's taken you two and a half years of fat camps and counselors and psychologists and doctors and behavioral coaches and trainers to get ready for this. For the past two and a half years, you've walked ten thousand steps a day. Every one of them was pointing you to now.*

I can't drive.

I've never been to a dance.

I completely missed middle school.

I've never had a boyfriend, although I did make out with this boy at camp once. His name is Robbie and he's repeating his senior year somewhere in Iowa.

Except for my mom, I've never had a best friend, unless you count the ones I made up for myself—three brothers who lived across the street from my old house. The ones I called Dean, Sam, and Castiel, because they went to private school and I didn't know their names. The ones I pretended were my friends.

My dad looks so nervous and hopeful that I grab my bag and push out onto the sidewalk, and then I'm standing in front of the school as people walk past me.

What if I'm late to every class because I can't walk fast enough, and then I get detention, where I will meet the only boys who will pay attention to me—burnouts and delinquents—fall in love with one of them, get pregnant, drop out before I can graduate, and live with my dad for the rest of my life or at least until the baby is eighteen?

I almost get back in the car, but my dad is still sitting there, hopeful smile still on his face. "You got this." He says it louder this time and—I swear to you—gives me a thumbs-up.

Which is why I join the crowd and let them carry me along until I'm waiting my turn at the entrance, opening my bag so that the guard can check it, walking through metal detectors, stepping into a long hallway that splinters off in all directions, bumped and jostled by elbows and arms. I think, *Somewhere in this school could be a boy I fall in love with. One of these fine young men might be the one who at long last claims my heart and my body. I am the Pauline Potter of Martin Van Buren High School. I am going to sex the rest of this weight right off me.* I'm looking at all the boys going by. *It could be that guy or maybe this one. That's the beauty of this world. Right now, that boy right there or that one over there means nothing to me, but soon we will meet and change the world, his and mine.*

"Move it, fat-ass," someone says. I feel the sting of the word, like a pinprick, like the word itself is trying to pop me the way it pops my thought bubble. I forge ahead. The great thing about my size is that I can clear a path.

JACK

Like the hair, the car is part of the image. It's a restored 1968 Land Rover that Marcus and I bought from an elderly uncle. It was originally used for farmwork before it sat rusting for forty-some years, but now it's part Jeep, part all-terrain vehicle, and one hundred percent total badass.

In the passenger seat, Marcus sulks. "Asshole." This is said low and to the window. Unfortunately for me, he got his license a month ago.

"You're adorable. I hope eleventh grade won't spoil your boyish charm. You can drive next year when I'm at college."

If I go to college. If I ever leave this place.

He holds up his middle finger in my direction. From the back, our younger brother, Dusty, kicks the seat. "Stop fighting."

"We're not fighting, little man."

"You sound like Mom and Dad. Make the music louder."

A couple of years ago, my parents got along pretty well. But then Dad was diagnosed with cancer. The week before he was diagnosed I found out he was cheating on my mom. He doesn't know I know, and I'm not sure Mom knows, but sometimes I wonder. He's cancer-clear now, by the way, but it hasn't been easy, especially on Dusty, who's ten.

I turn up the song, an oldie—Justin Timberlake's "SexyBack"— and I can feel myself settling once again into my zone. I've got four soundtrack songs that I wish would start blasting every time I walk into a room, and this is one of them.

We pull up outside Dusty's school, and he goes leaping out before I can stop him. I get out after him, taking the keys so Marcus can't drive off with the car.

This summer, Dusty started carrying a purse. No one talks about it—not my mom or dad or Marcus.

Dusty is halfway up the walk before I chase him down. I have to keep my eyes on him so I don't lose him. He has the darkest skin of the three of us, and his hair is the color of a copper penny. Technically, Mom is half black, half Louisiana Creole, and Dad is white and Jewish. Dusty is dark like Mom. Marcus, on the other hand, couldn't be whiter. Me? I'm just Jack Masselin, whoever the hell that is.

Dusty says, "I don't want to be late."

"You won't be. I just wanted to . . . Are you sure about the purse, little man?"

"I like it. I can fit everything in here."

"I like it too. It's a really damn cool purse. But I'm not sure everyone's going to dig it as much as we do. There might be some kids here who are going to be so jealous of that purse that they'll make fun of you." I see about ten of them walking past us right now.

"They won't be jealous. They'll think it's weird."

"I just don't want anyone to be rough on you."

"If I want to carry a purse, I'm going to carry it. I'm not going to not carry it just because they don't like it."

And in that moment, this scrawny kid with big ears is my hero. As he walks away, I watch the way he moves, straight as an arrow, chin up. I want to follow him all the way into school to make sure nothing happens to him.

7 Careers for Someone with Prosopagnosia

by Jack Masselin

● ● ●

1. Shepherd (assuming face blindness doesn't extend to dogs and sheep).
2. Tollbooth operator (assuming no one you know is taking the route you're working).
3. Rock star/boy band member, NBA player, or some other profession along these lines (where people expect you to have an ego so massive they won't be surprised if you don't remember them).
4. Writer (the most recommended job for people with social anxiety disorders).
5. Dog walker/trainer (see number one, above).
6. Embalmer (except that I might get the corpses mixed up).
7. Hermit (ideal, except the pay isn't very good).

LIBBY

I clear a path all the way to my first class, where I take a seat in the row closest to the door, in case I need to flee at some point. I *just* fit behind the desk. Under my shirt, my back is damp, and my heart skips a beat. No one can see it, though. At least, I hope no one can see it because there's nothing worse than being known as the sweaty fat girl. As my classmates trickle in, a few of them stare. A couple of them snicker. I don't recognize any of the eleven-year-old kids I once knew in these teenage faces.

But school is exactly what I expected, yet more at the same time. For one thing, Martin Van Buren High School has about two thousand students, so it is a place packed with commotion. For another, no one looks as shiny and polished as they do in the TV and movie versions of high school. Real teens aren't twenty-five years old. We have bad skin and bad hair and good skin and good hair, and we're all different shapes and sizes. I like us better than our TV selves, even though sitting here, I feel like an actor playing a part. I'm the fish out of water, the new girl at school. *What will my story be?*

I decide that what I've got here is a clean slate. As far as I'm concerned, this is me starting over, and whatever happened when I was eleven, twelve, thirteen doesn't exist now. I'm different. They're different, at least on the outside. Maybe they won't remember I was *that girl*. I don't plan on reminding them.

I look them in the eye and give them my father's new signature taped-up-corner smile. This seems to surprise them. A couple of them smile back. The boy next to me holds out his hand. "Mick."

"Libby."

"I'm from Copenhagen. I'm here for the exchange program." Even with crow-black hair, he is Viking-like. "Are you from Amos?"

I want to say *I'm an exchange student too. I'm here from Australia. I'm here from France.* But the only boys I've talked to in the past five years are the ones at fat camp, which is why I don't do anything but nod.

He tells me how he wasn't sure at first whether to come here, but then he decided it would be a good experience to see the heartland of the States and "the way most Americans live." Whatever that means.

I manage to say, "What's your favorite thing about Indiana?"

"That I get to go home one day."

He laughs, so I laugh, and then two girls walk in and their eyes go immediately to me. One of them whispers something to the other, and they take the seats in front of us. There's something familiar about these girls, but I can't place them. *Maybe I knew them before.* My skin prickles and I have that horror movie feeling again. I look up at the ceiling as if a piano is about to fall on my head. Because I know it's going to come from somewhere. It always does.

I tell myself to give Mick a chance, give these girls a chance, give this day a chance, give myself a chance most of all. The way I see it, I've lost my mom, eaten myself nearly to death, been cut out of my house while the whole country watched, endured exercise regimes and diets and the nation's disappointment, and I've received hate mail from total strangers.

It is disgusting that anyone would ever let themselves get so large,

*and it is disgusting that your father wouldn't do anything about it.
I hope you survive this and get straight with God. There are people
starving in the world and it is shameful that you would eat so much
when others don't have enough.*

So I ask you, What can high school do to me that hasn't already
been done?

With a minute to spare, we roll into the parking lot, into the last empty space in the first row of cars. Marcus drops his phone, and when he sits up again, it's as if he's a brand-new person. Like that, the Etch A Sketch in my brain is cleared, and I have to start over, adding up the parts:

Shaggy hair + pointy chin + eight-foot-long giraffe legs = Marcus.

The Land Rover's barely in park before he's out the door and calling to people. I want to say *Wait for me. Don't make me go out there by myself.* I want to grab hold of his arm and hold on so I don't lose him. Instead, I keep my eyes on him, not blinking because that will make him disappear. And then he morphs into the crowd, moving toward school like one of the herd.

The animal kingdom has crazy names for animal groups. A zeal of zebras. A murder of crows. An unkindness of ravens. And, my favorite, an embarrassment of pandas. What would this group be called? A horror of students? A nightmare of teens? Just for fun, I scan the faces going by, looking for my brother. But it's like trying to choose your favorite polar bear out of an aurora of them.

I sit for thirty seconds, enjoying the solitude: *30. 29. 28. 27 . . .*

This is it for the day until I'm home again. In this thirty seconds, I let myself think all the things I won't let myself think for the next eight hours. The song always starts the same way.

I have a fucked-up brain. . . .

LIBBY

Twenty minutes into class, no one is staring at me. Our teacher, Mrs. Belk, is talking and so far I'm able to keep up. Mick is whispering clever commentary just for my benefit, which makes him either my new best chum or my future boyfriend, or possibly the boy who will sex the rest of this weight right off me.

You belong here as much as anyone. No one knows who you are. No one cares. You've got this, girl. Don't get ahead of yourself, but I think you've got this.

And then I laugh at one of the things Mick says *and something goes flying out of my nose and lands on his textbook.*

Mrs. Belk says, "Settle, please." And keeps on talking.

I superglue my eyes to her, but I can still see Mick in my peripheral vision. I'm not sure he notices the thing I shot at him, and I don't dare look. *Please don't see it.*

He goes right on whispering as if nothing happened, as if the world is not about to end, but now I only want to close my eyes and die. This is not the foot I want to start on. This is not what I envisioned for myself when I was lying awake last night imagining my grand reentrance into teenage society.

Maybe he'll think this is some weird American tradition. Like, some bizarre custom we have for welcoming foreigners to our country.

I spend the rest of the class period focusing hard on what Mrs. Belk is saying, my eyes on the front of the room.

• • •

When the bell rings, the two familiar-looking girls turn around and stare at me, and I see that they are Caroline Lushamp and Kendra Wu, girls I've known since first grade. After I was rescued from my house, they were interviewed by the press, referred to as "close friends of the troubled teen." The last time I saw them in person, Caroline was a homely eleven-year-old who wore the same Harry Potter scarf every day, no matter how hot it was. Her other distinguishing factors were that she'd moved to Amos from Washington, DC, when she was in kindergarten, and she was self-conscious over her feet, which had these very long toes that curled like a parrot's. The thing I remember about Kendra is that she wrote Percy Jackson fan fiction on her jeans and cried every single day over anything—boys, homework, rain.

Caroline, of course, is now eight feet tall and beautiful enough to be a shampoo model. She wears a skirt and a tight little jacket, like she goes to private school. Kendra—whose smile appears to be tattooed on—is dressed all in black, and is just pretty enough that she could hostess at the Applebee's on the good side of town.

Caroline says to me, "I've seen you before."

"I get that all the time."

She stares, and I know she's trying to place me.

"I'll help you out. Everyone gets me confused with Jennifer Lawrence, but we're not even related."

Her eyebrows shoot up like rubber bands.

"I know, right? It's hard to believe, but I went on Ancestry.com and double-checked."

"You're the girl who was trapped in her house." She says to Kendra, "The fire department had to cut her out of there, remember? We were on the news?"

Not *You're Libby Strout, the girl we've known since first grade,* but *You're the girl who was trapped in her house and was the reason we got to be on television.*

Mick from Copenhagen is watching all of this. I say, "You're thinking of Jennifer Lawrence again."

Caroline's voice goes soft and sympathetic. "How are you doing? I was so worried. I can't even imagine what that must have been like for you. But oh my God, you lost so much weight. Didn't she, Kendra?"

Kendra is technically still smiling, but the upper half of her face is pinched into a frown. "So much."

"You look really pretty."

Kendra is still smile-frowning. "I love your hair."

One of the worst things a pretty girl can say to a fat girl is *You look really pretty.* Or *I love your hair.* I realize lumping all pretty girls together is just as bad as lumping all fat girls together, and I realize that you can be pretty and fat (hello!), but it's been my experience that these are things girls like Caroline Lushamp and Kendra Wu say to you when they're really thinking something else. These are pity compliments and I feel my soul die a little. Without a word, Mick from Copenhagen gets up and walks out of the room.

JACK

Caroline Lushamp is the closest thing I have to a girlfriend. This used to be because she was geeky and sweet, and, most of all, smart. When I first fell for her, she was the kind of smart that didn't make a show of it—that came later. She would just sit back and soak things up like a sponge. We'd get on the phone after everyone else had gone to sleep, and she'd tell me about her day—what she saw, what she thought. Sometimes we talked all night.

The Caroline of today is tall and gorgeous, but her biggest identifier is that she can part a crowd. She intimidates the hell out of everyone, even the teachers, mostly because she speaks up now—*always*—and tells it like it is. The main reason we're still at all on-again is history. *I know she must still be in there even if there's no sign of her.* This new Caroline arrived without warning, sophomore year, which means the old Caroline could (possibly) come back at any minute. The other reason is that she is generally easy for me to recognize.

I turn down my least-favorite hall, the one outside the library, the one where Caroline's locker is. When I was a freshman, I worked in the library, and if I run into any of the librarians, they'll all say hi and ask how my family is, and I'll be expected to know who they are.

As I walk, people are saying hi to me, and that's a nightmare too. I put on some extra swagger, half smiling at everyone, keeping it casual, but I must miss someone because I hear, "Prick."

The waters are treacherous. And also fickle. This is the first thing I learned about high school. One minute you're well liked, the next minute you're an outcast. Just ask Luke Revis, the most famous cautionary tale at MVB. Luke was *the man* our freshman year till everyone found out his dad served time in prison. Now Luke's in prison too, and you don't want to know why.

At this moment, the hall is full of potential Lukes. One kid being stuffed into a locker. Another kid tripping over someone's outstretched foot so that he goes flying into someone else, who shoves him, until he's bouncing from one person to another like a human volleyball. Girls trash-talking another girl right in front of her face so that she turns away, all red-eyed and crying. Another girl walking by with a big scarlet "A" swinging from her back, which leaves people snickering in her wake because everyone but Hester Prynne is in on the joke. For every single laughing person in this hallway, there are five who look either terrified or miserable.

I try to imagine what it would be like if the general high school public knew about me—they could literally walk right up and steal my shit or steal my car, then come back and help me look for it. This guy could pose as that guy or this girl could pretend to be that girl, and it would be really fucking hilarious. Everyone in on the joke but me.

I want to keep walking till I'm at the front entrance and then run the hell out of here.

I hear, "Wait up, Mass," and I start walking faster.

"Mass!"

Holy shit. Fuck off, whoever you are.

"Mass! Mass! Wait up, you fucker!"

This guy runs to catch up with me. He's about my height and stocky. His hair is brown and he's wearing a nondescript shirt. I glance at his backpack, the book he's carrying, his shoes, anything that might give me a clue as to who he is. Meanwhile he's launching into a conversation.

"Man, you need to get your hearing checked."

"Sorry. I'm meeting Caroline." If he knows her, this will work.

"Shit." He knows her. When it comes to Caroline Lushamp, most people fall into one of two camps—they're either in love with her or terrified of her. "No wonder you're somewhere else." The way he says it lets me know he belongs to Camp Terrified. "I just thought you might want to tell me to my face."

This is yet another nightmare—when they don't give you enough to go on.

"Tell you what?"

"Are you serious?" He stops in the middle of the hall, and goes red in the cheeks. "She's my *girlfriend*. You're lucky I don't beat the shit out of you."

This is almost certainly Reed Young, but there's a slight chance it could be someone else. I decide to keep it generic while trying to sound as specific as possible. "You're right. I am lucky, and don't think I don't appreciate it. I owe you, man."

"Yeah, you do."

I hear voices coming down the hall, loud and boisterous like a mob pillaging the countryside. People are dodging out of the way, and here come a couple of guys as big as the football field. They go, "What's up, Mass? Heard you had a nice time at the party." And they laugh hysterically. I may not recognize them, but these are apparently friends of mine. One of them rams his shoulder into some poor kid slinking past and then tells the kid to watch where he's going.

I say to the football field, "Dude, show some respect." And nod at Reed. Then I say to him, "Really, man. You're a good friend." This isn't exactly true, but he and I have been on the baseball team together since freshman year.

"Well. I still want to kick your ass, but don't let it happen again."

"Never."

He looks toward the library. A girl stands at the lockers opposite, talking on her phone. He shivers. "I wouldn't want to be you right now." And he bolts in the other direction, followed by the human football fields.

As I get closer to the girl, I can see the light eyes against the dark skin and the mole she paints on by her right eyebrow, even though everyone knows it's not real.

Run away while you still can.

She looks up. *"Seriously?"* she says, and yep, it's Caroline. She doesn't wait, just turns to go into the library, where I can see the librarians behind the desk, waiting for me to walk in there so they can make a fool out of me.

I grab her arm and spin her around and even though I don't want to, I pull her in and kiss the breath out of her. "That's what I should have done on Saturday," I say when I let her go. "That's what I should have been doing all summer."

Caroline's Achilles' heel is rom-coms and vampire romances. She wants to live in a world where the hot guy grabs the girl and just plants one on her because he's so overcome with desire and love that he's rendered brainless. So I touch her face, push her hair behind her ear, careful not to mess it up or she'll be madder. For some reason, eye contact, as a rule, is tough for me, which means I focus on her mouth. "You're beautiful."

Be careful. Is this what you want? We've been down this rabbit hole before, buddy. Do we really want to go down it again?

But there's a part of me that needs her. And hates that I need her.

I can feel her softening. If I know Caroline, this is the greatest present I could ever give her—letting her be the forgiver. She doesn't smile—Caroline rarely smiles anymore—but her eyes dart to the floor, fixing themselves on some invisible something there. The corners of her mouth turn down. She is thinking it over. Finally, she says, "You're the worst, Jack Masselin. I don't know why I even talk to you." Which is Caroline-speak for I love you too.

"What about Zach?"

"I broke up with him two weeks ago."

And like that, we're back together.

She takes my hand and we walk through the halls, and my heart's beating a little fast and I've got this feeling of *I'm safe.* Without even knowing it, she'll be my guide. She'll tell me who's who. We're Caroline and Jack, Jack and Caroline. As long as I'm with her *I'm safe. I'm safe. I'm safe.*

LIBBY

According to Mr. Dominguez, if he wasn't teaching driver's ed, he'd be repossessing cars. Not the cars of people who can't afford payments. No, he'd reclaim the cars of the people who are bad drivers, and then, like Robin Hood, he'd give those cars to an orphanage or to good drivers who can't afford their own set of wheels. It's hard to tell if he's serious because he has absolutely no sense of humor and he glares at everything. He is the sexiest man I've ever seen.

"A lot of schools are doing away with driver's ed. They send you out somewhere to take classes ..." The way he says *somewhere* makes it sound like a dark and terrible place. "But we teach you here because we care."

And then he shows us a film on underriding, which is when cars rear-end semitrucks and go plowing under them. At first, this boy named Travis Kearns is laughing, but then he utters one last "Goddamn" and goes quiet. Ten minutes later, even Bailey Bishop isn't smiling, and Monique Benton asks permission to go throw up in the bathroom.

After she leaves, Mr. Dominguez says, "Anyone else?" As if Monique walked out in protest and not clutching her stomach. "Statistics say you're going to die in a car crash before you're twenty-one. I'm here to make sure that doesn't happen."

My skin prickles. I feel like he's preparing us to go to battle, like Haymitch to our Katniss. Across the room, Bailey goes, "Oh my golly," which is her equivalent of "Holy fuck." Everyone looks ill except me.

This is because in that moment, as someone's head goes rolling off down the highway, I know the part I want to play here in this class and at MVB High. I'm not going to be a statistic—I've beaten statistics for most of my life. I'm not going to be one of those drivers who gets smashed under a truck. I want to be the girl who can do anything. I want to be the girl who tries out for the MVB Damsels *and makes the team.*

I raise my hand. Mr. Dominguez nods at me and my skin goes electric.

"How soon do we drive?"

"When you're ready."

Top 8 Things I Hate About Cancer
by Jack Masselin

● ● ●

1. It runs in families, which means even if you're my age, you can still feel like you've got a target on your back.
2. It runs in my family.
3. The way it can hit you like a meteor, completely out of the blue.
4. Chemo.
5. It's really goddamn serious. (In other words, do not, whatever you do, smile or laugh about something in an effort to lighten the mood.)
6. Having to bribe/bargain with God, even though you're not sure he exists.
7. When your dad gets diagnosed your sophomore year one week after you find out he's been cheating on your mother.
8. Seeing your mom cry.

LIBBY

I stop in the office of Heather Alpern on my way to fourth period. She is eating apple slices, long legs crossed, long arms draped like cats on the armrests of her chair. Before she was coach of the Damsels, she was a Radio City Music Hall Rockette. She is so beautiful that I can't look directly at her. I stare at the wall and say, "I'd like a Damsels application, please."

I wait for her to tell me there's a weight limit and that I am far, far beyond it. I wait for her to throw her beautiful head back and laugh hysterically before showing me the door. After all, the Damsels are high-profile. In addition to football and basketball games, they entertain at every big event in town—grand openings, parades, dedications, concerts.

But instead Heather Alpern rummages through a drawer and pulls out a form. "Our season technically started this summer. If we don't lose anyone, the next tryout period isn't until January."

I say to my feet, "What if you do lose someone?"

"We'll have auditions. We'll make an announcement and post flyers." She hands me the application. "You can fill this out and bring it back to me and I'll keep it on file. Just make sure to get your parents' permission." And then she smiles this beautiful, encouraging smile, like Maria in *The Sound of Music,* and I float out of there like I'm full of helium.

I bob and bounce like a balloon through the halls feeling as if I'm carrying the world's greatest secret. *You may not know this about me, but I love to dance.*

I am looking at the faces of everyone passing by and wondering what secrets they're keeping, when someone slams into me, a square-headed boy with a big, ruddy face.

"Hey," he says.

"Hey."

"Is it true fat girls give better blow jobs?"

"I don't know. I've never gotten a blow job from a fat girl."

People are passing by on all sides, and some of them laugh at this. His eyes turn cold, and there it is—the hatred a total stranger can feel for you, even if they don't know you, simply because they *think* they know you or hate what you are.

"I think you're disgusting."

I say, "If it's any consolation, I think you are too."

He mutters something that sounds like and probably is *fat whore.* It doesn't matter that I'm a virgin. I should have had sex a thousand times by now for all the boys who've been calling me this since fifth grade.

"Leave her alone, Sterling." This is from a girl with long, swinging hair and legs up to her neck. Bailey Bishop. If the Bailey of now is anything like the Bailey of then, she is earnest, popular, and loves Jesus. She is adorable. Everyone loves her. She walks into a room expecting people to like her, and they do, because how could you not like someone so thoroughly nice?

"Hey, Libby. I don't know if you remember me . . ." She doesn't link her arm through mine, but she might as well. Her voice still has the same lilt to it, every sentence ending on a high, happy note. She almost sounds as if she's singing.

"Hey, Bailey. I remember you."

"I'm just so glad you're back." And then she throws her arms around me, and I accidentally suck in some of her hair, which tastes like a cross between peaches and bubble gum. Exactly how you think Bailey Bishop's hair would taste.

We pull apart and she stands there grinning, eyes wide, dimples shining, and everything about her is too bright. Five years ago, Bailey was my friend, as in an actual friend and not one I made up. Five years is a long time. We barely had anything in common back then, so I'm not sure what we'll have in common now. But I tell myself, *Be nice. This could be the only friend you will ever make.*

She calls out to a girl walking past, and says to me, "I want you to meet Jayvee. Jayvee, this is Libby."

Jayvee says, "Hiya. What's shakin'?" Her hair is cut in a swingy black bob, and she's wearing a T-shirt that reads, MY REAL BOY-FRIEND IS FICTIONAL.

Bailey is beaming like a lighthouse. "Jayvee moved here two years ago from the Philippines." I wait for her to tell Jayvee this is my first year back at school after being a shut-in, but all she says is "Libby's new too."

Fourth period is advanced chemistry with Monica Chapman. Science teacher. Wife. And the woman who slept with my dad. As a rule, teachers are easier to recognize than students because of these three things: there are fewer of them than there are of us; even the younger ones dress older than we do; and we have license to stare at them on a daily basis (i.e., more time for me to learn their identifiers).

None of this helps me with Chapman. I've never had class with her before, and everything about her is *young* and also ordinary. I mean you'd hope that the woman your dad decides to cheat with on your mom is so remarkable that even a person who doesn't remember anyone would recognize her. But there's nothing about her that stands out. Which means she could be anywhere.

I choose a seat at the back, by the window, and someone sits down next to me. There's this look people get when they know you and when they expect you to know them, and he gives me this now.

"Hey, man," he says.

"Hey."

At some point, this cluster of girls breaks apart and one of them walks to the whiteboard at the front of the room. She looks around at everyone, introduces herself, sees me, and her face freezes, just for an instant, before she remembers to smile.

After everyone settles, Monica Chapman starts lecturing about the different branches of chemistry, and all I can think about is the branch she's not mentioning—the one that's responsible for her affair with my dad.

The way I found out was Dusty. He was the one who saw the text on Dad's phone. It was just sitting there, where anyone could see it. Dad had walked away, and Dusty was looking for things to collect—like me, he's always collecting things—and later he said to me, "I thought Mom's name was Sarah."

"It is Sarah."

"Then who's Monica?"

So the bastard didn't even bother to change her name on the phone. There it was, plain as day, *Monica.* To make matters worse, it wasn't his regular phone, but some phone he must have bought just to talk to her. Figuring out *which* Monica took a little more work, but you can take my word for it, it's her.

Right now she starts in on physical chemistry, and I raise my hand.

"Do you have a question, Jack?"

I think, *Do I ever.* If I can get the next words out of my mouth, it will be a miracle, because I feel like my chest is stuffed into my throat.

"Actually, I just wanted to tell you what I know about physical chemistry."

The guy next to me—who seems to be Damario Raines—nods at his desk, and some of the girls turn around to see what I'm going to say. They are identical to each other, and I wonder if they want to look exactly the same or if they even know they do. They're expecting me to say something clever. I can see it on them. Besides, no one else knows about what happened between Chapman and my dad. Marcus doesn't even know, and I want to keep it that way.

"Go ahead, Jack." Chapman's voice sounds perfectly normal, breezy and clipped, with a hint of Michigan or maybe Wisconsin.

"Physical chemistry applies theories of physics to study chemical systems, which include reaction kinetics, surface chemistry, molecular quantum mechanics, thermodynamics, and electrochemistry."

I smile this dazzling smile, one that competes with the overhead lights and the sun beating in the windows. I am going to blind her with this fucking smile so she won't ever be able to see my dad again. A girl two chairs over is grinning at me, chin in her hands, but the others look confused and a little disappointed. The Guy Who Seems to Be Damario says to his desk, "Man." And I can tell in that one word what a letdown I am.

"Actually, I think that's my favorite, electrochemistry. There's just something about a good chemical reaction, am I right?" And then I wink at Monica Chapman, who—for the next twenty seconds—goes speechless.

As soon as she can talk again, she gives us a pop quiz to "judge our aptitude," but really I think she's doing it to mess with me, because she grades them at her desk and then says, "Jack Masselin. Pass these back."

And it is on.

I get out of my seat and walk to the front of the room and take the quizzes from her. And then I stand there for a minute, trying to figure out what to do. The class is looking at me as I look at them. There are four kids who are definite IDs. Three, I'm fairly sure I don't know and am not supposed to know (but I'm not completely, totally sure). Eight are in the gray zone—better known as the danger zone.

Now, I can march up and down the aisles, trying to match the names of people I know with the faces. I can take all the shit that would be thrown at me as soon as it's clear that I don't know who everyone is. *Prick. Dumbass.*

Or I can do what I'm doing now—hold up the stack of papers and say, "Who here really wants to see what you got?" It was a pop quiz, after all, so it's not like any of us prepared for it. For good measure, I flip through the pages, and most of the grades are C, D, C-, C. As expected, no one raises a hand. "Who would rather take this opportunity to promise Mrs. Chapman you'll do better from here on out?" Almost all hands go up. These hands are attached to arms that are attached to torsos that are attached to necks that are attached to faces, which swim at me, foreign and unrecognizable. It's like being at a costume party *every single day* where you're the only one without a costume, but you're still expected to know who everyone is.

"If you're interested, I'm going to set them right here." I drop them onto an empty desk at the front and take my seat.

When the bell rings, Monica Chapman says, "Jack, I'd like a word with you."

I walk right on out the door like I don't hear, and go directly to the school office, where I tell them I need to change to the other advanced chemistry class, even though it's taught by Mr. Vernon, who is at least one hundred and deaf in one ear. The secretary starts in with "I'm not sure we can switch you because we'll have to reorganize part of your schedule . . ."

For a minute, I'm tempted to say forget it, I'll stay right where I am. Believe me, I'm more than happy to torment Monica Chapman for a semester. But I think about my dad losing his hair, about how paper-thin the chemo left him, about how frail he looked, like he might crumble away in front of us. I remember what it felt like to almost lose him. There's a part of me that still hates him, that maybe will always hate him, but he's my dad, after all, and I don't want to hate him any more than I already do. Besides, I actually like chemistry, and why should I ruin that for myself?

I lean on the counter. I give the secretary a smile that says *I've saved this up for you and only you.* "I'm sorry if it's inconvenient, and I don't want to be a pain in the ass, but if it helps, I know we can get Mrs. Chapman to sign off on this."

I decide to skip lunch. The thing that comes after it is gym, and I don't think there is a heavy girl on this planet, no matter how secure she is, who doesn't dread gym.

In the grand scheme of things, today could be worse. No one's banned me from the playground. So far I've only been mooed at and laughed at four or five times, and stared at a couple hundred times. A lot of people haven't looked twice at me, and a lot of them are treating me like anyone else. I've made at least one, maybe two, potential friends. I haven't had a single panic attack.

But the hardest thing is something I didn't expect—seeing people I used to know, people I grew up with, and knowing that while I sat in my house, they got older and went to school and made friends and had lives. It's like I'm the only one who stopped.

So I don't feel like eating. Instead I sit outside the cafeteria in the parking lot and read my favorite book, *We Have Always Lived in the Castle* by Shirley Jackson. It's about a girl named Mary Katherine Blackwood. Most everyone in her family is dead, and she lives with her sister, holed up away from society, trapped in her house, not by her weight but by a horrible thing she did once upon a time. The people of her village tell legends about her and are afraid of her and sometimes sneak up to the house to try to catch a glimpse of her. I'm pretty sure I understand Mary Katherine in a way no one else does.

I read for a few minutes, and then I close my eyes and tilt my head back. It's a warm, bright day, and even though I haven't been housebound in a while, I don't think I'll ever get enough of sunshine.

Gym is worse than I imagined.

JACK

Of course it's Seth Powell who says, "There's this game I read about."

Or maybe he saw it online, he can't remember.

"It's called Fat Girl Rodeo."

And he's laughing like it's the funniest damn thing he's ever heard. He laughs so hard he almost falls off the bleachers. "And what you do is you go up to some fat girl and you throw yourself around her like you're riding a bull . . ." He leans forward, covering his face, and then he kicks the bleachers three times like it's going to help him get his breath. When he finally looks up again, his eyes have gone squinty and wet. "And you hold on as tight as you can, really squeeze the shit out of her . . ." He doubles over and rocks back and forth. I look at Kam and Kam looks at me like, What a dumb motherfucker.

Seth sits up, shaking all over. "And whoever . . ." (These last words are the hardest to get out.) ". . . holds on longest . . ." (He's barely breathing.) ". . . wins."

I say, "Wins what?"

"The game."

"Yeah, but what do they win?"

"The game, man. They win the game."

"But is there a prize?"

"What do you mean a prize?"

Seth is pretty stupid, if you want to know the truth. I sigh like I'm carrying the world's burdens, like I'm freakin' Atlas.

"If you go to the state fair and you play the shooting gallery, they give you, like, a stuffed panda or some such shit."

"When I was eight." Seth rolls his eyes at Kam.

I rake my hands through the lion fro, making it bigger and badder. I talk very, very slowly, the way my dad does to foreigners. "So when you went to the shooting gallery at age eight, they gave you something when you won."

Kam takes a swig of the flask he always carries, but he doesn't offer us any. He snorts. "Like he ever won."

Seth is looking at me, but he reaches out and slaps Kam on the side of his head. I'll say this for him, he's got good aim.

Seth squints at me. "What's your point?"

"What do you get if you win the rodeo?"

"You win." He holds up his hands like what more is there.

It could go on this way for hours, but Kam says, "Losing battle, Mass. Let it go."

I look at Kam now. "Have *you* heard of Fat Girl Rodeo?"

He stands, takes another swig from the flask, and for a second I think he's about to offer it to me. Then he caps it and shoves it back into his pocket. "I have now."

And suddenly he's out of the bleachers and on the ground and jogging toward some girl, who looks like she's wearing an inner tube under her shirt. I don't recognize her, but of course I don't recognize anyone. Except for the inner tube, she could be my own mother, for all I know.

Seth's identifier isn't the fact that he's the only black kid in school with a Mohawk. His identifier is his stupid laugh. Because he's an idiot, he's always laughing, and I'd know that laugh anywhere. With Kam, it's the fact that he has this white-blond hair that makes him look like an albino. He's the only person I know with hair that color.

I have no idea who this girl with the inner tube is, and the whole time I'm watching, I'm thinking Kam's not really going to do it. He's just trying to make us think he's going to do it.

And then he's doing it. He's wrapped around the girl like cellophane, and at first you can tell maybe she's happy because it's Dave Kaminski, but the longer he holds on, the more upset she gets, till it looks like she's going to start screaming or crying or both.

I stand up. I want to tell him to stop. Seth's eyes are fixed on Dave and the girl, and his jaw goes slack before he starts pounding on his knee going, "Oh shit, oh shit, oh shit." And then he's laughing and says something to me that sounds like "You know she wants it." And the whole time I'm thinking to myself, *Say something, douchebag.*

But I don't. And right before she loses it, Kam lets her go. Then he breaks into a victory lap around the track.

"Fifteen seconds," Seth says under his breath. "It's a goddamn world's record."

LIBBY

Libby Strout is fat.

I am locked in the bathroom after school, black Sharpie squeaking against the ugly, ugly wall. There is an unused tampon lying on the floor and an empty lip gloss in the sink, even though the trash can is literally *right there*. A sign on one of the stalls says OUT OF ORDER because someone dropped (shoved) a math book in the toilet. It smells like air freshener and cigarettes in here, among other things. That old saying about girls being sugar and spice and everything nice? Not so true. All you have to do is visit the third-floor bathroom of MVB High School in Amos, Indiana, to figure that out.

Someone is pounding on the door.

I reach up one arm and write in thick letters as large as I can so that everyone will see.

Libby Strout is fat.
Fat and ugly.
She will never get laid.
No one will ever love her.

I catch sight of myself in the mirror, and my face is the color of beets, the ones Mom used to call "nice vegetables," even though she knew there was nothing nice about them. Mom always did that—made things nicer than they were.

Libby Strout is so fat they had to destroy her house to get her out.

Word for word, these are the things I overheard Caroline Lushamp and Kendra Wu saying about me in gym, as the other girls stood around and listened. And laughed. I add in one or two other lines, the meanest things I can think of, so that I don't have to hear it from anyone else. I write it so they don't have to. This way, there is nothing they can say about me that I haven't said myself.

Libby Strout is the fattest teen in America.

Libby Strout is a liar.

I step back.

These are the truest words of all, and until I see them I'm okay. But something about seeing them there, like someone else wrote them, makes me catch my breath. *Too far, Libbs,* I think.

Yes, I'm fat.

Yes, they had to partially destroy my house.

Maybe no boy will love me or want to touch me ever, even in a dark room, even after an apocalypse when all the skinny girls have been wiped off the earth by some horrible plague. Maybe one day I can be thinner than I am now and have a boyfriend who loves me, but I'll still be a liar. I'll always be a liar.

Because in about three minutes I'm going to open the door and walk down that hall and tell myself what did I expect, I knew this would happen, it was never going to go differently than this, they don't matter, high school doesn't matter, none of this matters, it's what's inside that counts. It's what lies beyond this. All those things they like to tell you. Besides, I stopped feeling a long time ago.

Except this is a lie too.

Sixty seconds later:

I walk out of the bathroom and bump right into a girl almost as big as I am. She's bawling her eyes out, and my first instinct is to get out of her way. She says, "What were you doing in there? Did you lock the door?" Actually, she shouts it.

"It must have gotten stuck. Are you okay?" I talk softly and calmly, hoping she'll follow my lead.

She's crying and hiccupping hard, and it takes her a minute. "Bastards." This is a little less loud.

I don't have to ask what, only who. I can imagine by the size of her what's happened. "Who?" I ask, even though I feel like I don't know anyone at this school.

"Dave Kaminski and his bastard friends." She pushes by me to the sink, where she bends over, washing her face, wetting down her hair, which is wound in tight black ringlets. She's wearing a Nirvana shirt and one of those candy necklaces you eat. I grab a paper towel and hand it to her. "Thanks." She pats at her face. "Dave Kaminski grabbed me, and when I told him to let go he wouldn't."

The Dave Kaminski I knew was a scrawny twelve-year-old with white hair who once stole his dad's Johnnie Walker and brought it to school.

"Where are they?"

"Bleachers." She's still hiccupping, but not as bad. She glances up at the wall and starts reading. "What the . . ."

My eyes follow hers. "I know, right? Look on the bright side. At least that's not your name on the wall."

JACK

Kam's still running laps when these two girls come walking out of the school. One of them hangs back, but the other marches across the football field. She glances up at us for a second, and our eyes meet. And then she heads straight for Kam.

At first, he doesn't see her, which is a miracle because this girl is enormous. But then I can tell he sees her, and he picks up speed, laughing and sprinting away. Seth is sitting straight up, like a dog watching a squirrel. Under his breath he goes, "What the hell . . ."

Just as the girl gets close, Kam takes off like he's on fire, and *the girl runs after him.* I'm on my feet now because it's the best damn thing I've ever seen. I mean, she is *flying.*

Seth starts clapping like a fool. "Oh *shit.*" He's hollering at Kam and laughing himself blue, kicking and stomping at the bleachers, and the whole time I am rooting for the girl.

"Run!" I yell, and I'm yelling it to her, though no one knows it. "Run! Run! Run!"

Finally, Kam hurdles the fence and races off down the street away from us. Like a fucking gazelle, the girl hurdles the fence right after him, and the only thing that stops her from catching him is a truck that goes barreling past at just that moment. She stands on the street and stares after Kam, and then she walks, not runs, back toward the school. She crosses the football field, and as she walks her eyes are on me again. She doesn't turn her head, just follows me with her eyes, and I am telling you she is pissed.

SIX YEARS EARLIER

LIBBY
AGE 10

I walk onto the playground, and Moses Hunt says to me, "Hey, if it isn't Flabby Stout. What's up, Flabby?"

I say, "You're flabby." Even though he isn't, but then neither am I.

He does a sideways look at the boys grouped around him, the ones who hang on his every move all the time, even when he's just making arm farts and repeating the swear words his brothers taught him. His eyes come sliding back to me, and he's about to say something, and I know whatever it is I don't want to hear it because no one could say anything nice with a mouth that looks like it swallowed a whole lemon, seeds and all.

He opens that pursed-up lemon mouth and says, "No one will ever love you. Because you're fat."

I stare down at my legs and stomach. I hold out my arms. If I'm fat, it's news to me. Plump, maybe. A little chubby. But this is the way I've always been. I take a good, hard look at Moses and the other boys and the girls over by the swings. As far as I'm concerned, I don't look that much fatter than any of them.

"I don't think I am."

"Well then, you're not only fat, you're dumb." The boys fall down with laughter. Moses's face bunches up like a fist, and he opens his mouth so wide it looks like all the pigeons in Amos could nest there. *"Go home, Flabby Stout. The sun can't shine when you come out . . . "* He's singing it to the tune of "Lullaby and Good-night." *"You're so big you block the moon. Go home, Flabby, go to your room . . ."*

I think, *You're the one that's dumb.* And I move past him. I'm aiming for the swings, where I see Bailey Bishop along with a hundred other girls. Moses steps in front of me. *"Go home, Flabby Stout . . ."*

I step the other way, and he blocks my path again. So now I move toward the jungle gym, where I can sit in peace, but he says, "I can't let you do that. You might break it."

"I won't break it. I've been on it before."

"But you might. Your flab has probably cracked the foundation. The next time you go on it, I bet that whole thing'll collapse. Maybe the playground too. You're probably cracking it right now just standing here. You probably killed your mom by sitting on her." The boys die over and over. One of them rolls along the ground, hooting his face off.

I'm not as tall as Moses is, but I stare directly into his dark, soulless eyes. All I can think is *For the first time in my life, I know what it's like to have someone hate me.* I can see the hate in there like it's lodged in his pupils.

I spend the rest of recess standing against the wall on the edge of the playground wondering what I've done to Moses Hunt to make him hate me and knowing that whatever it is, there's no coming back from it. It's my stomach that tells me *He will never like you no matter what you do, no matter how thin you are, no matter how nice you try to be to him.* This is a terrifying feeling. It's the feeling of something turning. Of coming to a corner and going around it and seeing that the street ahead is dark and deserted or filled with wild dogs, but you can't go back, only forward, right into the middle of the pack.

I hear a shriek, and my friend Bailey Bishop jumps off the swing in midflight, legs reaching for the earth, hair sailing for the sky, bright gold as the sunrise.

I wave but she doesn't see me. *Doesn't she notice I'm missing?* I wave again, but she's too busy running. I think, *If I were Bailey Bishop, I'd run too.* She has legs as long as light poles. *If I were Bailey Bishop, I wouldn't even look for me to see where I'd gone off to. I would just run and run and run.*

NOW

LIBBY

The girl's name is Iris Engelbrecht. These are the things I've learned in the past five minutes: She's been heavy since birth, thanks to a double whammy of hypothyroidism and something called Cushing's syndrome. Her parents are divorced, she has two older sisters, and everyone in her family is overweight.

"You need to tell the principal."

Iris shakes her head. "No."

We are back inside the school, just the two of us. I'm trying to lead us toward the main hall, toward where the principal's office is, but Iris is dragging her feet.

"I'll go with you."

"I don't want to make it worse."

"What makes it worse is Dave Kaminski thinking he can do that to you."

"I'm not like you." And what she means is *I'm not brave like you.*

"Then I'll just go." I walk away from her.

"Don't." She catches up to me. "I mean, thanks for chasing after him, but I want the whole thing to go away, and it's not going away if I tell. It does the opposite of going away. It gets so big I have to look at it all the time, and I don't want to. It's the first day of the school year." And again I can hear what she isn't saying: *I don't want this thing to follow me the whole year, even if I've got every right to kick his teeth in.*

• • •

My counselor, Rachel Mendes, meets me at the park. For two of the past three years, I've seen her every day. Back when I was in the hospital, she was the first person, other than my dad, who spoke to me like I was a regular girl. Later she became my tutor and also my caregiver, the one who stayed with me while my dad went to work. Now she's my best friend and we meet here once a week.

She says, "What happened?"

"Boys. Idiots. People."

There used to be a zoo in the heart of the park, but it was shut down in 1986 after the bear tried to eat a man's arm. All that's left of it is this wide stone bench, which used to be part of the bear's habitat. We sit on that and look out toward the golf course, and I'm fuming so much I'm worried the top of my head is going to blast right off.

"This boy did a cruel thing, and the person he did it to doesn't want to speak up."

"Is the person in danger?"

"No. The boy probably thought what he did was harmless, but he shouldn't have done it and he shouldn't get away with it."

"We can't fight another person's battles, no matter how much we want to."

But we can chase the bastards who terrorize them down the street. I think how much simpler life was when I couldn't leave the house. It was just *Supernatural* reruns all day long, reading, reading, reading, and spying on the neighbor boys from my window.

"How's the anxiety?"

"I'm mad, but I'm breathing."

"How's the eating?"

"I didn't stress-eat, but the day's not over." *And there's an entire school year left to experience.* Even though I've spent almost three years eating nutritiously and boringly without a hiccup,

Rachel and my doctors are worried I might end up spiraling into some wild, bottomless binge because I'm so deprived. What they don't understand is it wasn't about the food. Food was never part of the Why. Not directly, at least.

"Here's the worst thing of it," I say. "You know how far I've come and I know how far I've come, but everyone else just sees me for how large I am or where I was years ago, not who I am now."

"You'll show them. If anyone can, it's you."

Suddenly, I can't sit on this bench any longer. This happens sometimes—after all those months of being motionless, I still get overcome with the need to move my body.

I say, "Let's twirl."

And this is what I love most about Rachel. She just gets right up and starts twirling, no questions asked, no fear of what anyone else might think.

Christmas Eve. I'm four. My grandmother gives Mom and me these giant matching Christmas skirts—one in green, one in red. They're ugly, but they twirl, and so we wear them straight through New Year's, twirling all the way. Long after I outgrew the skirt, we twirled for birthdays, Mother's Day, anything worth celebrating.

Rachel and I spin till we're dizzy and then fall back down onto the bench. I sneak-check my pulse without her seeing because there's good breathless and bad breathless. I wait until I feel my pulse go steady, till I know I'm safe, and I say, "Do you know what happened to the bear? The one that was here?"

I can't blame him for trying to take someone's arm off. I mean, the man reached into his cage, and that cage was all the bear had in the world.

"The news report said they sent him over to Cincinnati for socialization."

"What do you really think happened?"

"I think they shot him."

On the wall above me, my great-great-something-grandfather stares at me from out of a giant frame, stern and wild-eyed. The stories paint him as a saintly man who lived to carve toys. If they're to be believed, he was a kind of selfless Indiana Santa Claus. But in his photo, he is one scary old son of a bitch.

He fixes those wild eyes on me as I leave a voicemail for Kam: *I'm sitting here at good old Masselin's Toys, wishing you well on your journey home. Let me know if you need money for a plane ticket back.*

I hang up and say to Great-Great-Something-Grandfather, "Don't judge a man till you've walked a mile in his shoes."

I'm in the store office returning emails, checking inventory, paying bills, work I could do in my sleep. Masselin's Toys has been in our family for five generations. It's survived the Great Depression and race riots and the downtown explosion of 1968 and the recession, and it will probably be here long after my dad is gone and I'm gone, long after the next ice age, when the only other survivors are cockroaches. Since birth, reliable, dutiful Marcus has been the one expected to take the baton from Dad. This is because for whatever reason everyone expects Great Things from Jack. But I know something they don't. *This will be me one day, living in this town, running this store, marrying, having kids, talking loudly to foreigners, cheating on my wife. Because what else am I possibly equipped for?*

My phone buzzes and it's Kam, but before I can answer, a man walks in (dark, wiry hair, dark eyebrows, pale skin, Masselin's store shirt).

My dad clears his throat. The chemo has left him with hearing damage in one ear and a throat that constantly needs clearing. He says, "Why did you quit advanced chemistry?"

How the fuck does he know this? It only happened a couple of hours ago.

"I didn't."

I'll tell you how he knows this. Monica Chapman probably whispered it in his ear as they were doing it in his car.

And before I can stop them, all these images go racing through my head of primeval naked body parts, some of them belonging to my dad.

He grabs a chair, and as he sits down I look away because I can't get these images out of my mind. "That's not what I heard." *As I was banging Monica Chapman all over the chem lab. As I was banging her against your locker, on top of your lunch table, on the desk of every teacher you will ever have.*

I say, maybe too loudly, "I just changed to the other class."

"What was wrong with the class you were in?"

And there it is. I mean, he must be kidding, right? Because there's no way he's actually *continuing to ask me about this.*

I can't avoid it. I have to look him in the eye—something that makes me even more uncomfortable than this conversation. "Let's just say I have a problem with the teacher."

Dad's shoulders stiffen, and he knows I know, and it is awkward as hell in there. Suddenly I don't give a shit about the emails or the inventory. All I care about is leaving because *why would Monica Chapman tell him anything if she wasn't still sleeping with him?*

. . .

This skinny kid with big ears sits at the kitchen table drinking milk out of one of the whiskey glasses my parents keep on the bar. Even though he's just a kid, the way he's sitting makes me think of an old man who's seen kinder times and better days. His purse is on the table.

I grab a glass, pour myself some juice, and say, "Is this seat taken?" He pushes the chair out to me with his foot and I sit. I hold out my glass and he clinks his against mine and we drink in silence. I can hear the tick of the grandfather clock from down the hall. We're the first ones home.

Finally, Dusty says, "Why are people so shitty?"

At first I think he knows about my conversation with Dad, or about me, about the person I am at school, but then my eyes go to the purse, where one of the ugliest words in the English language is scrawled across one side of it in black marker. The strap has been sliced in two.

My eyes go back to my little brother. "People are shitty for a lot of reasons. Sometimes they're just shitty people. Sometimes people have been shitty to them and, even though they don't realize it, they take that shitty upbringing and go out into the world and treat others the same way. Sometimes they're shitty because they're afraid. Sometimes they choose to be shitty to others before others can be shitty to them. So it's like self-defensive shittiness." Which I know plenty about. "Who's being shitty to you?"

Dusty holds up his hand and shakes his head, which tells me no, we won't speak of details. "Why would being afraid make someone act shitty?"

"Because maybe someone doesn't like who he is, but then here's this other kid who knows exactly who he is and seems pretty damn fearless." I glance at the purse. "Well, that can be intimidating and even though it shouldn't, it can make that first kid feel even worse about himself."

"Even if the other kid isn't trying to make anyone feel worse, he's just being himself?"

"Exactly."

"That's shitty."

"Is there anything I can do?"

"You just don't be shitty."

"I can't promise anything except that I'll never be shitty to you, little brother."

We drink like two old comrades, and after a while I say, "You know, I bet I could fix that bag for you. Or even build you a new one. One that's indestructible."

He shrugs. "I'm better off without it."

And the way he says it makes me want to buy him every goddamn purse in the world and start carrying one myself out of solidarity.

"What if I build you something else, then? What's one thing you've always wanted? Sky's the limit. Heart's desire."

"A Lego robot."

"One that can do your homework for you?"

He shakes his head. "Nah, I've got that covered."

I lean back in my chair and rub my jaw like I'm deep in thought. "Okay, you probably want one that can do your chores."

"Uh-uh."

"Maybe a drone, then?"

"I want one that can be my friend."

It's like a kick to the gut. I almost lose it right there, but instead I nod, rub my jaw, empty my glass. "Consider it done."

LIBBY

After dinner, Dad and I sit on the couch and I show him the most recent Damsels video, filmed two weeks ago at a festival over in Indianapolis. Sequins flashing, stadium lights blaring, crowd cheering. *All that color. All that life.* I'm not sure anyone else on earth appreciates it as much as I do.

He says, "Are you sure about this?"

"No. But I'm auditioning anyway. You can't protect me from everything. If I fall on my face, I fall on my face, but at least I've done it."

I hand him the application, which he flips through. He reaches for the pen that lies on the coffee table and signs his name. As he hands it back, he says, "You know, having you out in the world again is harder than I thought."

JACK

I'm in the basement, which is like a warped version of Santa's workshop, cluttered with cars and dump trucks, Mr. Potato Heads, walkie-talkies, and all things Fisher-Price. Discarded toys, but other stuff too—car parts, motorcycle parts, motors, fragments of lawn mowers and appliances. Anything I can turn into something else. Some projects are finished, but most are works in progress, the guts pulled out, pieces everywhere. This is where I take things apart and put them back together in new and stupefying ways. The way I wish I could do with myself.

The phone buzzes and it's Kam. "I ran all the way to Centerville, man."

I laugh the laugh of someone brave and manly. "Did the mean girl scare you?"

"Shut up. She was so fucking fast."

"Are you okay? Do you need to talk about it?" I use the voice Kam's mom uses when she's speaking to his little sister, the one who's always crying and slamming doors.

"That's it, dude. The golden ring."

"What?"

"Her. She's the prize. Or at least, the goal. Whoever can hold on to that one, wins."

"Wins what?"

But I already know what he's going to say.

"Fat Girl Rodeo."

The walls of the workshop start to close in around me.

"Mass?"

"Maybe I'm not so into this game."

"What do you mean you're not into it?"

I mean I don't want to have this conversation because I don't like where this is going.

"It just seems kind of lame. I mean, dude, *Seth* came up with it." When in doubt, always, always throw Seth under the bus.

"He didn't come up with it. He told us about it. A different animal altogether. Besides, it's fucking hilarious. What's wrong with you? She almost ran me over."

"Seth's a moron." More bus throwing as I try to think of a way to stop this before it ends in the humiliation of every heavy girl in school. They don't deserve it. The girl who hurdled that fence like a gazelle and chased Kam down the street doesn't deserve it. I say, "She doesn't deserve it."

"Jesus, you mad fucker. It's like you want to take her to prom. Should I order the limo now?"

"I'm just saying we can make better use of our free time senior year. Have you *seen* the freshmen girls?" When in doubt, mention girls.

"Since when are you such a pussy?"

I stop talking. My heart pounds like a drum. *Say something, douchebag.*

"We're doing this with or without you, Mass."

Finally I go, "Whatever, man. Do what you want."

"Thanks so much, I will. As long as we have your approval."

"Dick."

"Douche." Our pet names for each other. The ground between us feels a little more solid, but the rest of the world shakes, like it's built on a high wire miles above the earth.

What I Stand to Lose if I Tell My Friends to Fuck Off
by Jack Masselin

● ● ●

1. **Kam and Seth.** They may not be the greatest friends in the world, but they're the only ones I can reliably recognize on a semiconsistent basis. Maybe it's because I've known them longer than anyone else, or maybe it's because their identifiers are so easy to pick out in a crowd. For whatever reason, they stick. Which is probably why I became friends with them in the first place. Imagine moving to a town where you only know two people and *will only ever know these same two people,* no matter how many other people you meet.

2. **The carefully constructed world I've built for myself within the walls of Martin Van Buren High School.** I did not get to be Jack Masselin by pissing people off. And even though I may not always like Jack Masselin, I need him. Without him, I'm just some screwed-up kid with a screwed-up family and a questionable future. And if I know anything about high school, it's this: if you give people an excuse, they will feed you to the wolves. (Luke Revis, I'm looking at you.)

So yeah.

3. **Me.** I'd rather not lose me.

LIBBY

I lie on my bed—not the same bed I spent twenty-four hours a day on, back when I couldn't leave the house, but a new one we bought after I lost some weight. I pull out my headphones and find the song "All Right Now." I know it from season one, episode six of *Supernatural*. It's at the very end of the episode, when Dean tells Sam he wishes he could have lived a normal life.

A normal life is what I've wanted for as long as I can remember. It's what I tried to create in my mind, from my bed. When Dean-across-the-street learned to skateboard, I learned with him, and we would race each other for hours. When Dean and Sam played baseball in the yard, I played too, and when they built a potato cannon in the driveway, I helped spray-paint it and shoot potatoes over the roof. The four of us hung out in their tree house, and whenever Castiel's big brothers left him behind, I took him for ice cream and told him stories. Afterward, I would go back to my house and eat dinner at the dining room table with my dad *and* my mom, because, of course, it was all imagined, which meant I could make it anything I wanted it to be. Just like I could make me anything I wanted to be, including a regular-size girl.

I turn the song up loud enough that it feels like it's in me, running through my veins just like blood. As angry as I was today, I don't remember feeling anxious. No heart palpitations, no nervous sweats. The cafeteria didn't spin. My head didn't feel like it was being squeezed by two enormous hands. My lungs breathed normally, evenly, all on their own.

The Damsels application lies next to me. Under *What trait or asset do you possess that you could bring to our team that we might not find in other candidates?* I wrote, *I'm big, eye-catching, and can dance like the wind.* Nowhere on the application does it ask for my weight.

I watch as George attacks the comforter and think, *Yes. All right now. That's me. Nothing will ever be okay again, not in the same way, but I'm getting used to it. Maybe I will get that normal life after all.*

JACK

I sit at my computer for a long time, trying to figure out what to say. I can bullshit my way through school essays, but I'm not a writer. This has never been a big deal until this exact moment.

Here's the thing. For all their faults, my parents are good people. Okay, Mom more so than Dad. They've taught my brothers and me to be good people too, and even though we may not always act that way, it's still inside us, inside me. Enough so, at least, that I don't want some innocent girl getting shamed and humiliated because of my jackass friends.

And what if they do something worse than the rodeo calls for?

What if they try to kiss her?

What if they try to cop a feel?

In my mind, I run through every worst-case scenario, and all of them end with this girl crying her heart out.

I rest my head on the desk. I feel like crying my own heart out right now.

Finally, I'm like:

To hell with it.

I lift my head and just start writing.

I'm not a shitty person, but I'm about to do a shitty thing. And you will hate me, and some other people will hate me, but I'm going to do it anyway to protect you and also myself . . .

THE NEXT DAY

LIBBY

Iris Engelbrecht decides to join me in the cafeteria. For some reason—maybe it's our combined size—she walks five steps behind me.

"You still back there, Iris?"

"I'm here."

She can make even those two words sound miserable and defeated. She is the Eeyore of Martin Van Buren High. And she talks about weight *a lot*. I definitely am not interested in becoming the Official Spokesperson for Fat Girls, which is exactly what Iris seems to think I am, along with Badass Fat Girl with Attitude. This is ten times worse than the Sassy Fat Girl or the Fat Girl Best Friend. This is a role that comes with a lot of expectations, and the last thing I want is to feel responsible for helping someone else maneuver high school.

I'm heading over to where Bailey Bishop sits with Jayvee De Castro at a table by the window, when I spy Dave Kaminski, white head covered by a black beanie. Iris tugs on my sleeve. "I want to get out of here."

I turn around and start walking in the opposite direction, poor Iris bumping along behind. And I run smack into one of Dave Kaminski's friends, one of the guys from the bleachers. He's tall, long-limbed, and lanky, with gold-brown skin and this dark brown hair that explodes in all directions like the sun.

Before I can get out of his way, he goes, "Sorry." And there's something serious and troubled in his eyes, like he just lost his best friend.

"No, I'm sorry." And I step to the side so I can go around him. But then he's stepping to the same side. So I step to the other side, and so does he, and I'm thinking how ridiculous we must look when I hear Dave Kaminski somewhere over my right shoulder going, "HOLY SHIT, IT'S *ON*!"

For a second, I think this boy is going to pass out right in front of me. He says again, "I'm sorry." And then he throws himself on me and holds on like his life depends on it.

I'm so surprised, I can't even move. Instead my mind goes spinning back in time to a family vacation when I was nine. My mom and dad and cousins and aunts and me at the beach in North Carolina. It was a hot day, and we were all swimming. I had this pink-and-yellow checked bathing suit I loved. I was treading water in the shallows and a jellyfish attached itself to my leg while I was swimming. I mean, the little monster wouldn't let me go and they had to carry me out of there and *pry it off,* and I thought I was going to die.

Well, this little monster is holding on just as hard, and at first I can't do anything but stand there. It's like the world goes blank and still, and so do I. Everything just

s
l
o
w
s

d
o
w
n.

And stops.

Just stops.

For the first time in a really long time, I feel panicked. Chest clenching. Breath coming too fast. Palms damp. Neck hot.

And then something snaps me back into reality—maybe the sound of shouting and clapping and booing. Or is it mooing? Whatever, I'm suddenly back in the school cafeteria with this boy draped on me like a sweater, arms wrapped around me tight.

"No."

I recognize my own voice, but I sound far away, like I'm on the other side of the school, over by the library.

It's clear that this is some kind of horrible game. Hug the Fat Girl or Velcro Yourself to the Fat Girl. This is worse than being banned from the playground, and I'm suddenly so mad I'm shaking. My whole body goes hot, which I'm sure he must notice, seeing as how he's as attached to me as my arms and legs.

I think, *I didn't lose three hundred pounds and give up pizza and Oreos just to be shamed in my school cafeteria by this jackass.*

"NOOOOO!" It comes out like a roar.

For someone so lanky, he's strong, and I summon all the strength I have to peel him off like a Band-Aid.

And then I punch him in the mouth.

JACK

I'm lying on the cafeteria floor, and the girl is standing over me. My jaw feels knocked loose, like it's over somewhere in Ohio. I give it a rub to make sure it's still attached, and my hand comes away covered in blood.

I say, "What the hell?" My words are garbled. *Jesus, I think she broke my voice box.* "Why did you punch me?"

"WHY DID YOU GRAB ME?"

My eyes go to her backpack, to the letter sticking out of the pocket I just managed to shove it into. I want to say *You'll understand later,* but I can't speak because I'm wiping the blood from my mouth.

I may not know who anyone is, but every face in that cafeteria is turned toward us, eyes staring, mouths hanging open or gums flapping. The girl is still standing there, and from the floor I say, "I'm getting up. In case you're thinking of punching me again."

A hand comes toward me, and it's attached to a tall white guy wearing a stupid black beanie. I hate hats because sometimes the only identifier is someone's hair, and a hat erases that, which erases them. I'm not sure whether I should take the hand, but no one else is offering one, so I let him pull me up. As he does, the son of a bitch starts laughing.

The girl turns on him. "You're a jackass."

He holds his hands up like she's pulled a gun. "Hey, I'm not the one that grabbed you."

"Maybe not, but I'm sure you had something to do with it." Which tells me this might be Dave Kaminski.

Then another girl is there, dark and angry, with a mole by one eye, and she gets right up in the face of the girl I grabbed. "YOU HIT HIM? YOU STUPID COW! HE WASN'T HURTING YOU!" And only Caroline Lushamp can get her voice that high and loud.

I say, "I deserved it. I shouldn't have grabbed her." And suddenly I'm defending my attacker.

"*She* did this to *you?*" A kid appears, pointy chin, shaggy hair. I'm searching his face for signs of who he is, but everyone is coming at me all at once, and this is my nightmare because I don't know who anyone is. People are pulling at me, and wanting to know *What happened, am I okay, it's going to be okay, don't you worry, Jack.* I want them to get off me and go away because I'm supposed to know them and I don't, and I might as well have amnesia. They are freaking me out and I want to tell them to fuck off. She's the one who deserves the attention, not me. It's my fault, not hers.

"What the hell happened, Jax?" The pointy-chinned guy is Marcus, my own brother, because this is what he used to call me when we were kids.

But I can't be sure, can I? Even babies recognize the people they know. Even dogs. Even Carl Jumers, who still—how many years after grade school?—has to count on his fingers, and last year ate a cat turd because he was dared.

One of the security guys appears, pushing people away. And also a teacher (gray hair, beard), who tries to restore order in the crowd. As he's telling them there's nothing to see here, go back to your business, another girl comes walking up, fast.

"Jack Masselin, what happened?" She's examining my face, and at this point I'm not sure where I'm bleeding from. Do I know this person? There's nothing about her that looks familiar, but then someone goes, "It was him, Ms. Chapman. He grabbed her."

I jerk my chin out of her hand. I say, "It's *Mrs.* Chapman," and I look her right in the eye. In that moment, I'm like, *Come on, lady. Show me what you got. Show me what makes you so special.* I mean, there must be something incredible here, right? Why else would my dad put his family on the line and risk everything?

But the only one who stands out from the staring, jabbering crowd of them isn't my own brother or the woman who's wrecking my parents' marriage. It's a girl I don't even know, the largest girl here.

LIBBY

Principal Wasserman is a wiry jumping bean of a woman. A plaque behind her desk says she's been a principal for twenty-five years. I sit across from her, next to the boy and a woman who must be his mother.

Principal Wasserman says to me, "Your dad should be here any minute."

Suddenly I feel like I'm going to throw up because I've just gone reeling back in time to the worst moment of my life. I was in fifth grade, in the middle of a school assembly, when the principal found me and led me out of the auditorium in front of everyone. She took me to the office, where my dad was waiting along with a school counselor. A big box of Kleenex sat on the corner of the principal's desk, and that was what I focused on. It was such a big box, as if they'd created it especially for that moment.

"Your mom is in the hospital and we have to leave now."

"What do you mean?"

He had to repeat it three times before I could understand, and even then I thought it was a terrible joke, that they'd all conspired for some reason to play this really cruel trick on me.

"Libbs?"

I look up as my dad walks in. "Are you okay?"

"I'm okay."

Someone brings in a chair for him, and then the principal tells everyone what happened in the cafeteria.

The boy's mom is staring at her son like he's Rosemary's baby. She says, "There's got to be some sort of explanation as to why *on earth* you would do such a thing."

My dad says to her, "I'd like to hear the explanation that could make me understand this."

The principal speaks over them. "I want to hear from Jack and Libby."

Everyone looks at us.

"He grabbed me."

"How did he grab you?"

"He launched himself at me and held on like I was a flotation device and he was the last man off the *Titanic*."

This boy, Jack, clears his throat. "That's not exactly how it happened."

I raise an eyebrow at him. "Really?"

But he's not looking at me. He's too focused on trying to seduce Principal Wasserman. He leans forward in his chair and talks in this low, drawling voice like he's conspiring with her. "It was stupid. The whole thing was stupid. Is stupid. I've just . . ." He glances at his mom. "The past couple of years haven't been so easy." He looks at Principal Wasserman in this superintense way, like he's trying to hypnotize her. "I'm not saying there's any excuse for what I did, because I doubt there's anything I can say to you to justify what happened out there . . ."

He's a snake charmer, this one, but lucky for me, Principal Wasserman isn't a fool. She cuts him off and turns to me. "I'd like to hear what precipitated the punch in the mouth."

My dad goes, "You punched him?"

As evidence, Jack points to his face.

I say, "He grabbed me."

"Technically, I hugged her."

"It wasn't a hug. It was a grab."

Principal Wasserman goes, "Why did you grab her, Jack?"

"Because I was being an idiot. I didn't mean anything by it. I wasn't trying to scare her. Wasn't trying to bully her. I wish I had a better reason, believe me." His eyes are going, *You will forgive me. You will forget this ever happened. You will love me as all the others do.*

"Did you feel threatened, Libby?"

"I didn't feel great, if that's what you're asking."

"But did you feel threatened? Sexually?"

Oh my God.

"No. Just humiliated."

Even more so now, thanks.

"Because we don't take sexual assault lightly."

Jack's mother leans forward in her chair. "Principal Wasserman, I'm an attorney, and I'm as concerned as you are—if not more so—about what's transpired here today, but until we—"

Principal Wasserman says again, "I want to hear from Jack and Libby."

Next to me, I can feel the life go out of this boy. I glance over at him, and he looks like a shell, like someone came along and sucked away every ounce of his blood. For whatever moronic reason he grabbed me, I know he didn't mean it *like that.*

So I say, "It wasn't sexual. At all. I never felt threatened in that way."

"But you hit him."

"Not because I felt assaulted."

"Why did you hit him, then?"

"Because he grabbed me in a totally nonsexual but still really annoying and humiliating way."

The principal folds her hands on her desk. Her eyes are fixed on us like she'd turn us to stone, if only she could. "Fighting on school property is a serious charge. So is vandalism." And it takes me a minute. She holds up a scan of a photograph, which I don't need to look at because I already know what's there. She says to Jack, "Do you know anything about this?"

He leans forward to study the picture. Sits back again, shaking his head. "No, ma'am, I do not." *Ma'am.*

My dad leans in. "Let me see that, please."

As he takes the piece of paper, Principal Wasserman says, "I'm afraid someone has defaced one of our school bathrooms with derogatory comments about your daughter. I assure you it is going to be dealt with. I don't take something like this lightly either." She looks at Jack again. His mom looks at him. My dad looks at him, his jaw tensing so much I'm worried it will crack in half.

I will myself to become invisible. I shut my eyes, as if this might help. When I open them again, I'm still in the chair and everyone is staring at me. I say, "Sorry?"

My dad waves the scan. "Do you know who did this?"

I want to say no. Absolutely not.

"Libbs?"

Here's my choice—I can lie and say no. I can tell them Jack did it. Or I can tell the truth.

"Yes."

"Yes, you know who did it?"

"Yes."

Everyone waits.

"It was me."

It takes them a minute.

The boy whistles.

His mom says, "Jack."

"Sorry. But." He whistles again.

Principal Wasserman's face has fallen, and I can imagine her sitting down with her husband tonight, telling him how kids have changed, how we break her heart, how it's a good thing she's almost retired because she doesn't know that she can do this much longer.

My dad says, "Why, Libby?"

And maybe it's the way he says "Libby" instead of "Libbs," but for some stupid reason, I'm about to cry. "Because someone was going to write it."

And suddenly I feel naked, like I might as well be laid out on a dissecting table, insides exposed to the world. There's no way I can ever explain to anyone other than my dad the importance of being prepared, of always being one step ahead of everyone and everything.

"Better to be the hunter than the hunted. Even if you're hunting yourself."

My eyes meet Jack's. "Something like that."

"And then I come along to prove your point."

He holds my gaze for a few seconds, and then we both look away. We sit there, the five of us, in the most awkward silence of my life, until the principal says, "There are several different punishments I could give you. Suspension. Expulsion. In some cases, schools in Rushville and New Castle have even called in local police to make arrests."

Jack goes, "How about we let my punishment be that the entire school saw a girl kick my ass."

"Or we can prosecute you for bullying," she says to him.

Jack's mother, the attorney, nearly falls off her chair. "Before we talk about prosecuting—"

Principal Wasserman speaks over her. "And you, Libby, for fighting."

"It was self-defense!" My voice booms out, too loud and high. "When I punched him, I mean." Although the bathroom was about self-defense too.

The principal nods at Jack. "Had he let go of you by the time you hit him?"

"Only because I pulled him off me."

She shakes her head and sighs for three days. "I'm not going to make my decision right now. I want to talk to witnesses. I need to look at your records, weigh the options. But I want to make it clear that I have a zero-tolerance policy when it comes to violence, bullying, or anything that even *hints* at sexual harassment." She narrows her eyes at Jack, then at me. "I'm not too crazy about vandalism either."

We're told to wait outside Wasserman's office. The security guard and the bearded teacher go in as we come out, along with a couple of kids, God knows who, maybe my own brother. Libby and I sit side by side on a bench. I watch the door leading out of here, into the main hall, and all I can think is *Don't let Monica Chapman walk in, not with my mom in there.*

Libby looks at me. "Why did you do it?"

I want to say *Read the letter,* but right about now that letter seems like the second-worst idea I've ever had.

"Haven't you ever done something mean or stupid without thinking it through? Something you instantly regretted as soon as you did it?" She doesn't answer. So I say, "Sometimes people are just shitty. Sometimes they're shitty because they're afraid. Sometimes they choose to be shitty to others before others can be shitty to them. Like self-defensive shittiness."

Because my brain is damaged. Because I'm damaged.

"Why me? Or should I ask?"

"You shouldn't ask." There's no way in hell I'm saying the words "Fat Girl Rodeo" to her.

She rolls her eyes and looks away. "You don't think they'll suspend us. Or expel us?" She says this toward the other side of the room.

"No. This isn't my first . . ." I almost say "rodeo" but stop myself. "We'll be okay." Although honestly, I'm not so sure.

Her eyes meet mine again and I smile at her, even as I'm hating myself, and my lip starts bleeding.

"Does it hurt?"

"Yeah."

"Good."

An hour or so later, the door to the principal's office opens, and Principal Wasserman (short gray hair, glasses) waves us back in. Two men lean against the windowsill—one of them is a giant and the other is pretty skinny. Libby's dad fixes me with a look. He is broad-shouldered, like Charles Bronson, and I feel the need to say, "I'm sorry, sir."

Libby and I drop into our usual chairs. I catch my mom's eye, and she shakes her head (she wears her hair one of two ways, and today she is Mom-with-Hair-Up). I may not be able to recognize faces, but I can tell when someone is disappointed and furious, and my mom is both. I think of all the times Mom has told me to stay out of trouble, that people will be harder on me because of the way I look. I know I've let her down, and she will say I've let myself down.

The gray-headed woman props her elbows on the desk and leans forward. "I'm not going to suspend you or expel you. Not this time. Instead the two of you will perform community service together, only instead of doing this for the community, it will be community-type service for the school. We're putting you in charge of painting the bleachers and the locker rooms. Mr. Sweeney will supervise." The giant nods at us.

"The two of you will also meet with a counselor every day after school for the next few weeks. The Conversation Circle is being used effectively at more and more schools across the country, and I believe it will also be effective here. It's important that you learn from the experience and each other. Mr. Levine"—the skinny guy waves—"specializes in some of the most prevalent issues affecting teens today, including bullying, prejudice, and sexual harassment."

I clear my throat, which still feels raw. "I don't think it's fair to punish her for something I instigated. I'd rather serve the time for both of us."

Libby goes, "You are unbelievable."

"What?"

"You don't get to be the villain *and* the hero."

Principal Wasserman says, "Thank you, Jack, but Libby broke the rules as well."

As we leave, I try to say "I'm sorry" again, but Libby's father wraps his arm around her shoulders and steers her away.

In the parking lot, my mom says, "We'll discuss this at home, Jack Henry." My full name. Something she hasn't called me in years. She drives off without another word.

I go directly to Masselin's, hoping to slink in and bypass everyone—namely my dad. I'm barely settled behind the office desk when he comes walking in. "I heard what happened today. What the hell were you thinking?"

I tell him I don't know, that it was meant to be a prank, but it ended up being a really stupid idea, and I wish I hadn't done it, and all the other things I've spent the past few hours saying over and over.

"Your mother and I are disappointed in you."

As if he needs to tell me this. I want to say *I'm disappointed in you too.* But instead I say, "I know. I'm sorry."

When I'm finally alone, I turn on my phone. It immediately blows up with voicemails and texts. There's Caroline, Seth, Bailey Bishop, Kam, and about a hundred other people, including Marcus, who know all about what happened.

Bailey Bishop is crying because she can't believe I would do something so hurtful to another human being. Caroline talks mostly about herself, but my brother actually wants to know if I'm okay and what happened with the principal.

Kam's message says, *Congrats, princess. You win. Choose the place so we can take your sorry ass out for a victory meal. But hey, do me a favor and don't get your ass kicked by any other girls before then.* Followed by an entire minute of laughter.

LIBBY

The radio is playing, but the volume is low, and my dad is talking on and on. When he brings up homeschooling again, I say, "You don't need to worry about me. I can take care of myself."

"You really punched him?"

"Right in the mouth."

And then he laughs.

"Are you *laughing*?"

"I think I am."

"You're not supposed to laugh. You're supposed to tell me violence never solves anything and take away my phone or something."

"Don't punch anyone again. And if it makes you feel better, give me your phone." And he just keeps on laughing.

And now I'm laughing too. And for the first time in a long time, I feel normal, weird as that sounds. We feel normal. Which makes me think what happened today wasn't so bad after all, and maybe all the humiliation and the upcoming hours of community service and counseling are worth this single moment.

As we pull up to our house, Dad says, "Don't let that boy get in your head. Don't let him take away what you've worked so hard for."

"I won't. I'm getting up tomorrow and going back to school." I look down at my shoes and the quote written there. " 'You can't stop living.' "

JACK

I find Dusty in his room, playing video games. He's got his headphones on, and I can hear the music blasting through them—the Jackson 5, which he only listens to when he's feeling his absolute worst.

I wave at Dusty, and finally he looks up and mouths, "What?"

I mime removing headphones. I make it elaborate and exaggerated, hoping he'll laugh. He ignores me.

I start to dance. Dusty can't resist dancing. The song is "Rockin' Robin," and I don't hold back. I just go for it. I'm twisting and grooving across the floor. I'm in a music video. I'm Michael Jackson in his prime. I am the man.

"I'm the man," I say, loud enough so he can hear. I shake out the lion fro, making it as big as possible.

"You're not the man." He says it too loud, the way you always do when you're listening to the Jackson 5 at full volume through headphones.

"I am the man." I'm doing dance moves, ones he taught me. I purposely do them wrong because he won't be able to help himself. He makes me sweat it for another thirty seconds, and then he's up and the headphones are off and he starts showing me the correct steps.

We finish the song, dancing in unison, and it's awesome, but then the song is over, and Dusty drops onto his bed and gives me this look that lets me know we're only in unison on the dance floor, nowhere else.

Just to drive the point home, he goes, "You're not the man."

"I guess not." I sit next to him and we both stare at the floor.

"So which is it? Which reason made you do this shitty thing?"

I think through all the reasons I listed before—*Sometimes they're just shitty people. Sometimes people have been shitty to them. Sometimes they're shitty because they're afraid. Sometimes they choose to be shitty to others before others can be shitty to them. Sometimes someone doesn't like who he is, but then here's this other kid who knows exactly who he is, and that can make that first kid feel even worse about himself.*

"Maybe all of them. But I meant what I said. I'll never be shitty to you."

Then he looks at me, and he might as well knock me in my split lip because he goes, "You need to make it right."

"I know."

My dad finds me in the kitchen, eating standing up, and this is something we don't do anymore. It's one of the food rules we follow, along with don't eat in front of the TV, don't eat too fast, and stop eating when you're sixty percent full.

When I see him, I set the plate down. Wherever the ache is coming from—my heart, my stomach—the food isn't reaching it.

When my mom went away, I went empty too. Like all of me just flooded out and disappeared. In the hospital, I held her hand until my grandmother came in, and my dad, and the rest of my family. All of them sweet and loving and brokenhearted, but none of them like my mom. Not even all together. They didn't begin to add up to her.

My dad's eyes go to the plate, but he doesn't comment. Instead he says, "Bailey Bishop is here to see you."

Bailey stands in the center of my bedroom, head turning, hair catching the light like it's trying to grab all of it and keep it for itself.

"It's been a long time." She leans down to rub George under his chin, and surprisingly he lets her. *Traitor,* I think. Bailey says, "Didn't you have him back then?"

"I got him when I was eight." My mom and I picked him out, or rather he picked us. We went to a rescue event, and George got free of his cage and packed himself into my mom's purse. "He was supposed to die four years ago, but he's not ready."

The last time Bailey was at my house, we were ten. I had invited her and Monique Benton and Jesselle Villegas for a sleepover. The four of us stayed up all night and talked about boys and told each other our deepest, darkest secrets. Bailey's was that she tried to give her baby brother away when he was born. Mine was that I sometimes spied on the boys who lived across the street. This was before Dean, Sam, and Castiel became my only friends.

Bailey straightens and focuses all of her Bailey-ness on me and says, "I'm sorry I never came to see you. I should have come to see you. When you were in here. Well, not in here, but in your old house."

This throws me completely, and I stand there like a lump. *How does she get to be so nice and also have hair like that?* Finally, I go, "That's okay. I mean we weren't best friends or anything."

"But we were friends. I should have come."

Should I hug her? Should I tell her it's okay? Should I tell her she should have come to see me a long time ago, way before I was trapped in my house, when my dad first pulled me out of school and let me stay home?

She says, "I have to tell you something, and it's horrible, but I don't want you to have to hear about it at school." All of a sudden, she looks like she's going to cry, and at first I think she's going to tell me she's dying or maybe I'm dying.

And then she tells me about the game. How I was the grand prize in something called Fat Girl Rodeo, and how that news has spread across social media like a virus. Everyone is infected, and my two thousand classmates and many, many strangers are all weighing in (get it?) about whether they're Team Libby or Team Jack.

Someone's posted a picture of me, which they must have

snapped just after it happened, because there I am in the cafeteria, looking mad as a hatter, fist still clenched, Jack Masselin sprawled at my feet. You can't see his face, but you can see mine (dangerously red, slightly sweaty). Caption: *Don't mess with Mad Lbs.* "Lbs" as in pounds, of course. There are seventy-six comments, and only a few of them are nice. The rest say the usual: *If I was that big, I'd want to kill myself.* And: *She's pretty for a fat girl.* And: *Just looking at her makes me want to never eat again.* And simply: *LOSE WEIGHT, YOU FAT WHORE.*

This is exactly why I don't do social media. So many mean comments and snarky comments and bullying disguised as *I'm only expressing my opinion, as the Constitution of our great country requires me to do. If you don't like it, don't read it. Blah blah blah.*

I have this overwhelming urge to throw Bailey's phone away and my phone away, and then go up and down the street collecting phones so I can throw them away too.

Bailey says, "Maybe I shouldn't have said anything." She chews on a fingernail and squints up her eyes, and I can see the tears in them.

"I'm glad you did." I mean I'm not happy, obviously, but I was going to find out somehow and being told by the world's kindest person is probably the best way to do that.

I turn my phone off, and then I shut down the computer so I can't read about myself anymore. I say to Bailey, "I am sick of reading about myself." She nods in her eager-to-please Bailey way. I start pacing, which means I'm about to start talking. A lot. "For one thing, there's only so much new material you can get from the fact that I'm overweight. We get it, people. Move on."

Bailey nods like crazy. "We get it."

"And this whole 'pretty for a fat girl' thing. I mean, what is that? Why can't I just be pretty period? I wouldn't say, 'Oh, Bailey

Bishop, she's pretty for a skinny girl.' I mean, you're just Bailey. And you're pretty."

"Thank you. You're pretty too." And unlike Caroline and Kendra, I know she means it.

"And what is this whole 'fat girl equals whore' bullshit?" She flinches. "Sorry. 'Fat girl equals whore' garbage. What is that? Why am I automatically a whore? How does that even make sense?"

"It doesn't."

"If everyone who had something to say about me spent as much time on, I don't know, *practicing kindness* or *developing a personality or a soul,* imagine how lovely the world would be."

"So lovely."

I go on and on, Bailey as my cheerleader, until I run out of steam. I sink down onto my bed and say, "Why are people so concerned with how big I am?" She doesn't answer, just takes my hand and holds it. She doesn't need to answer because there is no answer. Except that only small people—the inside-small kind—don't like you to be big.

JACK

I've never built a robot before, but I'm determined. I watch a couple of YouTube videos. Consult a couple of books. By the time I'm done, I've decided it's going to be the best damn Lego robot ever.

For my eighth birthday, I asked for a hammer, screwdrivers, and wire cutters. I got my first soldering iron when I was nine. No one knows where this urge to build comes from, except that my dad has always been pretty handy, so maybe I get some of it from him. I just know that ever since I was little, making things out of thin air is what centers me, like the way other people turn to yoga or morphine. It's why we have a pizza oven and a pitching machine in our backyard, a catapult in our garage, and a weather station on the roof. When I'm working, I see the object as a whole before it ever exists, and I build my way there. It's the exact opposite of my everyday life.

But right now all I see are the pieces, which is exactly like my everyday life. Red ones here, blue ones there, white and yellow and green and black. At some point, I lie back on top of them, right on the cold concrete floor. It's uncomfortable as hell, but I tell myself, *You don't deserve comfort, asshole.*

I wonder what Libby Strout is doing right about now. I hope she's not thinking about me or today. I hope somehow she can think about something else. Anything else.

I hear footsteps on the basement stairs, and a woman appears, first her legs, then the rest of her. I assume it's my mom, because what other woman would be in the house unless Dad's decided to bring Monica Chapman in here? I look for the identifiers. This is Mom-with-Hair-Down. Her mouth is wide. She's clearly black. I try to build my way to her face, but even after I locate enough pieces to tell myself *Okay, that's her,* it's not as if the image of her snaps into place for me, and it's not as if it sticks around. I suddenly feel old and so, so tired. It's exhausting, constantly having to search for the people you love.

She says, "I don't need to tell you how disappointed I am in you. Or how angry."

"You do not." I look up at her from the floor.

"We have to hope they don't decide to press charges. You may not see yourself as black, and you may not think people see you as black, but it's a fact that our society treats kids of color more severely than others, and I do not want this following you for the rest of your life." We're both quiet as I think about my dismal, dead-end future. She says, "What are you doing?"

"I was preparing to build a Lego robot for little man, but right now I'm contemplating what an asshole I am."

"That's a start. How are you going to make this better?"

"I don't think there's any making it better, is there? There's just making it as good as I can after the fact."

"Is there anything you want to talk about? Anything you need to tell me?"

"Not tonight." *Maybe not ever.* My phone buzzes on the floor next to me.

"Get your call. You can tell me tomorrow."

Maybe.

She adds, "I love you anyway."

"I love you anyway too."

LIBBY

It's almost nine when Bailey leaves. I'm still fired up, so I dance for a while, and then I decide to do homework. I dump the contents of my backpack onto my bed and sort through my papers and notebooks and pens and gum wrappers, and all the miscellaneous rubbish I've stuffed in there, including *We Have Always Lived in the Castle,* which I carry everywhere.

Buried in the mess is a white letter-size envelope.

What's this?

I rip it open and start reading.

I'm not a shitty person, but I'm about to do a shitty thing ...

At first I think he's making it up. I read the letter again. And again.

You know how it's easy to believe everything is about you, especially when something goes wrong? *Why me? Why do I have the worst luck ever? Why is the universe so mean? Why does everyone hate me?* My mom used to say sometimes it's actually about the other person and you just happen to be there. Like sometimes the other person needs to learn a lesson or go through an experience, good or bad, and you're just an accessory in some way, like a supporting actor in whatever their scene happens to be.

Maybe, just maybe, this whole nightmare is more about Jack

Masselin than it is about me. Maybe this whole thing happened to teach him a lesson about how to treat other people.

I sit and think on that for a while. This was the thing Mom did—looked at all sides of things. She believed that situations and people were almost never black-and-white.

Ten minutes later, I'm reading everything I can find on prosopagnosia, which leads me to an artist named Chuck Close, neurologist/author Oliver Sacks, and Brad Pitt. According to the Internet, they all have face blindness. I mean, *Brad Pitt*.

What if the entire world was face-blind?

If everyone had prosopagnosia, there'd be hope for the homely. No one would ever say "You're too pretty to be fat" or "She's pretty for a fat girl" because looks would stop mattering. Would people still care if you were overweight or too thin? Tall or short? Maybe. Maybe not. But it would be a step in the right direction.

At fat camp, we had to try to put ourselves into the skin of other people, just like Atticus told Scout: *You never really understand a person until you consider things from his point of view . . . Until you climb inside of his skin and walk around in it . . .* Skin's so fascinating anyway—I mean the way it expands and shrinks. I used to weigh twice what I do now—that's *two times* more—and my skin fit me then and it fits me now. Weird.

I try to put myself in Jack Masselin's skin and imagine what he sees when he looks at me. Do I look different, in some way, from everyone else? Or do I blend in? Then I imagine that I'm the one with face blindness. *What would the world look like?*

I pull up a new document. I write:

Dear Jack,

    Thanks for explaining your douchiness. I don't think

prosopagnosia gives you the right to be a jerk, but I'm at least glad you're not rotten to your core. Maybe there's hope for you.

Libby

p.s. I have questions.

JACK

On the other end of the phone Kam says, "I wish you could have seen it. The look on her face when you threw yourself around her, and then when you just hung out there and wouldn't let go."

I force out this kind of halfhearted laugh that sounds like I'm being strangled. "Man, I bet she looked surprised."

"As surprised as that chick in *Psycho* when Norman Bates interrupts her shower. So what did Wasserman say?"

"Oh, she was really fucking thrilled. Community service and counseling. *For weeks.*"

"Shit."

"I know."

"But it was worth it."

"Says the man who doesn't have to do it."

He's laughing again. "But wait, it gets better."

Great.

"Remember the girl who got cut out of her house a couple of years ago?"

"What about her?"

"That's her."

"Who?"

"Libby Strout. She's the one you rodeoed."

I feel like I've been punched in the face again.

"Are you sure?" I try to sound like I don't really give a shit, but here's the thing—I do give a shit. I give five million shits, which is why I feel like I'm going to be sick all over these Legos.

"Oh, I'm sure." He's laughing.

I do my strangle-laugh again, only it sounds worse this time.

"Man, you sound rough."

"I think she broke my throat."

"So do you remember her?"

"Yeah. I do."

Outside, the neighborhood is asleep. I climb out my window and into the tree that acts as a ladder to the roof. I snake all the way up it until I'm there, and then I walk to the edge, over by the gutter. My weather station is anchored near the chimney, battered and lopsided. When I was six, I fell off the roof and cracked my head open. Without thinking, I reach up to feel the scar.

I run my fingers along it as I stare across the street. If I stand here long enough, I can see it—the gaping hole where the front wall of her house used to be.

THREE YEARS EARLIER

I dream that the street's on fire. And then I wake up to sirens. I lie still and listen as they come blaring toward the house. It's end-of-days dark in here, but suddenly the ceiling flashes red and the sirens wind to a stop. I'm up and out of bed and grabbing shit off my dresser and bookshelves before I even know what's happening.

On my way out, I fall headfirst into the hallway, where I hear but don't see my dad, who says from the black recesses of his bedroom, "It's not us. Go back to bed."

But the dream was *so damn real* that I'm still half in it, and I keep right on going. Outside, the air is cold but smells clean. No fire, no smoke. I'm still holding the shit I grabbed—my granddad's watch, my retainer, a stack of baseball cards, my phone charger (but no phone)—and of course there's no jacket.

It's the house across the street. Rolling up in front is this line of fire trucks, an ambulance, two police cars. I figure it must be drug lords or a meth lab or maybe even a terrorist. I think it would be really damn cool to have a terrorist on our street because Amos, Indiana, is one boring-ass place.

"Whose house is that?" It's Mom behind me.

"Strom, Stein . . ." This from Dad.

"Strout," says Marcus, who's twelve, almost thirteen, and *knows everything*.

I say before he can, "The Strouts moved out years ago." The house has been empty since then. You never see anyone coming or going.

"No, they didn't." My other brother—Dusty, seven—is hopping on one leg. "Tams and me went over last week and looked in the windows."

"Dusty." Mom shakes her head.

"What? We wanted to see the fat girl."

"We don't say 'fat.' It's not polite."

"Teacher says 'fat' is an adjective just like 'beautiful' or 'handsome.' It's only people that make it a bad word by saying 'Listen up, fatso,' or 'Hey, look at that fat-ass.'"

Mom frowns at my dad like, *He's your fault,* and he says, "Dustin," in a warning tone, but I can tell he's trying not to laugh.

I say, "Mrs. Buckley?" Dusty stares up at me, still on one leg. He nods. I nod. "That's about right." Mrs. Buckley is a very large woman.

"Jack." Mom sighs. My mom is always sighing. "Let's go. Back inside. It's cold. You've got school tomorrow." If we don't stop her, she'll list a hundred and one reasons why we need to get off this lawn.

Just then another fire truck comes roaring up, siren blaring, and then this white truck comes lumbering along behind and this one's pulling a crane.

A *crane.*

We watch in silence as the firefighters and police and these construction workers, who suddenly seem to be everywhere, set up giant spotlights. The front door to the house opens and closes, and people are moving like ants, scrambling across the yard and disappearing inside and blocking off the street. By now, all the lights on the street are on and every lawn is covered with gawkers. We're directly across from it all, front-row seats.

A man walks toward us, hands in pockets, glancing over his shoulder at all the commotion. He says to me, "Can you believe this?" He nods over at the house.

"I really can't," I say, and then Dad goes, "I thought that house was empty." He says it to the man, who falls in beside him, and they stand side by side, watching. There's an ease to it that makes me think my dad must know him, and then my mom calls the man Greg and asks about his daughter Jocelyn, the one at Notre Dame, and that's how I know it's Mr. Wallin, our next-door neighbor.

I stand there surrounded by the fire trucks and the spotlights and that giant crane, ruminating on my brain and how it's so weirdly, strangely different from Marcus's or Dusty's or the brain of anyone else I know. It's *so* weirdly, strangely different that for the past year I've been writing about it—not my life story, but a sort of *This is me, this is what I think* log because I like to understand how things work. Other brains are simple and uncomplicated, and there's room in them for Mr. Wallin and his daughter Jocelyn, whereas my brain seems to be made for bigger things. Baseball. Physics. Aeronautical engineering. Maybe president. This is the reason I don't watch a lot of TV or movies. I tell myself my brain is too busy thinking important things to keep track of the characters.

I watch as a news van rolls in, all the way from Indianapolis, and think again, *Terrorists.* I mean, what else could it be?

LIBBY
AGE 13

It's the feeling of being suffocated.

What being strangled must be like.

My world has tilted away and gone light and floaty, and maybe it's actually more like floating in space. I try to move my head. My arms. My legs. But I can't.

When I was little, my mom read me this story about a girl who lived in a garden and was never allowed outside the walls. The garden was all she knew, and to her that was the whole world.

I'm thinking about this girl now as I'm trying to breathe. I see my dad's face but he looks a hundred years away, like I'm circling the moon and he's down on earth, and I'm trying to remember the name of the story.

I suddenly need to remember. This is what happens when people die. They start to disappear if you don't watch it. Not all at once, but a piece here, a piece there.

Think.

The father was Italian.

Rappaccini.

Rappaccini's daughter.

Did the girl have a name?

I try to raise my head so I can ask my dad, but he says, "Stay very still," from way down on earth. "Help is coming, Libby."

Not Libby, I think. *Rappaccini's daughter. I am here in my gar-*

*den, and the world has stopped, and my heart has stopped, and I am
all alone.*

Then I hear something that brings me back to this planet, this
town, this neighborhood, this street, these four walls. The sound
of the garden being torn away, the sound of my world crumbling.

JACK
AGE 14

Five hours later, the top half of the house has been demolished by a team of sledgehammers and circular saws. The emergency workers have erected scaffolding and a long, wide bridge up to the second-floor window. They've fitted supports to keep the roof from collapsing, and when the sun comes up, they unroll this black tarp and circle the house with it—for privacy, I guess.

It's clear that something needs to come out of there, and whatever it is, it's big.

I sit on our roof so I can see right over the tarp. An enormous stretcher—I'm not sure what else to call it—is hauled out of the truck and rolled up onto the bridge. The emergency workers are racing back and forth, and a handful of them anchor the stretcher in place. And then the crane goes cranking forward and reaches its claw into the bowels of the house.

The tree outside my bedroom window suddenly starts to shake and a head appears. This skinny little kid pulls himself up next to me. "Move over," he says.

I make room for him, and together we sit there. We watch as the claw comes up and out, and inside the claw is a pair of arms and a pair of legs.

"Is she dead?" Dusty whispers.

"I don't know."

The arms start waving and the legs begin kicking. It's like King Kong clutching Ann Darrow. "Not dead," I say.

The crane sweeps around till it's above the bridge and all that scaffolding, and then lowers itself over the stretcher. Very gently, like it's playing a game of pickup sticks, the crane releases the arms and legs until I can see that they belong to a girl.

The largest girl I've ever seen.

"Told you," Dusty says.

The sky is bright and blinding. It's like I've never seen it before, and oh, it's so beautiful and I'm alive! I'm alive! If I die right now, at least I've seen the sky like this—all blue and brilliant and new.

My chest is still clenching, but some of the clenching releases and it's because these nice men and women are here and I'm not dead and I'm not going to die in there, in that house. Not to say I won't die here in the yard, but at least the air is fresh and I can breathe and there are trees and sky and birds and over there a cloud, a fluffy one, and there is the smell of something, flowers maybe. I want to say *Look at me, Dean, Sam, Cas! I'm out here just like you.* And then I think how they're my only friends, even though they don't know it. And oh my God, I'm crying again, but then I must pass out because when I wake up I'm being bumped all around, and I'm in the back of a truck, not even an ambulance like a regular person. I stare up at dingy metal instead of blue, and all at once I feel humiliated. How many people did it take to break me out?

I try to ask my dad, who sits back against the rattling metal wall, head jostling up and down, but his eyes are closed, and I can't speak and suddenly I think, *What if I never speak again?*

Dad opens his eyes and sees me staring at him, and he smiles, but he's not fast enough. My chest is clenching tighter and tighter, and I don't want to be here in this truck. I want to be in my bed, in my room, in my house. I don't want to be out here, in this world.

I want to say *Take me home, please, if there's anything left of it,* but then something sweeps over me, and it's this kind of quiet, peaceful feeling, and that's her, that's my mom. I breathe slower, to try to make it last, to try to keep her with me. *Live live live live . . .* I think it as hard as I can before everything goes black, and as I drift off I remember.

Rappaccini's daughter.

Beatrice.

Her name was Beatrice.

JACK
AGE 14

When I get home from school that day, a security vehicle is parked in front and a guard sits behind the wheel, sound asleep. I check to see if anyone is looking and then I walk right in.

There's only half a living room. The sofa is oversize and drooping in the middle like a hammock. A framed picture lies faceup on the floor, and it's of a man and a woman and a little girl. The girl is out of focus, and you can tell she's laughing. In the photo, she's just a regular-size kid.

The kitchen is a typical kitchen. For the most part, it's intact, only a little dust. I go to the fridge first because I can't help it, I want to see what's in there. I expect a banquet suitable for Henry VIII, but it's just your run-of-the-mill stuff—eggs, milk, deli meat, cheese, diet sodas, juice. On the outside of the door is a single magnet: OHIO WELCOMES YOU.

I walk through the whole house. It's smaller than ours, and it doesn't take me long to find her bedroom. Even though part of the front wall is missing, I don't go in because it doesn't feel respectful. Instead, I stand in the doorway. The walls—the ones that are left—are lavender, and there are bookshelves, floor to ceiling, on every single one. The books look like they might spill out and overtake the room, maybe the whole house.

The bed is the focal point of the room and looks specially built. It's a king-size bed that pretty much fills all the space. It sits on top of this metal—steel?—platform, and beside it is a single pair of slippers. It's the slippers that get me. They look delicate, like they were made for a girl Dusty's age. The sheets have daisies on them, and they're thrown all around, as if a tornado's blown through. One of the pillows lies on the floor. A stack of books sits by the bed, and it takes me a second to see that these are six copies of the same book, *We Have Always Lived in the Castle* by Shirley Jackson, although the bindings are different. I think, *She must really love that book.*

When I leave, I try not to touch anything except for one copy of the Shirley Jackson book and the Ohio magnet, both of which I take. I don't know why. Maybe it makes me feel closer to the girl who lives there. Outside, the guard is still sleeping, and I rap on the glass to wake him up. When he rolls down the window, I say, "Stay alert, buddy. I imagine everything they own is in that house, and they've been through enough without losing it to looters." Of course the book and magnet don't count.

I knock on the door of Marcus's room and then walk on in. His walls are covered with posters—mostly of basketball players. There's a hoop attached to the closet door. A gangly, shaggy-haired kid hunches on the floor in front of his computer. He's playing a video game—the shoot-everyone-and-blow-shit-up kind.

I do what I usually do—look for the signs that this is my brother. The pointy chin, the messy hair, the mopey expression. I look for the pieces and put them together because this is how I know it's him.

"Can I ask you a question?"

"What?" He doesn't take his eyes off the screen.

"How do you remember people so well? How do you tell them apart?"

"*What?*"

"Take Squinty."

"Her name's Patrice."

"Whatever. Patrice. How do you pick her out of a crowd?"

"She's my girlfriend."

"I know she's your girlfriend."

"Do you know what she'd do to me if I couldn't pick her out of a crowd?"

"Yeah, but what is it about her that tells you it's her?"

He pauses the game. Stares at me for, like, a whole minute. "I just look at her. I just know. What's wrong with you? Have you gone crazy?"

My eyes move past him to the walls of basketball players. I want to ask if he can tell them apart without their jersey numbers or names on the back. When I look at him again, he's still staring at me, only his features have shifted so that he's brand-new. I say, "Never mind. I'm just messing with you."

I go back into my room and dig out the old composition notebook I keep hidden away in a drawer and start flipping through it. This is where I sort out the projects I build—drawing them, planning them out. But in between the brainstorms and sketches and blueprints and lists of materials needed, there are passages like these:

Went to Clara's Pizza with the family. Got lost coming back from bathroom. Took me a while to find them. Dad finally had to wave me down.

I was so wiped out after Saturday's game (we won in straight innings) I didn't even recognize Damario Raines when he came up to congratulate me.

Every few pages, entry after entry. Nothing earth-shattering or alarming until you start adding them up. As I'm reading them now, a feeling settles over me like a blanket, but not the warm, comforting kind. More like a thick and scratchy blanket thrown over the head just before you're shoved into the trunk of a car.

There is something wrong with me.

Of all the people in the world, I feel like the girl would understand. I sit there the rest of the night thinking, *I hope she makes it.* And even though the news is protecting her identity, and all I know is her last name, I write her a letter to tell her this, tuck it into her favorite book, and go online to find the mailing address for the local hospital.

Dr. Weiss is thin and tall and probably couldn't gain weight if he tried. He's worried I'm trying to kill myself. I tell him, "If I wanted to kill myself, there are faster ways to do it."

He stands beside my hospital bed with his arms crossed. His face is hard to read because he does this thing where he can frown and smile at the same time. He says, "Your father says you've been housebound for six months."

"It depends on when you start counting. For five months and twenty-four days, I've been too large to get through the door. But my last day of school was two years ago."

"There are two important things we need to understand here: why you had this panic attack and why you gained the weight. That's what we need to address. It will be a process and it will take time, but we are going to get you healthy again."

I glance at my dad, in the armchair across from me. He knows as well as I do what the Why is. It's everything changing when I was ten. It's the bullying and the fear. So much fear of everything, but mostly death. Sudden, out-of-the-blue death. It's also me being terrified of life. It's the giant emptiness in my chest. It's touching my face or my skin and feeling nothing. This is the Why of me staying home in the first place. And the Why of me eating. And the Why of me ending up here. But that doesn't mean I want to die.

· · ·

On the day before I leave the hospital, the nurse brings me a package, no return address. Most everyone else is sending me letters, not packages, which is the only reason I open it. That and the fact that my dad isn't here to take it away before I can.

Inside is a handwritten note without a name or signature, and a copy of my favorite book. One of my actual very own copies of my favorite book, with my initials on the cover and my highlights throughout.

I thought you might want this. Unlike the other letters, this one is nice. *I want you to know I'm rooting for you.* For the first time in a long time, I touch my skin and feel something.

When Rachel Mendes—tutor and caregiver—arrives, I lay the book down and tell her the thing I've been wanting to say but no one will hear. I pull up one of the news articles on my new phone, my first phone, the one my dad bought me so I can call him if I need anything.

I enlarge the picture of me, taken the day I was rescued from our house. "This girl," I tell Rachel. "That's not what I look like. That's not who I am." I have a feeling Rachel will get this because she pretended to be straight all through high school, even though she figured out she was a lesbian when she was in eighth grade.

I say it again, "That's not me."

Her eyes light up. "Great. Let's see if we can find her."

NOW

LIBBY

I throw open my locker before first period, and something flutters out and lands on my shoe. It's a piece of paper folded in thirds. I stare at it for a while because it's been my experience that pieces of paper folded in thirds are not a good thing.

I finally pick it up and hold it inside my locker, where no one will see.

America's Fattest Teen Rescued from House

It's an article from the Internet, and there I am, in a blurry photo, being wheeled across the front lawn by emergency workers.

On the other side is a giant picture of my giant face taken yesterday in the cafeteria. Beside it someone's written, *Congratulations on being voted MVB High's Fattest Teen!*

I close the door and rest my forehead against the metal of the locker because my head is going hot and I feel dizzy, which is sometimes how it starts. *Is this what she felt the day she drove herself to the hospital? Is this how it began for her?*

The metal cools me for only a second, but then it's hotter than my skin and I'm worried I'll burn myself. I concentrate on lifting my head till it's sitting upright on my neck once again. The hallway tilts. I open the locker door and focus on the jacket hook, my books, my little corner of the universe. I breathe.

• • •

In first period, Mick from Copenhagen is talking to me, but I'm too busy to listen because I'm writing my resignation letter from school.

> **Dear Principal Wasserman,**
>   **Thank you so much for this educational opportunity. Unfortunately, I will not be able to continue here at MVB High because it is overrun by imbeciles.**

I cross this out and write,

> **because of an unfortunate epidemic of imbeciles.**
> **Unfortunate epidemic of imbecility?**

I say to Mick from Copenhagen, "Which sounds better to you? 'An unfortunate epidemic of imbeciles' or 'an unfortunate epidemic of imbecility'? Or do you think it sounds stronger to say a place is 'overrun by imbeciles'?"

He laughs, and lines like the sun's rays frame the corners of his eyes. "Libby Strout. I'm amazed by you. You turn the hell out of me on."

At least that's one person.

JACK

As far as days go, this is pretty much the worst one ever.

You think it's funny to harass women?

You think bullying is funny?

Eating disorders aren't funny, asshole.

I want to go, *The whole reason I fucking did this was not to piss you people off.*

I'm also getting a lot of:

That was hilarious. You're fearless, man.

Good one, dude. You're awesome.

And:

Nice lip, Mass. What's the other guy look like? Oh wait—the other GIRL.

Hey, Masselin, don't piss off [insert name of tiny freshman girl], she might kick your ass.

The only good news is that I can't tell who's yelling things at me as they pass me in the hall.

Caroline Lushamp holds my hand between first and second period, and when someone shouts at me she says, "Just ignore them." Suddenly, she's the sweet Caroline of years ago, and I concentrate on the feel of her hand in mine.

Throughout the day, more printed-out articles show up in my locker. I try to tell myself to look on the positive side—at least my peers are using the Internet for something other than social media and porn. But honestly, it's not very comforting. By fourth period, it's clear that everyone, even the janitors, knows me as the Girl Who Had to Be Cut Out of Her House. I'm Indiana's high school version of Typhoid Mary. In each class, I sit alone, like fatness is catching.

Moons ago, when I was getting all that hate mail, my dad talked to an attorney who told us to hang on to everything just in case something terrible happened, like I was murdered. That way there would be a paper trail to possible suspects.

News reporter: Do you feel worried? Do you fear for your safety?

Me: You know, I'm glad you asked that. Maybe I should be scared right now, but I honestly think the people writing these letters need to be pitied more than feared. It's been my experience that the people who are most afraid are the ones who hide behind mean and threatening words.

I stuff the articles in my backpack. I don't think anyone at MVB is planning to kill me, but you can never be too safe.

I return to the cafeteria even though this is the last place on earth I want to be. I walk in, and six hundred heads turn at once. Six hundred mouths start buzzing. Twelve hundred eyes follow me as I walk. I feel my breath abandon ship like it's saying *Every man for himself! Good luck to you, you're on your own.* I move on without it, taking one step, two steps, three steps. I'm counting them the way my trainers and counselors taught me to do.

It is thirty-seven steps to the round table by the window, where Iris, Bailey, and Jayvee De Castro are sitting. I clutch the back of the chair, and it feels so solid and comforting that I almost remain standing, gripping it with all my might. But then I lower myself into the seat and say, "Well, that was fun."

Bailey says, very low, because, let's face it, the people around us are trying to listen, "I've known Jack Masselin since seventh grade and I can't believe he would do this. I mean, okay, he's not exactly a model student, and there was that one time junior year— his junior year, our sophomore year—when he and Dave Kaminski kidnapped a freshman and locked him on the roof outside the second-floor boys' bathroom—"

"Walt Casey." Jayvee shakes her head, and her bob makes a *swish swish* sound. "Poor Walt."

Iris freezes midsip. "What's wrong with Walt?"

"He's just . . . off." Jayvee frowns across the cafeteria at a boy I assume must be Poor Walt Casey, sitting by himself. As if he's trying to illustrate her point, he starts picking his nose.

Bailey keeps right on. "But I mean, if you'd told me something like that happened and asked me to guess who was behind it, I never would have guessed Jack Masselin. Never. There are a lot of other people I would have guessed before him. Dave Kaminski being one, and Seth Powell. And the Hunts, of course, and Reed Young and Shane Oguz and Sterling Emery . . ." On and on, naming every boy in the history of the universe.

"I think he's really sorry he did it."

They look at me.

"He wasn't thinking. He did this stupid thing and he feels pretty bad about it."

Iris goes, "You're defending him?"

"I'm just crawling around inside his skin."

Jayvee says, "Atticus Finch." She holds up a hand so we can high-five. "If it was me he did that to, I'd go super-ninja on him." Jayvee would go super-ninja on anyone who pissed her off.

"Haven't you ever done something you regretted?" I look right at Bailey.

Jayvee says, "Does last year's school picture count?"

I poke at my food—at this lunch my dad so carefully prepared—and then shove it aside. I can't eat. Not in here where everyone is staring at me. Iris says, "Did you hear about Terri Collins? She's moving to Minnesota."

Jayvee's hair goes *swish swish swish*. "Poor Terri."

I say, "She's a Damsel, right?"

Jayvee holds up a finger. *"Was."*

JACK

In the cafeteria, Kam and Seth and the other idiots I call friends can't talk about anything else. Seth is giving those who missed it a play-by-play.

"Shit, Mass," one of the idiots says, and you can hear the admiration in his voice, see it there on his face.

I hitch up one corner of my mouth, as if I'm just too fucking cool to smile all the way, and hold up my hands like, *Whatever, man, all in a day's work.* "That's why I'm me and you're you, baby." I slap Seth five and go back to watching the large girl by the window, who I'm pretty sure is Libby Strout.

At some point I feel Kam staring at me. "Whatcha looking at?"

"Nothing."

He turns and looks toward the window, hangs out there for a few seconds, then turns back to me.

"You know, sometimes I can't figure you out. Are you as dickish as the rest of us? Or is there a heart beating in that underdeveloped chest of yours?"

I fake-grin. "I couldn't possibly be as dickish as the rest of you."

And this is why I like Kam, in spite of himself. He's no dummy, and someday, about fifteen or twenty years from now, he may even become a nice guy. Which is more than I can say for the rest of them.

Seth and the others are congratulating me on how goddamn

hilarious I am, and I'm feeling smaller and smaller, when a girl comes over, trailed by a group of girls, and they all look exactly the same. Same hair. Same lip gloss. Same clothes. Same bodies. The leader goes, "Why don't you pick on someone your own size, Jack Masselin?" And empties her Diet Snapple on my head.

Someone yells, "Not the hair! Anything but the hair!" Laughter.

I jump to my feet, dripping everywhere, and now people are applauding. The girl goes storming away, and Kam says to me, "If you're only picking on people your own size, I'm afraid that's going to limit you to freshmen." And then he pulls out his flask, unscrews the top, and—for the first time ever—offers it to me.

"I hope that's orange juice." It's a woman's voice, over my shoulder.

I'm looking at Kam, and he goes, "Of course, Mrs. Chapman. Vitamin C is not only crucial to our development, it protects us from scurvy."

Monica Chapman shakes her head at Kam and then, in front of everyone, turns to me and goes, "I wanted to make sure you're okay." She's eyeing my wet clothes and the puddle of Diet Snapple at my feet.

"I'm super, thanks."

"I know today can't be easy." To her credit, she lowers her voice, but this actually makes it worse. Like she's conspiring with me. As if we're the ones with the secret. "There's nothing that bonds people more than judging someone else, and even when we've done something wrong, it often doesn't warrant those judgments . . ."

And now she's talking about her, not me. I feel the rubber band compressing my cold, dead heart snap in two, and without a word, I'm outta there.

LIBBY

I escape outside into the fresh air and let out all the breath I've been holding for the past hour. *You returned to the crime scene and you survived.* Now that I can breathe again, it's coming in a rush, and I feel dizzy from so much oxygen in my chest and in my brain. It's important I keep my blood pressure low and steady. It's a matter of life and death. I am serious. Life. And. Death. Because this could be how it starts—soaring blood pressure followed by dizziness followed by goodbye, Libby.

It can run in families.

Like that, the time machine that lives in my head teleports me back to that day. I'm standing beside my mom's bed and wondering how something like this—her, unconscious in that bed—could happen.

"She looks peaceful," my dad said on the ride to the hospital. "Like she's sleeping."

In the ICU, my mom was connected to all these tubes and wires, and a machine was breathing for her. I didn't know what to do, so I sat by her and then I took her hand, and she was still warm, but not as warm as usual. I squeezed her fingers, but not too hard because I didn't want to hurt her. Her head was back, her eyes open, like she was just waking up. She didn't look peaceful. She looked empty.

I said, "I'm here. Please don't go. Please stay. Wake up. Please wake up. Please don't leave me. Please please please. If anyone can come back, it's you. Please come back. Please don't go. Please don't leave me alone." Because if she went away, that's what I would be.

Outside the school, the sky is a mix of white and blue, but the cool air feels like a kiss against my hot, hot skin.

I dig a marker out of my bag. I find a blank space on one sneaker. I write: **You just hold your head high and keep those fists down. (Harper Lee, To Kill a Mockingbird)** I tell my brain to focus on the good—the fact that no one tried to ride me like a bull in the cafeteria today, the fact that I seem to have three actual friends, and the fact that Terri Collins is moving to Minnesota. *The Damsels will need to replace her.* Yet I can't seem to shake the feeling that everyone belongs here but me.

I think about Mary Katherine Blackwood from *We Have Always Lived in the Castle.* I've always loved her and felt sorry for her because she's quirky and weird, just like me, and—I've told myself—misunderstood. But right now I have this unsettling, someone's-hiding-in-the-closet feeling, like maybe I was wrong. Maybe it's better that she's locked away from the rest of the world. Maybe she's not cut out to live like other people with other people. Maybe she belongs in that house forever.

JACK

In the ocean of people, I see this very large girl coming toward me, and it's her—Libby Strout. A group of girls elbows each other, and even though they're whispering, I can hear them say something about Fat Girl Rodeo. They stare at Libby, and that's the moment it hits me, square in the face. This is what I've done to her—painted a giant red target on her back.

As they're gawking, she stops in front of me and hands me a note. "Here." This sends the girls into a giggling fit, and I can already hear the gossip mill churning.

LIBBY

After school, I walk down a flight of stairs off the main hall to the creepy basement, which is where the old basketball court is, the one they used years ago before they built a million-dollar sports complex that seats ten thousand people. Jack Masselin leans back on the bleachers, legs stretched in front of him, elbows propped on the riser behind him, chatting with Travis Kearns from driver's ed, a smiling girl with long brown hair, and a boy with a smooth, shaved head who I think is Keshawn Price, basketball star. They're hanging on Jack Masselin's every word, and he looks up, sees me, and keeps right on talking.

Or maybe he doesn't see me. Although I am the largest girl in here.

I sit apart from them, on the front row. This gym can fit probably six hundred, and there's something about it that feels sad and neglected, which, of course, it is. With every laugh coming from the group above me, I feel more and more invisible. Two other kids wander in, but I don't know their names. The girl sits next to me, about a foot away, and the boy takes a seat one row up. The girl leans over and goes, "I'm Maddy."

"Libby."

"Is this the Conversation Circle?"

But right then Mr. Levine moseys in. "Hello, hello. Thank you all for being here today." He stops in front of the bleachers, hands on hips. He's wearing an orange bow tie and matching orange sneakers, and except for the gray hair, he looks like he could be one of us.

He says, "Let's get this out of the way. I'm not going to talk to you about the importance of tolerance, equality, and realizing that we're all in this together because I don't think you're stupid and completely lacking moral fiber. I think you're smart individuals who did really stupid things. Who wants to start?"

We all sit there. Even Jack Masselin goes silent. Mr. Levine keeps on. "How about 'Why are you here?' The real reason, not 'Principal Wasserman made me do this.'"

I'm waiting for someone to say something. When no one does, I say, "I'm here because of him." And point at Jack.

Mr. Levine shakes his head. "Actually, you're here because you vandalized school property, and because you punched him."

One of the guys goes, "Nice."

Jack says, "Shut up."

"Gentlemen. And I use that term loosely." Mr. Levine says to me, "You could have walked away."

"Would you have walked away?"

"I'm not the one he grabbed."

"Okay." I take a breath. "How about I'm here because I lost my temper. Because when someone grabs you out of the blue and won't let go, you panic, especially when everyone's watching you and no one's doing anything to help you, and everybody but you seems to think it's funny. I'm here because I didn't know if it stopped there or if he was going to do something more than just hold on."

Everyone is staring at Jack, at me. Mr. Levine is nodding. "Jack, buddy, feel free to jump in."

"I'm good."

That's what he says. *I'm good.* Lounging there with his bored expression, and that giant explosion of hair, too full of himself to participate.

"If he doesn't have anything to say, I'll go again." If there's anything I'm good at in this world it's being counseled. I've had years of it, and I know how to talk about myself and the Whys of things. Even in front of a room of strangers.

Mr. Levine says, "Great. The floor is apparently all yours, Libby."

"After they cut me out of my house, I was in the hospital for a while, and even when I was strong enough to go home, the doctor kept me there because he said I couldn't leave till I understood the Why. Why was I there. Why did I gain all that weight."

Mr. Levine doesn't interrupt, but you can tell he's really, truly listening. So is everybody else, even Travis Kearns. I keep talking because I've been over this a hundred times, so much that it's barely a part of me anymore. It's just a truth that lives outside me in the world. *Libby got too big. Libby was cut out of her house. Libby got help. Libby got better.* If there's anything I've learned from counseling and losing my mom, it's that it's best to just say what's on your mind. If you try to carry everything around all the time, pretty soon you end up flat on your back in bed, too big to get up or even turn over.

"So the Why was a lot of things. It was inheriting my dad's Hulk-size thighs and slow metabolism. It was being bullied on the playground. It was my mom dying and the way she died, and me being afraid and me feeling alone and worrying, always worrying, and Dad being sad, and Dad loving food and loving to cook, and me wanting him to feel better and also wanting me to feel better."

I hear a "Damn, girl," from Keshawn before Mr. Levine says, "Well done, Libby."

A couple of the kids applaud.

"Thank you." For some reason, this means something, not the applause, but Mr. Levine. What he thinks of me matters. "I was housebound for a while, so I had a lot of time to think about it. And I've had a lot of time to think about it since."

We all look at Jack, but he says nothing.

Mr. Levine turns back to me. "So why did you punch him?"

I want to go *Look at him. He's perfect. He's never had a bad day. Okay, he has this strange disorder that keeps him from recognizing people, but no one's ever called him fat or ugly or disgusting. No one's sent him hate mail or told him he would have been better off killing himself. His parents never received hate mail just for having him. Also, he has parents. I doubt he knows what it's like to lose someone he loves. People like us, we can't touch him because he's too good for you and me and the rest of these kids and this punishment. Not to mention his friends utterly suck.*

I want to say *Why* wouldn't *I punch him?*

But I don't really have an answer other than "I was mad."

And I know it's not enough because of the look on Mr. Levine's face. I've seen it before. It's the look counselors get when they analyze you, when they know the answer before you do, but they're not going to tell you because you have to think of it yourself.

JACK

When it's my turn, I say, "The real reason I'm here is because I'm king douchelord of the universe."

The guy with the bow tie who must be Mr. Levine goes, "In English, please, Jack."

I hunch forward and stare at the floor. I look like I'm trying to come up with just the right words, which I am. But the main reason is so I can avoid eye contact. Sometimes I want to close my eyes and forget that I can see. Because sometimes being face-blind feels a lot like being regular blind.

Mr. Levine says, "What's your Why?"

"I don't have a Why, only an Oh Shit and a What Was I Thinking." I crack a grin at him, and then I catch Libby's eye. I stare at her and she stares back. *She's read my letter. She can out me right here.* I wait for her to say something. When she doesn't, I clear my throat. "For what it's worth, I wish I hadn't done it." It's the first honest thing I've said all day.

Afterward, she finds me in the parking lot, half in the Land Rover, phone to my face.

"So when did you put it in there?"

"What?"

"The letter."

I say into the phone, "I'm going to have to call you back," and hang up on Caroline just as she goes, *Who are you talking to?* I say to Libby, "When I grabbed you."

"Did you think a letter was going to magically make everything okay?"

"Did it?"

"What do you think?"

"You can't blame a guy for trying."

I flash her a smile, but she shakes her head and waves a finger at my face. "Don't do that."

"All right. Let's be real, then. You said you've got questions. Ask me anything." My phone buzzes in my pocket.

"How long have you known about the face blindness?"

"I figured it out around fourteen. It wasn't this kind of overnight revelation, though. It was more like this process. I had to put the clues together, so it took a while."

"So you can see my face, but you can't remember it."

"Something like that. It's not like faces are a blank. I see eyes, noses, mouths. I just can't associate them with specific people. Not like how you, as in Libby, can take a mental snapshot of someone and store it away in your mind for next time. I take a snapshot, and it immediately goes in the trash. If it takes you one or two meetings to be able to remember someone, it can take me a hundred. Or never. It's kind of like amnesia or like trying to tell everyone apart by their hands."

She glances down at her hands and then at mine. "So when you turn away and then you turn back, you're not sure who I am?"

"Intellectually, I get that it's you. But I don't *believe* it, if that makes sense. I have to convince myself all over again *This is Libby.* I know that sounds crazy." *What's crazy is standing here talking about this to someone other than myself.*

"Is it true it's hard to watch TV or movies because you can't keep the characters straight?"

"Like people, some shows and movies are harder than others. Monster movies and cartoons are easy. Crime shows aren't so much. I'm always wondering, *Where's the bad guy?* And *Who the hell is that?*"

I'm looking at her, and I'm charged with all this crazy, heart-pounding adrenaline. It's almost as if she's interviewing me, but I don't mind because it's the first time I've talked about this with anyone, and it's kind of feeling a lot like *freedom,* like *Here's a person who might actually be able to get who I am.*

"How is it, you know, to have it?"

"It's like having a circus in my mind and always jumping through hoops. It's like being in a crowded room where at first you don't know anyone. Always."

Her eyes go bright and kind of intense. "Like coming back to school five years later and you're trying to figure out if you knew him or her or them, but everyone looks different, and so the people you knew before are just . . . people."

"Right. You don't know their histories and details, all the things that make them who they are now. And you're the only one who feels that way."

"While the rest of them go to class and go to lunch like, *Oh, look at me, I've been doing this forever. I know you and I know you and time never stopped, and here I am.*"

"Yeah."

Her eyes are large and the lashes are long. The color of her eyes is this very clear light brown. Like amber or whiskey. I'm having a hard time seeing the girl in the crane in this girl here. Even though the girl in front of me is big, she's much more delicate in person.

She goes, "Do you ever wonder if it's everyone else who sees the world differently? Like, maybe you see people the way they're supposed to be seen?"

"Identifiers. That's what I call it. Everyone has at least one thing that stands out."

"Is that why your hair's so big?"

"My hair's big because it's so damn awesome, baby."

She makes this *hmm* sound as if she doesn't quite believe it, and then she tilts her head to one side, scrunches up her forehead, and says, "I feel like I know you. You know, from way back when."

My pulse speeds up. It starts buzzing the way my phone is buzzing. I'm thinking, *You don't know me, you don't know me,* like I have some power over her mind and, whatever happens, she cannot find out I was there that day she was rescued from her house. If she does find out, she might think I'm making fun of her *because* I saw her being rescued from her house, that this is why I grabbed her.

She says, "Did you go to Westview Elementary?"

"No, ma'am." Before I can say anything else, my phone buzzes again.

"Do you need to get that? Someone really wants to talk to you."

"They can wait."

She's still studying me, but finally she shakes her head as if she's clearing the slate. "I'm having that 'I feel like I know you' feeling a lot these days."

"You're in good company. Or maybe shitty company, depending on how you look at it." I smile. She almost does, but stops herself. "With face blindness, I seem to constantly lose the people I love."

She goes quiet for a second. "I know what that's like." And walks away.

• • •

I drive home and collect my little brother, and we scavenge the garage for robot materials. This is where I store the wreckage from all the creations I've built and later taken apart.

I say, "Hey, little man, how was school today?"

"Okay."

"Real okay or fake okay?"

"Somewhere in between."

LIBBY

I meet Rachel in the park. We sit on our usual bench and she says, "So why did you punch him?"

Because I'm ready for my normal life. I just want to move forward like everyone else without being grabbed in cafeterias as if I'm some sort of prize heifer at a rodeo.

I tell myself, *This is the person you can say anything to, the person who knows you better than anyone.* But all I come up with is "I was mad."

And then I think of three more questions I want to ask Jack.

The next afternoon, Mr. Levine is practicing free throws when we all walk into the gym. He says, "You're here. Excellent. Keshawn, Travis, Jack, and Libby, you'll be playing Natasha, Andy, Maddy, and me."

"Playing what?"

"Basketball, Mr. Thornburg." And he throws the ball to Keshawn, who catches it one-handed.

"Shouldn't it be all of us against Keshawn? You know, just to make it more even."

"Quiet up, Mass." Keshawn sinks a basket from the door, which is no surprise. During the time Rip Van Libby was sleeping, he's become Mr. Basketball three years running.

"This isn't about winning or losing. It's not a competition. This is about teamwork." We all stare at Mr. Levine, who's doing this crazy back-and-forth shuffle-dance, like he's in a boxing ring. "Everyone in this room needs to learn how to play well—or at least better—with others."

Of course Keshawn wins the tip-off. We run up and down the court, and except for him, we all suck, even the athletes among us. It's sad and embarrassing really, and the only thing we're learning is how to humiliate ourselves in front of our peers.

Every single time Keshawn makes a basket, he acts like he's just won the state championship. He's barking orders at his team and dribbling behind his back and through his legs and making these impossible jump shots, and honestly it's like playing with LeBron James, if he were a six-foot-six-inch baby. At some point, Mr. Levine grabs the ball from him and says, "This is not Keshawn hour. It's about helping out your teammates. It's about *we're all equal.* It's about pulling together." He sinks a perfect three-pointer. "Take a time-out, Mr. Basketball."

"What?"

"You can sit on the bleachers for a few minutes. It's not going to kill you."

"Man." Keshawn goes dragging off, the slowest human on earth. We wait for him to leave the court, and, two years later, he finally sits down.

Natasha rolls her eyes. Shakes her head at the ceiling.

Mr. Levine says, "If it'll make you feel better, I'll sit out too. Even numbers. Whatever's best for the group, right, Keshawn?"

Keshawn looks at him, then past him at Natasha, who raises a single eyebrow. He says to Mr. Levine, "Sure."

So now we're three and three. We keep the lead until Jack passes the ball to Andy, who's on the other side. After Andy shoots and scores, Keshawn is on his feet. "WTF, Mass?" Only he doesn't spell it out *and* he shouts it.

Mr. Levine says to him, "Language," at the same time Jack mumbles something about the ball slipping.

When it happens again, I think Keshawn's going to LOSE IT.

Jack says, "Hey, man, just trying to do my civic duty."

Andy goes, "What does that mean?"

Jack shrugs. Does this kind of cocky half-smile. "I'm just saying it looked like your team could use some help."

Andy throws the ball at him, a little too hard. Now they're having some sort of standoff, bristling at each other like two cats in an alley. "Why don't you keep the ball, Masselin? I'll get it back in about sixty seconds."

Mr. Levine goes, "Enough, both of you. Jack, stop wasting time."

For the next few minutes, Andy and Jack are each trying to win the game single-handedly. Andy is shouting at Natasha and Maddy, and Jack isn't even passing anymore, just moving the ball from one end of the court to the other and taking every shot. Until Natasha gets him cornered, and Jack has to get rid of the ball. To Andy. *Again.* The following thirty seconds go like this: Andy does a layup and walks by Jack, ramming him in the shoulder. Jack says, all sarcastic, "You're welcome." Andy gets in his face like he wants to take a swing. Jack stands there, like he wants Andy to punch him. Mr. Levine gets in between them and rattles off this speech about getting along and playing out our feelings.

That's the moment I look at Jack, and he looks at me. And I know what's going on here. He's getting Andy confused with Travis. Same build. Same height. Same hair. Same color shirt. I try to imagine that Andy and Travis are strangers to me, that I'm face-blind, that every time I look at them and then look away, I have to put them back together.

I tell myself, *Let it be, Libbs. Let nature do what it's going to do. After all, doesn't he deserve to be shamed in front of not only these people but all people everywhere?*

And now we're playing again, and suddenly I'm yelling at Jack, "Hey, pass it to me." Even though I am the worst shot in this room, maybe in the world.

But instead of passing me the ball, he drives down the court himself. The next time he gets the ball, I jump up and down and wave my arms in his direction. "I'm wide open over here." He shoots me this look, and I think, *Fine, if you don't want my help.* But then he's called on a foul. We stand next to each other, watching Maddy shoot free throws, and I say, "Just give me the damn ball before Mr. Levine makes us stay an extra hour."

A minute or so later, Jack throws me the ball. As I start to dribble, Maddy steals it away, but when he throws it to me the next time, I aim for the basket. By some miracle, I make it.

JACK

I hold the door open as everyone files out into the parking lot. We won by thirteen points, and Keshawn is carrying Natasha like she's his NBA trophy.

As Libby brushes past, I think of sunshine. It's her shampoo or her soap, or maybe it's just her. I think, *Did she smell like sunshine before she was cut out of her house, or did this come after, once she was back out in the world?*

She looks up at me and says, "You should really tell someone what's going on with you."

"I already did." I'm irritated because now here's this girl saving my ass. Like I am a person in need of saving. Which, apparently, I am.

"Someone other than me. It's not like you're the only one who has this. I know that may be what it feels like to you, but statistically it's not *that* rare. At least, it's not as rare as being so super-fat you got stuck in your house. Have you been on the Prosopagnosia Research Centers site? Because they have this wallet card you can carry with you and give to people to explain what you have. I'm not saying that's the answer, but maybe it's a start."

I call Caroline as I'm driving away. "Hey, beautiful."

"Come over."

"I can't."

"What do you mean you can't?"

"I've got work."

"Later, then."

"I'm busy tonight. I'll take you out tomorrow night. We'll do it up big. We'll paint the town. A night you'll never forget."

"What are you busy with? Or should I ask *who*?"

"I'm building Dusty's Christmas present."

"It's *September.*"

"I'm *building* it."

She goes completely quiet.

"Caroline? Babe?"

"I wish you'd never grabbed that girl. That Libby Strout."

"Believe me, that makes two of us. I like to think I'm above that kind of shitty behavior, so you can imagine how disillusioning it's been for me."

"All this detention time is eating into *us* time. It's beginning to ruin my life."

Uh.

I want to say *Can you put nice Caroline on the phone?* but instead I say, "Sorry, babe. I promise I'll make it up to you."

My dad and I are driving home on National Road, heading past the college, when this wave comes over me, and I feel the hollow in my heart that's been there ever since my mom died. Loss does that, hits you out of the blue. You can be in the car or in class or at the movies, laughing and having a good time, and suddenly it's as if someone has reached directly into the wound and squeezed with all their might. I can see my dad and me driving home, this same direction, that night we lost her. We pass us on the road, and I can see our faces through the windshield. We are ghosts.

I look at my dad now, and he glances at me. "What is it, Libbs?"

I almost say it.

It's her. Always. It's the suddenness of life changing in an instant that makes me anxious when I sleep and makes me tell myself to breathe when I'm awake.

"It's nothing."

I lay my fingers on my wrist, so that it looks like my hands are just resting on my lap, when what I'm doing is checking my pulse. *Breathe. Stay steady. No reason to get worked up.*

"It was nice of Bailey to come over. She was always a sweet girl."

"She is."

"You know you can have friends over to the house anytime you want."

"So can you. Mom wouldn't want you to be alone." I can almost hear her. *Give me a respectable mourning period, Will, but don't stop living your life.*

"I'm not alone." He gives me this crazy-looking grin.

"I won't be here forever." *No one ever is.*

"I'm good."

I don't fully believe him, though. And then I decide to let both of us off the hook. "Have you ever heard of face blindness?"

"Face blindness?"

"Prosopagnosia. It's when you can't tell faces apart, so you don't recognize your family or friends."

"Is this for a school project?"

Jack Masselin asked me not to tell and, against my better judgment, I intend to honor that. "Yes," I say.

JACK

Instead of checking inventory or filling orders, I sit at the Masselin's office computer and search for *Prosopagnosia Research Centers*. The site says they're located at Dartmouth, Harvard, and University College London, headed by a man named Brad Duchaine. I've heard of it and him, but I've never really explored the site, so I spend some time on there, reading more about this thing I almost definitely for sure have.

Not surprisingly, prosopagnosia can create serious social problems ...

Reports of prosopagnosia date back to antiquity ...

One of the telltale signs of prosopagnosia is great reliance on non-facial information such as hair, gait, clothing, voice ...

Most of this I know by now. I visit a few of the links to Face to Face, the biannual newsletter, and then I take the Famous Faces test, which tests my ability to recognize celebrities. The president, Madonna, Oprah. Even though I've taken tests like this before, the only one I get right is Martin Luther King, Jr., and that's just because I guess.

I click on the contact page.

If you believe that you are prosopagnosic or have other types of recognition impairments and are interested in becoming involved with research, please contact us using our form. We will try to get you involved with studies that we are conducting or we can put you in contact with researchers in your area.

I open the email client, and it's logged in to my dad's account. There, right there, where anyone can see it, is a new, unopened email from Monica Chapman. Sent eleven minutes ago. While I was sitting here researching my damaged brain. Subject: **Re: Jack**. As in me. As in my dad and Monica Chapman are in some way discussing me.

I stare at the subject line, at her name, at my dad's name, at my name.

If I open it, here's what will happen: I'll know more than I already do, which means I'll only be adding to the secrets I'm already carrying around.

And then I open it.

And wish I hadn't.

I saw Jack, and he seems so angry. Has he ever talked to anyone? I know he's got Levine after school, but maybe you should think about getting him some one-on-one help. I can suggest somebody. The counselors here are actually pretty good, but I know other ones as well. We'll figure this out. You don't need to do it on your own. I love you. M.

I look down and my hands are shaking. I wait to spontaneously combust, like Knight Polonus Vorstius of Italy, who burst into flame after drinking too much wine.

When I don't, I write:

Dear M. If Jack is angry, it's because of you and us. The only thing that's going to help him is removing us completely. Maybe I should stop being so selfish. If I really loved you, I would end my marriage or at least come clean to my wife. I owe her that. Maybe I owe you that too. Maybe our love is the biggest love there's ever been, although I doubt it. But whatever, I just need to stop being such a pussy. No wonder he's so angry. Love, N.

I don't send it, but I leave it open for my dad to see.

I do a search for books on prosopagnosia and the brain, and I order every one of them, charging his credit card. I sign in to my email account and write a letter to Brad Duchaine.

My name is Jack. I'm a high school senior and I'm almost positive I'm face-blind. I'm not sure how much longer I can keep this up. Everyone in my life is a stranger, and that includes me. Please help.

I send it, and immediately want to take it back. But now it's out there. So all I can do is wait and hope that maybe, just maybe, this man can tell me what to do.

LIBBY

I still have the copy of *We Have Always Lived in the Castle* that some Good Samaritan sent to the hospital. I keep it on the little table beside my bed and use the letter that was sent with it as a bookmark.

I want you to know I'm rooting for you.

Sometimes we need to hear that, even from a stranger. I think of all the people I'm rooting for—my dad, Rachel, Bailey, Iris, Jayvee, Mr. Levine, Principal Wasserman, Mr. Dominguez, my classmates in the Conversation Circle, maybe even Jack.

And then I get out my Damsels application, read it through to make sure I've answered every question and filled out every line, tuck it neatly into my backpack, and dance.

JACK

During dinner, no one really talks except Dusty, who wants to audition for his school's production of *Peter Pan*. Marcus is screwing around with his phone under the table, and Mom's not even yelling at him. I'm too busy pretending we're all friends here and I don't want to knuckle-punch my own father, and he's too busy pretending *Mistress? What mistress?*

He finds me later in the bathroom when I'm brushing my teeth. He walks in and says, very low, "You shouldn't have gone into my email. I'm sorry you saw what you thought you saw, but there's the matter of respecting my privacy. There's more to it than you know, so what you read there—it's out of context. But I'm sorry."

He says it nicely because Nate Masselin is a nice guy and it's important for him to be liked, especially postcancer. I can tell he's waiting for me to forgive him and move on the way everyone else does, and that pisses me off.

I take my time brushing, rinsing, wiping my mouth on a towel. Finally, I look at him. I'm taller than he is by a good inch, not counting my lion fro. I say, "You can't use cancer as an excuse for shittiness anymore." And of course I'm talking to me too, although he doesn't know that.

· · ·

I dream that I'm flying from airport to airport, and each one is mobbed with people. So mobbed, I can't breathe or move, and every face is blank—no nose, mouth, eyes, eyebrows. I'm searching for someone I know, for anyone who looks familiar, and the more I search, the more my chest tightens and the less I can breathe.

But then I see her. *Libby Strout.* She's lowered from the ceiling by a crane, larger than life, larger than anyone, and she's the only one with a face.

SATURDAY

JACK

The locker room is enormous. It smells like feet and piss, or like Travis Kearns, whose main identifier is the fact that he sometimes reeks like a skunk because of all the weed he smokes. It's pretty much the last place you want to spend a Saturday. But here we are, the seven of us and Mr. Sweeney (enormous belly, mullet, side-burns, slight limp). We spread out, and I purposely take a corner by myself because I don't want to talk to anyone.

At noon, we break for lunch. Sweeney gives us forty-five minutes to eat outside on the bleachers we'll be painting next weekend, and I take a seat away from everyone else. The bleachers are old and weatherworn, and just the sight of them makes me lose my appetite. Painting these bleachers is one more thing added to the shit pile that is my life. I pop the top on my soda and close my eyes. The sun feels good. *Soak it in, brave soldier,* I tell myself. *While you can.*

I almost drift off, but I hear someone yelling "Leave me alone," over and over, and it's a voice I recognize, bellowing and foghorn-like. I open my eyes and see a big guy lumbering past the school and there's this group of guys following him. They're all around my age, white, kind of interchangeable. I don't recognize any of them, but the foghorn voice sounds like it belongs to Jonny Rumsford.

I've known Jonny since kindergarten, back when he was just Rum for short. He was always bigger than everyone else, a kind of gentle giant. For as long as I've known him, kids have been following Rum around, heckling him for being a little slow, a little simple, a little clumsy, like a pack of hyenas targeting a buffalo.

I'm watching these guys now, and they're yelling stuff at him, even though I can't hear what. The Boy Who May Be Rum's shoulders are all hunched up, like he's trying to pull his head into his neck or maybe right down into his chest. And then one of the guys throws something at him and hits him on the back of the head. Suddenly, I'm seeing myself like everyone else does—I'm one of those heckling, yelling hyena kids, throwing things at people who don't deserve it.

I set my sandwich down, and I take off like I'm being launched to the moon. At first, May/May Not Be Rum thinks I'm running straight for him and he freezes, clearly terrified. The guys are laughing and throwing shit—rocks, trash, anything they can find—and I run right into the herd of them. They don't even have time to think. One lands on his ass in the dirt, and suddenly they're not laughing anymore.

"Did he do anything to you?" I point at Rum. *"Did he?"*

"What the hell, Mass?"

Of course they know me. I'm probably friends with these scumbags.

"Tell me one thing he did to you."

One of the guys gets up in my face, and he's as tall as I am and wider by a couple of feet. But I don't back down because I'm at least three heads angrier. "Seriously, Mass? You're gonna give us shit? What did that fat girl do to you? Huh? Tell me one thing *she* did."

Another guy goes, "Yeah, how's detention, jackass?"

I don't think. I act. Maybe because I'm angry. At everyone. At myself. I feel like I could take on the whole world right now. I say to Rum, "Go home, Jonny. Get out of here." And then I turn around and punch the first guy I see. He drops to the ground, and another one comes at me, and I haul off and punch him too. Even when my hand feels broken, even when I can't feel my knuckles anymore, I keep pounding on these guys. And at some point, it's as if I leave my body on the ground and float up into the sky, where I watch the fight like it's happening to someone else.

Some part of me thinks, *What if that's it? What if whatever malfunction in my brain that's causing this face blindness is spreading, so that I can't even recognize where I am or what I'm doing? What if my brain is completely broken and I never get back down there to me again?*

I'm not sure how much time passes, but at some point I'm aware of something or someone tugging at my arm. I turn around and I'm on the ground again, and it's Libby Strout. She's yanking me back.

One of the guys says to Libby, "Don't hurt me, Flabby Stout! Don't hurt me!" He pretend-cringes, his hands up in front of his face.

She goes, "Don't call me that."

"What's that, Flabby?"

I say, "I know you're not talking to her." All cool and collected.

"She knows who I'm talking to."

And I don't like the way he says it, so I punch him. Then this tall black guy with a smooth, shaved head is there, and he's glaring at the herd of hyenas. "You better run. My boy here, he's gonna kill you, and if he don't, I will." This can only be Keshawn Price.

Those boys go walking away, and the Guy Who Must Be Keshawn stands watching them. "Son, you're as stupid as you look."

LIBBY

We've got fifteen minutes left of lunch, and Jack Masselin drops onto the bleachers, lip bleeding onto his shirt. As he stares off into the tree line, I'm watching him, trying to put myself in his skin again.

I think about going home and what it would be like if my dad walked in and I couldn't recognize him. Or if my mom miraculously came back from the dead and I didn't know it was her. If I'm putting myself in the skin of Jack Masselin, I'm feeling pretty lonely. And maybe scared. How would I know who to trust?

I sit down beside him and say, "It's Libby again." Even though I probably don't need to because it's pretty obvious in this group, even to someone with face blindness.

He's staring out at the street, like he's itching for another fight. The blood is dripping down his chin and onto his shirt, and he's not doing anything to wipe it away. I hand him a napkin.

"No thanks."

"Take it. You don't want Sweeney to see."

He swipes at his chin with the napkin, winces a little, and then holds his soda can against it like an icepack. He cocks an eye at me. "Was that about me?"

"What?"

"'Flabby Stout.' Did I do that? With the rodeo? I want to know exactly how shitty I should feel right now."

"That wasn't about you. That was about Moses Hunt being Moses Hunt—the exact same Moses Hunt he was in fifth grade."

"Moses Hunt. Great."

The Hunt brothers are as notorious as the James Gang. There are at least five of them, maybe more, because their parents just breed and breed. Age-wise, Moses falls somewhere toward the bottom, although he looks forty thanks to all the hard living, the missing teeth, and the fact that he's so mean.

Jack says, "Are you okay?"

"We just have history. Part of me wishes I'd let you kill him, but otherwise yes, I'm okay." Rattled, but okay. Heart pounding, chest clenching, but okay. "Thanks for standing up for me." Jack shakes his head and stares off toward the street again. We sit there a minute, Jack watching the street, me watching him. Finally I say, "If you're not careful, you're going to run into someone angrier than you."

"I doubt that person exists." And this isn't charming Jack Masselin. This is a boy who is burdened by life. I make myself sit there, inside his skin. I do it for Atticus and for my mom.

"If you're not careful, you'll eat too much and get stuck in your house. Trust me. You think no one understands and you're alone, and that makes you angrier, and *Why don't they see it? Why doesn't someone say, 'Hey, you seem burdened by the world. Let me take that burden for a while so you don't have to carry it around all the time.'* But it's on you to speak up." And then I shout, "Speak up if you've got something to say!"

The other delinquents turn and stare at me, and I wave.

"You're a very wise woman."

"I am, actually. You'd be amazed. But I've had a lot of time to read and watch talk shows and think. A LOT. So much time to think. Sometimes all I did all day was just wander around in my mind."

"So what makes you angry?"

"Stupid people. Fake people. Mean people. My thighs. You. Death. Gym class. I worry about dying all the time. Like, all the time."

He shifts the can so he can see me better.

"My mom died when I was ten. She got up that morning like it was any other morning and I went to school and my dad went to work, and I only told her I loved her because she said it first. She drove herself to the hospital. She was feeling dizzy. By the time she got there, she wasn't feeling dizzy anymore, but the doctors ordered some tests anyway."

He sets the soda can down but doesn't say a word.

"One minute she was talking to them, and the next minute she wasn't. It all happened in an instant. Conscious." I snap my fingers. "Unconscious. The doctors said the thing that caused it was a cerebral hemorrhage in the right hemisphere of her brain. Something just burst."

"Like an aneurysm?"

"Kind of. I was pulled out of assembly, and my dad came to get me. We went to the hospital so I could say goodbye. My dad had to tell them to turn off the machines, and half an hour later, she died. One of the nurses said to me, 'It can run in families.' So I was convinced it was going to happen to me. It still might." I check in with my heart rate. *Yes, it seems okay.* "I went to bed that night thinking, *Last night she was here. This morning she was here. Now she's gone, and not for a few days, but forever. How can something so* final *happen in an instant? No preparation. No warning. No chance to do all the things you planned to do. No chance to say goodbye.*"

His eyebrows are drawn together in a V, and he's looking at me like he can see straight into my heart and soul.

"Now you're the only one who knows something about me."

"I'm sorry about your mom."

"I'm sorry too." I stare at my lunch and realize I'm not hungry. In olden times, I would have eaten every last bite because it was in front of me. "I think that makes us even."

"Does it?"

"You're not punching me, if that's what you're thinking."

He laughs. "It's not." In a minute he goes, "What do your shoes say?"

I hold my leg out to show him. "Just quotes I like from books."

He points at the most recent one, written in purple marker, the one that says, *More weight.*

"Where have I heard that?"

"Giles Corey. From *The Crucible.* He was the last person put to death in the Salem witch trials. Those were his final words, a kind of FU to the people who were pressing him to death with stones."

Mr. Sweeney appears and yells for us to get back inside.

As we're collecting our trash and walking toward the doors, Jack goes, "Moses and who else?"

"The ones bullying Jonny Rumsford?" He nods. "His brother Malcolm and also Reed Young."

"Malcolm?" Now I nod. "Shit. He's the meanest of them all."

"I think the other two must be seniors."

"Thanks." He shoves his hands in his pockets.

"You're welcome."

The light catches his wild, wild hair and holds it. And *wham!*

Suddenly.

Just like that.

I'm completely conscious of his *guyness* next to me. His long legs. The way he walks, fluid, easy, like he's made to walk through water. But at the same time with purpose, which makes him seem taller than he is. There aren't a lot of guys my age who walk like this. *With swagger.*

It's as if I've suddenly discovered he's male. My face is hot and my back is damp and I'm thinking about Pauline Potter, sexing off all that weight, and I'm staring at his hands and I'm like, *Stop staring at his hands. What are you doing? He's the enemy! Well, maybe not the enemy, but you are absolutely not going to think of him like that.*

I realize he's talking and so I come zinging back to attention. He's saying, "I want you, Libby Strout. I've always wanted you. It's the reason I grabbed you."

Or maybe he's actually saying, "You can't tell, but I'm smiling on the inside."

I say, "I'm smiling back." I try to keep my face a blank, even though I don't have a split lip. But I can't help it. For some reason, I smile so everyone can see.

JACK

It's midnight when I walk Caroline to her door. On the step, I grab her by her waist and pull her in, and her body is rigid, like she's made of broom handles and marble. I want to ask her what it is that makes her like this, all uptight and controlling and mean. I wonder where geeky Caroline is right now, if the other day was real or a fluke and this newer, shinier Caroline has really swallowed her whole. *Is there anyone in there?* I want to say. Instead I pull her in tighter and wrap both arms around her, and try to squeeze geeky, awkward, nice Caroline out of there.

"Ow," she says. "You always do that too hard." She pushes me off her. "People might like her more if she didn't have such a chip on her shoulder."

"Who?"

"Libby Strout." She has been talking about Libby all night—at dinner, during the movie, on the ride home.

I laugh because, coming from Caroline, this is *hilarious.*

"Why is that funny?"

"It's not. But you know, pot. Kettle."

"No, I don't know." She crosses her arms. "Tell me more."

Smooth it over. Tell her what she wants to hear.

But I don't because suddenly I can't do it anymore. She's exhausting and I'm exhausting, and we're exhausting. I've been telling her what she wants to hear for the past four years.

I say, "You know what? I'll talk to you later."

"If you walk away, Jack, don't come back. You don't get to do that and come back."

"Thanks. Got it."

I feel this weird nervous energy, like I'm doing something big and life-altering. I tell myself, *You need her,* as I get back into the Land Rover and drive away.

I head straight to the scrap yard, where I jump the fence and wander through and no one bothers me because it's late and dark and I'm the only one here. It's amazing what you can find—old license plates, old screws, a metal bumper. For me, the greatest item of all is gears. Whether they're small or big, it doesn't matter—gears are like the power source for almost all machines, the thing that decides their force and speed.

I dig for a while, and it's peaceful, like I'm the only living soul for miles. But my mind's not in it. My heart's not in it. Too much of my life feels like this already—trying to recycle something old into something new and better, disguising someone else's trash as some fresh, shiny thing.

In the driveway of my house, I pull out my phone. Thirteen texts and one voice mail from Caroline, sent over the past hour. A text from Kam. Another from Seth. I open my email and wait for it to load. I'm thinking about Libby Strout when I see it. The email. Delivered at 6:35 p.m.

A reply from Brad Duchaine of the Prosopagnosia Research Centers at Dartmouth.

MONDAY

LIBBY

Before first period, Heather Alpern and the Damsels are running drills on the football field. I stand on the sidelines and watch them, and I can't move because *there they are.* I'm starstruck. The Damsels are sixty-five years old this year. They were originally created by two students who loved to dance, and the first-ever team was made up of twenty girls. They wore skirts to their knees, which some people found shocking, and white gloves, and they performed with pom-poms and flags. Now there are forty members, thirty-nine without Terri Collins. At the end of the school year, everyone in Amos will turn out for the Damsels Showcase, which is held in Civic Auditorium, the town's performing arts center. *And I want to be on that stage.*

I'm in a good mood until third period. After all, I have faced Moses Hunt without the sky falling. I've made up my mind to be a Damsel. And I've walked around in Jack Masselin's skin and been, yes, the bigger person.

I'm practically whistling as I go to my locker. Iris follows me, wanting to know why I'm so happy. And then I open the door.

The letters fall out like confetti. They are everywhere, across the hallway, like a carpet. People are trampling them as they pass, and I'm on my knees trying to collect them before anyone can see them and connect them with me.

Iris bends over, helping me. She opens one up and reads, " 'You aren't wanted.' " She opens another. " 'You aren't wanted.' " I grab the letters from her so she won't stand there reading every single one. There must be a hundred of them. "Are these for you?"

"That's my guess, Nancy Drew."

"Who would do this?"

But I know it's rhetorical because Iris Engelbrecht, more than anyone else, knows what people are capable of.

When I don't answer, she says in her matter-of-fact Eeyore voice, "You need to tell someone. Take them to the principal. Come on. I'll go with you. Let's go right now. They can write us a pass for next period."

I'm stuffing the letters into my backpack. "I'm not going to the principal with this." And I sound as hurt, angry, and upset as I feel.

"Weren't you the one who told me to be brave?"

"I never told you to be brave."

"You told me if I didn't speak up, Dave Kaminski would think he could go on doing things like that to me."

"This is different."

"No, it's not. You have to let them see they can't do this to you. Let's go."

I can feel the fluttering in my heart start to steady itself. This is another effect Iris has on a person. She's the human equivalent of Valium.

I slam the locker door closed, shoulder my backpack, and start walking, the weight of all those letters drilling me into the ground. Iris trudges along behind me, still talking. "Okay, I get it. I guess you can look on the bright side instead. It won't last forever. Eventually they'll find someone else to focus on, and then this whole Fat Girl Rodeo thing will be forgotten."

As if on cue, a group of boys goes by, hollering in my direction. Things like "Saddle up, fellas! Who wants a turn?"

"Bastards." This is from Iris, because instead of speaking I'm doing the thing I used to do when I was younger—trying to will myself small, as if by concentrating really, really hard I might start shrinking until I'm the same size as everyone else. An acceptable size, whatever that is. One that won't make all other people feel so uncomfortable.

Iris bumps my arm with hers, as if she's trying to remind me she's there and I'm not alone, but for some reason it ticks me off. I never volunteered to be her savior and protector. I can't even protect myself. She starts singing the Cowardly Lion's "If I Only Had the Nerve" verse from *The Wizard of Oz,* and as irritating as it is, I have to admit she's got a really pretty singing voice.

Bump.

Bump.

Bump.

I stop walking. "Why do you want to be my friend anyway?" I talk right over her singing. "Is it because I stood up for you that day? Is it because I make you feel less freakish by comparison? Or is it because when you're with me everyone leaves you alone for once and focuses on me?"

Her eyes go wide and then narrow, and Iris Engelbrecht is staring at me like she thinks I'm a bastard too. "It's because when you're not being a jerk? Like this? I like you. Because except for that jerkiness? You're who I want to be." And she walks away.

"Beggars can't be choosers," Kendra Wu crows as she strolls by with Caroline Lushamp.

I stand there, my hand on the classroom door, and yell, "What's that supposed to mean?"

They're still heading away from me, but Caroline turns to face me, as graceful walking backward as she is walking the regular way. "What she's trying to say is that you might not want to burn your bridges when you're standing on an island." And then she smiles the meanest smile I've ever seen.

In driver's ed, Mr. Dominguez says, "Libby? Whenever you want to join us."

"Sorry." I stop staring into space.

Bailey passes me a note. *Are you okay?*

Instead of answering, I sit there and pretend I'm paying attention, and even when Mr. Dominguez says, "Next week, we're ready to start driving"—the moment I've been waiting for all my short, sad life—it's like I'm sitting in another room, at another school, far, far away.

I'm in the bathroom after third period when two guys walk in, both white, both nondescript, except that one is a fucking mountain and the other is about my height. They shut the door. This is bad news because for as long as I've been at MVB, that door has never been closed.

"What's up?" I do the head nod, act casual, but even though I can't recognize their faces, I recognize the emotion. They're mad as hell. I saunter toward the exit, trying to look as carefree as one can in this particular situation, but the smaller one blocks my way.

"When you messed around with my girlfriend, I let it go, but when you jump me and my friends for no reason and try to beat the living shit out of us? You don't do that, man. You don't screw with the people I love."

This tells me it's almost definitely (probably) Reed Young, and that right there behind him is definitely (probably) Moses Hunt. I'm feeling reckless enough to go, "So you're saying you love him?" I nod at Moses.

And they both lunge for me. I can't afford another fight, so I duck and Probably Reed goes sprawling while Probably Moses ricochets into the wall, and then I throw open the door and I'm out of there. I don't run. Hell no. But I burn a path in the floor all the way down the hall.

For as long as people have been around, we've relied on facial recognition for survival. Back in caveman times, whether a person lived or died could come down to being able to read a face. You had to know your enemy. And here I am, barely able to make it out alive from a high school bathroom.

LIBBY

Mr. Levine (electric-blue bow tie, electric-blue sneakers) is sitting on the risers waiting for us as we walk into the old gym. We take our usual seats and after we have a chance to get settled, he bounces to his feet. "We're going to try something different." Which is what he says every day.

So far, we've sung songs, run a kind of obstacle course (stopping at each station to talk about a specific feeling or ways in which we might change our behaviors), and performed a scene from a *Star Trek* episode (about two enemies having to work together to survive). Mr. Levine calls these "teen-building exercises."

But this time he walks out of the gym.

We wait. When Mr. Levine doesn't return, Travis Kearns says, "Can we leave?"

And then the gym goes dark, the only light coming from these narrow windows way up by the ceiling. A second later, the room starts spinning with these spiraling globes of light—pink, orange, green, yellow, blue. It's what I imagine a European disco was like back in the 1970s.

"What the—"

But Travis doesn't finish because a song booms out over the speaker system, so loud I almost cover my ears. It's the sappiest eighties ballad you've ever heard, and all that's missing is a DJ and a corsage pinned to my shirt.

Mr. Levine comes back in and says, "On your feet." He waves his hands like he's some sort of conductor and we're his orchestra. "Up. Up. Time's a-wasting. Let's work on building that self-esteem."

One by one, we stand. Keshawn and Natasha kind of jokingly start slow-dancing. When they stop, Mr. Levine says, "Keep going. Yes, it's really that simple. Now the rest of you."

Travis Kearns asks Maddy, who's pretty but shy. She stares at her feet the whole time. Even though there aren't enough girls to go around, no one asks me. Andy Thornburg starts waltzing with an invisible partner *because dancing alone is apparently better than dancing with me.* My chest flutters, the first sign of panic.

Mr. Levine says, "Ask her to dance, Jack."

"What?"

"You heard me."

Jack looks at me and I look at him.

"Before the song ends, please."

We keep standing there, and now my palms are damp—the second sign of panic. The next thing will be this strange compression in my chest and head, as if I'm being squeezed by a giant boa constrictor. Gradually, everything will grow dim and distant, and I'll shrink until I'm a regular-size person, and then keep shrinking until I'm small enough to squash under someone's shoe.

Finally, Mr. Levine pulls out this remote and clicks it, and *the song starts over.* Everyone groans. "I can do this all day. My phone is fully charged, and there are a lot more songs just like this on there. Worse ones, even."

I look at Jack and he looks at me, and the lights are flashing across his face, turning his eyes green, brown, blue, gold, like he's a chameleon changing colors.

He offers his hand. I take it. Because we have to. *This is not the way I imagined my first school dance.*

We fumble our hands together and stand as far apart as possible, like someone's holding a ruler—more like a yardstick—between us. We shuffle back and forth as if we're both made of wood, staring at the ceiling, the floor, the walls, the other kids, anywhere but at each other.

The song only gets cheesier as it goes on, and the lights are swirling and strobing, and his eyes are flashing green/brown/blue/gold, and suddenly I'm thinking about my palms. Like how sweaty they are. I can just hear Jack Masselin going back to his friends, telling them all about my sweaty palms and what it was like to dance with the fat girl.

Jack says, "This may scare me off school dances forever."

My first instinct is that he's talking about me or maybe my damp hands, so I go, "Well, I'm not exactly having the time of my life."

"I didn't mean *you're* scaring me off. Although you're kind of scaring me off now."

"Sorry." As I realize he means the song and the lights and Mr. Levine, standing there like the world's most attentive chaperone.

We're now kind of swaying, and it's not *so* bad. It's the first time we've touched where I wasn't either punching him or stopping him from punching someone.

I say, "This is my first school dance."

"Ah."

"Well, it's the closest I've ever come, at least. Not to put any pressure on you."

"No pressure. Just extreme performance anxiety. Every guy's dream."

"You're not a terrible dancer."

"My confidence is soaring now."

"It's just not exactly how I pictured it."

"Okay, so what can I do to change that?"

"Uh . . ."

"You look really pretty tonight."

In the second it takes me to realize he's playing, my legs grow into the floor like roots. Jack tightens his grip on me and kind of nudges me into motion again.

He says, "Especially in that dress. The color really brings out your eyes."

"Uh." *Think.* "The sales clerk called it Hershey brown." *Ugh. What?*

"Actually more like amber."

And he's looking into my eyes as if I'm the only thing he sees. I tell myself, *He's such a good actor,* as these little goose bumps spring out at the base of my spine and go shooting up my back, across my shoulders, and down both arms.

Suddenly we're dancing closer, and I'm aware of not just his hands but each individual finger connecting to my body and his legs bumping against mine. I want to lean in and get a whiff of him and rest my head on his shoulder or maybe make out with his neck. Afterward he'll walk me home and kiss me on the doorstep, sweet at first, and then hungrier and hungrier till we fall into the bushes and go rolling off across the yard.

All at once, the song ends and a fast song begins, and my eyes fly open. We immediately break apart, and *Jack wipes his hands on his jeans. Ack.*

Mr. Levine goes, "Don't stop! It's a dance-off. Go, go, go!" And he's dancing like a crazy man. For a moment, all we can do is gawp at him. I mean, it's a *spectacle.* The man is all legs and arms and flopping hair. "The longer you don't dance, the longer we're here. I'm getting at least three songs out of you." And he starts it over.

Jack Masselin goes, "Shit." And then begins to move. *Of course,* I think. *Of course he can dance.* Because he's their leader, they all start dancing. First Andy and then Keshawn, Natasha, Travis, and even Maddy. Jack Masselin is not my leader, so I'm still standing there.

Once again, Mr. Levine starts the song over. "I'm going to keep doing that till we're all moving."

It's one thing to twirl in the near-empty park with Rachel, but it's another to start shaking and jumping on school property in front of my counselor and my fellow classmates, delinquents though they may be. In that moment, my Damsels dream wavers because the audition will be so much worse. The audition means Heather Alpern and her squad captains—including Caroline Lushamp—sitting at a table, watching me. If I'm able to get past the potential humiliation of that moment, *how will I ever perform in costume for the school?*

But ahhhhhhh, this song. It's so . . . I realize I'm kind of tapping my foot and bouncing my head. *No,* I think. *Libby, you can't.* But the song is . . . oh my God. I feel my hips start to move a little. *No, no, no. Don't do it.*

But I'm alive. I'm here.

We never know how long we have. We're never guaranteed tomorrow. I could die right now, right here.

It could be over in an instant.

She woke up like it was any other day, just like I did, just like Dad did. We thought it was a regular, normal day. None of us knew we were waking up to the worst day. If we'd known, what would we have done? Would we have held on to her tight and tried to keep her here?

The song starts over. Keshawn goes, "Come on, Libby. Damn."

What would Mom want me to do right now? If she could see me, what would she say?

And then Jack Masselin is suddenly breaking out these moves,

Keshawn and Natasha are doing some sort of routine, and Mr. Levine is kicking his legs out like he's Heather Alpern, former Rockette. Even shy little Maddy is shaking her shoulders.

Stay still. Wait out the song. Don't you do it, Libby.

But I can feel my body taking over my mind, and this is what happens. *The dance is in me.* All at once I'm in there, waving my arms, waving my booty, swinging my hair. I jump a little, and when the gym floor doesn't collapse, I jump some more.

Jack starts jumping too, and before I can stop myself, I spin off into a twirl. Jack shouts, "What's that dance called?"

I say the first name I think of: "The Merry-Go-Round!"

I twirl and twirl, and then Mr. Levine is twirling and Jack is twirling and all the others are twirling, just like the lights, until the gym turns upside down.

Heather Alpern is still in her office. She says, "Libby, isn't it?" Her voice is warm, like honey.

"I heard that Terri Collins is moving, and I wondered if there was going to be an audition for the Damsels." I'm still flushed and *entirely electrified* from the dancing. I want to climb onto her desk and make it my stage and audition right here, right now, but instead I hand her my application.

"Thanks so much for this." She smiles, and I have to look away because she's just that lovely. "I'll be announcing tryouts next week."

Outside, it's starting to rain. The parking lot is empty and my dad isn't there, so I stand up against the building where I won't get wet, even though the last thing I ever want to do is stand against a building like I'm fifth-grade Libby Strout, banished from the playground.

In a minute, this old Jeep-looking thing comes rolling up. The driver's window rolls down and Jack Masselin says, "Need a ride?"

"No."

"Do you want to at least wait in here?"

"That's okay."

But then the sky cracks in two and water comes flooding down. I run for the car, and he throws open my door, and I climb in as gracefully as possible, which unfortunately means I'm slipping and sliding all over the place, shoes squeaking against the floor mat, hair sticking to my face. I slam the door closed and here I am, panting and enormous and soaked to the skin, in the front seat of Jack Masselin's Land Rover. I'm conscious of everything dripping. My hair, my hands, my jeans. This is one of those times when I can feel myself taking up too much space.

I say, "Nice car." The interior is a kind of burnt orange-red, but it's all pretty basic and rugged. One thing is clear, though: *I am in the vehicle of a cool guy.* "It looks like something you'd take on safari."

"Thanks."

"Truck? Car? What do you call it exactly?"

"How about the baddest mo-fo in Amos?"

"Let's not go crazy."

JACK

I'm getting the heater going and now the windows are fogging.

She says, "I thought everyone was gone."

"I was driving away and saw you come out. I thought you might need a ride or at least some shelter."

"My dad's usually on time." She pulls out her phone and checks it, and I can see the worry in her, even though she's trying to blink it away.

"He'll be here."

We sit watching the rain pour down. The music is playing low and the windows are steaming. If this was Caroline, we'd be making out.

And then I'm thinking about making out with Libby Strout. *What the hell?*

I tell myself, *This is the girl you saw LIFTED OUT OF HER HOUSE BY A CRANE.*

But then I'm thinking about making out with her a little more. *Stop thinking about making out with Libby Strout.*

I go, "Let me ask you something. If there was a test you could take to find out if you have what your mom had, would you take it?"

She tilts her head to one side and studies the dash. "After she died, my dad took me to see a neurologist. He said, 'I can run a battery of tests on you to see if you have any aneurysms in your brain. If you have them, there's a chance we can pin them off so they don't become problems down the line. But there's no guarantee that they'll be fixable.' My dad and I went home and talked about it. I was too young to understand it all, so he was the one who made the decision."

"Did you do it?"

"No."

"What about now? Would you do it now?"

"I don't know."

And even though we're talking about aneurysms, I'm *still* thinking about making out with her. So I say, "Jesus, woman, you can dance."

She smiles.

I smile.

She says, "I just handed in my Damsels application."

"Really?"

She arches an eyebrow. "Sorry, is that shocking to you?"

"Only because I can't picture you dancing in formation. I'm not getting the whole wielding-flags-and-wearing-the-same-costume-as-thirty-other-girls vibe. I see you as a do-your-own-thing girl. If you ask me, you're better than the Damsels."

"Thanks."

She unzips her backpack and pulls something out, and at first it looks innocent—just a crumpled-up sheet of white paper. But then I read what's written there: *You aren't wanted.*

"Where did you get this?"

"My locker."

"Do you know who put it in there?"

"No. But does it matter?"

And I know what she means. No, it doesn't. Not really. The point is that it was sent at all, that anyone would think that or say that to her.

"People can be great, but they can also be lousy. I am often lousy. But not completely lousy. You, Libby Strout, are great."

"I don't know about that, but this right here is one reason I'm auditioning." She takes the paper from me and waves it. "They can tell me this all they want, but I'm not listening." She crumples it up and shoves it back in her bag.

I say, "I've got something to show you too."

And then I go into my phone and pull something up and hold it out to her.

She reads the email out loud. " 'Dear Jack.' " And I like the way she says my name. I mean, I really like it. " 'Thank you for reaching out. We would be very interested in testing you. If you aren't able to make it to Hanover, we suggest being in touch with Dr. Amber Klein, Department of Brain Sciences, Cognitive Neurology, Indiana University, Bloomington. Best, Brad Duchaine.' "

She looks up. "Is this about the prosopagnosia?"

"Yeah. I wouldn't have written to him if it hadn't been for you."

"Are you going to do it?"

"I don't know." *Yes.*

"Wouldn't you need your parents' permission?"

"I'll be eighteen soon."

"When?"

"October first."

She hands the phone back to me, studies the dash again, then looks at me with wide amber eyes.

"So let's go."

"What?"

"As soon as you turn eighteen. Let's go to Bloomington."

"Really?"

"Why not?"

Before I know what's happening, my eyes are reaching for her and hers are reaching for mine. Across the seat, our eyes are holding hands. We sit like this until the sound of a horn makes us jump.

I wait until they drive away before heading to Masselin's, where I'm in such a good mood that I'm civil to my dad. It stings a little to see how surprised he is by this, so I go one step further and talk to him about the robot I'm building for Dusty. It's going to be as tall as Dusty, maybe taller. It's going to talk. It's going to be the best damn robot ever.

To his credit, my dad is polite and asks questions. We don't mention Monica Chapman. We don't mention the email. And for a minute I think, *Maybe this is where we stay. Right here in this small radius where it's safe. Maybe we can just stay right here, safe like this, forever.*

Two hours later, when I get back in the Land Rover, it still smells like her. *Sunshine.*

LIBBY

After dinner, my dad and I watch TV with George. Dad is eating grapes one at a time, tipping his head back and throwing them into the air, catching them with his mouth as George swats at them. I lean my head back and catch one in my own mouth. I savor it the way I'm supposed to savor food that's good for me. I bite it a little, and it bursts into an eruption of goodness.

I was on fire today. I lit up the old gym. You should have seen me! I'm making up for every lost moment when I couldn't move or get out of bed. The dance is in me! Just wait till they see me at the Damsels audition. I'm going to nail it. I'm going to dance my heart out for all the world to see.

"The Masselin boy. Everything okay there? Is he leaving you alone?"

"He's not bothering me." *Not in that way, at least.*

"Libbs, you know you can talk to me about anything."

And I feel myself going bright red. *What if my dad can read my thoughts? What if he can see how I am, at this exact moment, undressing Jack Masselin while I eat these grapes?*

"I know, Dad."

For the first time in my life, I don't want to talk to him. Not about Jack and not about the letters. If I do, I become something he has to worry about, and I've already been something he has to worry about for too long.

"I'm thinking of ditching school on October first." One of the things my dad made me promise after my mom died was that I would always let him know where I was, and I figure I can at least tell him this much. "A friend of mine needs to go to Indiana University to take part in a research study."

"Who's this friend?"

"Just someone from school." I don't tell him it's Jack. I figure it's enough that I'm sitting here telling *my father* I want to skip school. "He's going through some things right now. I want to be there for him."

"Do you have any tests that day? Anything big that you'd be missing?"

"Not that I know of."

"Is this a . . . is it a . . ."

"Date? No."

I don't think so. I mean, it isn't. But it makes me wonder: *Could it turn into one?*

"No," I say again. "It was my idea to go."

I almost say, *I'm thinking about getting tested too. I know we talked about it after Mom died, but now that I'm older I think I might want to. Maybe that way I won't worry as much.* I throw myself a grape and miss my mouth. *Or maybe I'll worry more, depending on what I find out.* I pick the grape off my shirt, and then frown at the shirt. "Do you think we could go shopping?"

He raises an eyebrow. "For your non-date?"

"You wouldn't actually have to go. You could just let me borrow money. Or I could get a job."

"No jobs. Not right now. One thing at a time."

"So can I borrow some money, then?"

"You realize you've just asked me if you can skip school *and* borrow money in the same conversation? You realize I'm the world's best dad?"

"I do."

He tilts his head back and I throw him a grape. I throw George a grape and he smacks it across the room. I throw myself a grape and this time I catch it like a pro.

In my room, I pick up my phone and settle back against the headboard. I call Bailey because this is what real friends who aren't imaginary do. When she answers, I say, "What do you think of Jack Masselin?"

"As a person or as a guy?"

"Both."

"I think he's basically a good person who sometimes lacks judgment. As a guy, I think he's cute and funny, and he knows it, but he's not as jerky as a lot of them. Why?"

"Oh, I'm just wondering."

"I'm not telling you how to feel, Libbs, but he and Caroline are one of those forever couples. I mean, even when they're not together, they're together, and if it was me, I wouldn't want to go near him. You'd just set yourself up for heartbreak."

"I'm not saying I'm interested."

But am I?

I change the subject to Terri Collins and the Damsels, and Bailey tells me about this boy she likes who lives in New Castle. We talk for a while, and afterward I go on Iris's Instagram account, where I like every single one of her most recent posts. I choose one randomly and comment on it, and I almost leave it at that. But then I decide to call her. I go straight to voice mail and leave a rambling apology. She calls me back immediately, and even though I don't want to, I answer because I am not an island.

JACK

At home, I find Mom-with-Hair-Up in her study, deep in work, law books open, laptop humming. I rap on the door. "Oldest son, reporting for duty."

She gives me a Mom look. "Did you manage to make it through the day without assaulting anyone or having to see the principal?"

"Yes, I did." I raise my arms in a triumphant V, like I just crossed a finish line.

"Well done. Let's see if we can have more days like this." She holds up one hand, fingers crossed, while the other hand marks her place in one of the books. "By the way, a package came for you. I left it on the island in the kitchen. What did you order?"

"Just stuff for school." I'm hoping she'll take this as evidence that I'm a new and improved Jack, lesson learned.

Her phone rings, and she shakes her head. "Go ahead and get pizza or something for dinner, unless your dad can throw something together."

"I don't think he's home yet."

Her face goes blank, and before she can say anything and because she works hard and he's a louse, and because she doesn't deserve to feel bad about anything, I jog around the desk and kiss her on the cheek. "You're welcome to all this swag, Mom. I've got so much to spare. Here's a little more to help you with your case." And I hug her. It's not much, but it makes her laugh, even as she's pushing me away.

• • •

I open the box in my room. Two titles by Oliver Sacks, a text-bookish volume on visual perception called *Face and Mind,* and a biography of prosopagnosic painter Chuck Close, who's made a name for himself painting faces and is a total badass. He's in a wheelchair, with a messed-up hand, *and* he's face-blind, but he creates these paintings that are really damn awesome. This is how he does it:

He photographs the face.

He maps the face by making a photographic grid of it.

He then builds the face piece by piece on canvas, using oils, acrylics, ink, graphite, or colored pencils.

According to him, it's always about the face.
Only about the face.
Because the face is a road map of life.

LIBBY

I text Jayvee. Our conversation begins, as always, with Atticus
Finch.

Me: **Let's say Atticus Finch is your father.**

Jayvee: **Am I Scout or Jem?**

Me: **Either. Or Jayvee. Jayvee Finch.**

Jayvee: **Of the Filipino Finches. Continue.**

Me: **Let's say there's an illness that runs in the family, and when you
were little, Atticus decided you shouldn't be tested for it.**

Jayvee: **Atticus is usually right. Is there a cure?**

Me: **Not really.**

Jayvee: **Am I questioning Atticus now that I'm all grown up and wom-
anly?**

Me: **Maybe.**

Jayvee: **How old am I now?**

Me: **Our age.**

Jayvee: **I'd assume old Atticus had his reasons. He's Atticus Finch,
after all.**

Five seconds later:

Jayvee: **But there's something to be said for making your own
decisions.**

How to Build a Robot
by Jack Masselin

● ● ●

1. Collect as many Lego pieces and other materials as possible.
2. Draw up schematic of design.
3. Ignore "how to build a Lego robot" websites because this is for Dusty and he deserves something original that has never been created before.
4. Rewatch *The Day the Earth Stood Still* (the original, not the remake) for procrastination-designed-as-inspiration-gathering purposes.
5. Take everything you can find of any value from the scrap yard.
6. Order missing parts (if impossible to find at scrap yard)—microcontroller, breadboard, circuit board, battery, jumper wires, gear motors, power jack, speaker, infrared receiver, rotation servos, various brackets and hardware, motorized scroll saw, etc.
7. Create sketches that will tell the robot what to do. Basically, program its brain.

When I was six, I climbed up on the roof of the house, trying to be a superhero. I was Iron Man in my Iron Man suit, only in reality I was wearing a T-shirt and a pair of swim trunks, which meant that instead of flying I dove headfirst into the earth and cracked my skull open. Sixty-seven stitches. Did I recognize people before that? I can't remember.

8. Give it a good brain. A complete, fully functioning, normal, regular brain.

ONE WEEK LATER

JACK

October first is a Tuesday. I play sick and hide the keys to the Land Rover so Marcus can't take it to school. When a tall boy with shaggy hair comes into my room and starts yelling at me, I figure it's him. "I know you've got the keys, you faker."

I cough loudly.

He starts digging through my shit—bookshelves, drawers, closet. He's picking my jeans up off the floor and searching the pockets.

I hack away like I've got tuberculosis until a woman appears at the door and wants to know what in the Great Fanny Adams is going on.

In answer, I cough myself ragged, which makes her point to the door and tell the tall/shaggy boy to get the hell downstairs. NOW. The woman says, "Do you need anything before we go?"

"I'll be okay." I don't actually mean to, but I sound like a martyr. I cough a little more.

And then she's gone, and I lie still, listening to the leaving sounds that are happening downstairs.

I hear the front door slam, and I lie there another minute. I hear a car engine kick in, and then I'm up and at the window, counting the bodies down below. The woman climbs into one car with this little kid, and a man with thick dark hair gets in another car with the tall/shaggy boy. I watch them pull away and turn in opposite directions at the end of the block, first one and then the other. Like that, I fly into motion. I'm grabbing the keys from beneath the mattress, pulling on clothes, running down the stairs, shoving a bagel in my mouth, jumping in the Land Rover, and heading across town to Libby's.

Libby's neighborhood is street after street of these new houses that look identical, one after the other. There's nothing to distinguish her house from the rest of them except for the girl who lives there. She's waiting for me on the curb, wearing this purple dress, and it reminds me of something an actual *woman* would wear, tucked here, loose there, fitted there. Her hair is down and lit up by the sun.

I can see beauty. The more symmetrical the face, the more average the person looks to me because there's this *sameness* to them, even if other people think they're hot. A person has to have something unique about them. Libby's face is symmetrical, but her beauty has nothing to do with sameness. I recognize it as she swings the door open and climbs into the car. She's graceful, especially for someone so large. She kind of swoops in like Tarzan, kicks off her shoes, and wiggles her toes. Her toenails are purple too.

I say, "You look great."

She cocks her head at me. "Are you flirting with me, Jack Masselin?"

"I'm just stating the obvious."

She pulls her hair off her neck, and I want to say *Don't do that. You'll disappear before my eyes.* But then you can tell she rethinks it—maybe she remembers that I've told her this before—and lets it fall back around her shoulders.

Then she hands me something wrapped in Christmas paper and about fifty bows. "Happy birthday. If you can't tell, I like Christmas paper best."

"You didn't have to do anything."

"I wanted to. Open it."

I tear off the wrapping and the bows go flying. She picks one up and sticks it to her hair, right over her left ear. She picks up another and sticks it to the knee of my jeans. I pick one up and stick it to the end of my nose and then stick one on the end of her nose.

She says from behind the bow, "Open, please."

It's a book. *We Have Always Lived in the Castle* by Shirley Jackson. At first, I'm thrown. I wonder if she knows. She must know I was the one who sent this to her at the hospital. I look at her, but she's got this wide, open smile on her face, and I can see that no, she doesn't know.

I flip through the book. It's not the same copy I sent her years ago, but it's still well worn and well read.

"I wasn't sure what to get you because what do you get the boy who has everything, including face blindness? So I thought I'd get you something I love. It's my favorite book. You don't have to read it, but the girl, Mary Katherine—Merricat, they call her—she reminds me of, uh, me, I guess. And . . . I don't know. I thought you might relate to her too."

"I'll read it." I smile at her. "Thank you."

She smiles at me. "You're welcome."

And we're having what feels like a moment. Suddenly, the air isn't just filled with bows; it's filled with some sort of electric current that links her seat to mine.

She does the impossible—slices through the current by speaking first. "So are you ready for this?"

"As I'll ever be."

. . .

At first I'm amped. I talk her ear off, telling her about every online test I've taken and this guy with prosopagnosia named Bill
Choisser who lives in San Francisco and is an old bearded dude
who wrote a book about face blindness, which he's posted on the
Internet for all to read. All about the impact being face-blind has
on school, work, relationships, life.

But the closer we get to Bloomington, the quieter I get. I can
feel the air going out of me. *What am I going to find out? Will
Dr. Amber Klein be able to help me? Should I be going to New
Hampshire instead to see Brad Duchaine? What if this whole trip is
a waste of time? What if they tell me I've got some serious illness?
What if I find out it isn't face blindness, but cancer of the brain?*

"I can almost *feel* you thinking right now."

I look at her.

"Did you forget I was in the car with you?"

I'm so deep in the forest of my mind that yeah, I almost did.

"Sorry."

We pass a sign: BLOOMINGTON . . . 10 MILES. I feel my stomach
drop and land somewhere around the gas pedal.

"Does this thing have a radio?"

"Does it have a radio. What do you think, woman? Christ almighty." I hit a button and music fills the Land Rover, taking up
all the space around us. I try to concentrate on the words, on the
melody, but then she starts searching through songs, and this feels
like my brain—fragments of words, fragments of melodies, fragments of moments, fragments of things.

Finally, she finds a song she likes, and then she *cranks* it.

"*Disco?* Are you fucking kidding me?" I reach for the radio,
but she smacks my hand away. I reach around her hand, and she

smacks it again, and then it's not about turning off the music, it's about touching her, and our hands are flirting. Finally, she grabs my fingers and holds on to them. And that electric current is sparking out of my thumb, my pinky, and the fingers in between. I cough because *What the fuck is happening?* I say to the car, "I'm so sorry this had to happen to you, baby. I'm sorry you ever had to hear this. I'm sorry I ever had to hear this. I'm sorry I'm still hearing it."

Libby hollers, "What? I can't hear you over my own singing and this amazing beat!"

Now she's singing as loud as she can AND dancing. She lets go of my hand and yells, "Spontaneous dance party!" and goes on singing, but now she's dancing bigger and broader, like she's onstage somewhere.

"I love to love, but my baby just loves to dance, he wants to dance, he loves to dance, he's got to dance."

"What the f—?"

"The minute the band begins to swing it, he's on his feet to dig it, and dance the night away. Stop! I'm spinning like a top, we'll dance until we drop . . ."

It's pretty much the corniest song I've ever heard, but Libby is *into* it. She's grooving all over the seat, shaking her shoulders, shimmying toward me and away. She winks at me and belts it out louder, and she's a terrible singer. So I start singing along with her, kind of self-defensively.

And then we're dancing in unison—heads bobbing to the right, to the left, shoulders forward, shoulders back. Now we're yelling the words, and I'm pounding on the steering wheel, and she's got her arms in the air, and it's the best song I've ever heard, and now I'm smiling at her.

And she's smiling at me.

And it's a moment.

A definite moment.

She says, "Watch the road, Casanova." But she says it in this soft voice that I've never heard her use before. "Just remember, whatever we learn today, these tests don't change anything."

I like the way she says *we*, as if she's in this with me.

"You're still Jack Masselin. You're still a pain in the ass. You're still you."

LIBBY

I am having a moment with Jack Masselin. If you'd asked me a couple of weeks ago or even two days ago if I could imagine such a thing, I would have laughed until I laughed the breath right out of me. This is the thing about life outside the house, though: you never know what might happen.

I think he feels it too, but I'm not sure.

He'd better feel it too.

It had better not just be me over here, by myself, on my own, having a moment *over* him as opposed to *with* him.

I act like *La la la, no big deal, let's go to Bloomington, let's see if you're really face-blind.* But inside my chest, my heart is clenching and unclenching and skipping beats and fluttering like it's about to burst its way out of there and fly around this car. I fix a smile on my face and stare out the window and think, *Oh, heart, you traitor.*

JACK

The lab is busy. An assistant leads us to Dr. Amber Klein (light brown hair, sharp cheekbones, glasses). She is dressed all in black, her sleeves rolled over her elbows, and her hair swept up in a kind of no-nonsense way. She's probably around forty. The lab is also black, floors, walls, ceiling. The room is divided into cubicles by curtains—black, of course—and it feels like we've wandered onto the set of a music video. Libby wears purple and I'm in green, and we stand out like beacons.

Dr. Klein offers us chairs behind one of the black curtains, so it's as if we're enclosed in a small room. She boots up her laptop and says, "I understand you need to be home by late afternoon?" She's wearing an actual watch, and she checks it now: 9:54 a.m.

"There's a bit of a curfew situation." I smile at Libby and she smiles at me. She's still wearing the bow over her left ear, but her smile reminds me of the one my mom wore during Dad's chemo appointments. Like she's determined to make the most of things for the sake of him/me, when she knows how hopeless it really is.

"I'm going to run you through a series of tests." Dr. Klein sits down and starts clicking away at the keyboard.

Libby says to me, "I'm actually going to wait outside. I saw a Starbucks nearby. Just text me when you're done." She takes my phone and types her number in. When she hands it back, I feel this weird panic.

She hesitates over my shoulder. "Unless . . . I mean, I can

stay . . ." But I can tell that she doesn't want to stay, and I wonder if maybe it's the whole doctor/brain setting that's bugging her.

"Nah, I'm good."

I watch her go, hair swinging.

Dr. Klein says, "Does anyone in your family have prosopagnosia?"

"I'm not sure. Why?"

"Face blindness is often genetic, but there are three categories of prosopagnosia: acquired, developmental, and congenital. It can also be a symptom of other disorders, such as autism. Did you ever experience a fall or a childhood illness of the brain?"

"I fell off the roof when I was six."

"Did you hit your head?"

"Could something like that cause face blindness?"

"Yes. It's not as common as developmental prosopagnosia, but it's possible."

"I banged it pretty hard. I had to have stitches." Instinctively, I reach for the thin raised line along my scalp.

She types away, and as she does, it hits me: *This woman is going to dig around in your brain. You can't hide from her.*

She wants to know what kind of tests were done after I fell, and then she wants to know if I was able to recognize faces before the age of six.

The honest answer is *I don't know.* Yeah, I had every test imaginable to see what damage had been done to my brain. But did I know people by their faces back then? I'm not sure.

She says, "Certainly your parents would have noticed a difference if you suddenly had trouble recognizing everyone."

"I think I've always been good at compensating and covering up. I mean, even back then. Maybe I could recognize people before, but I was so young . . ."

"Did your parents notice behavioral changes?"

"My mom said they expected me to become this cautious kid, but I got louder. She says that's when she started going gray."

I give her a smile, but she's busy typing. I sit there looking around, telling myself to *man up, son, stop feeling nervous.* In a minute, she folds her hands in her lap and begins talking. "I'm not sure how much research you've done, Jack, but one of the earliest documented cases of prosopagnosia dates from 1883 . . . Lewis Carroll was rumored to be prosopagnosic. The next time you read *Alice in Wonderland,* you might see the clues . . . I'm sure you're familiar with identifiers. As you know, hairstyle and clothing can change on a daily basis. We've met a lady who identifies people by their wedding rings because this is an identifier that rarely changes . . ."

She's about to see everything you're hiding.

Suddenly, I feel naked. I actually have to look down at myself to make sure I'm still wearing clothes.

The first test is famous faces. This is similar to one I took online—photos of celebrities with their hair and ears removed. Dr. Klein says, "Okay, Jack. The clock isn't ticking here, so feel free to take as much time as you need."

She turns the laptop around so that I can use it. A face appears on the screen. It's just an oval with eyes, a nose, a mouth. If I look at it long enough, it doesn't look like a face at all, but a planet pocked by craters and shadows. One by one, I type in the names, but to be honest I'm making shit up.

When I finish, we go right into the next test. Dr. Klein says, "The system that processes reading emotions on a face is separate from the system that reads features. Can you typically tell if a person is angry or sad or happy?"

"Almost always. I can't recognize faces, but I can read them."

"That's because there is a visual processing system that exists only for face recognition, and specifically only human faces. Your dog or your cat is actually identified by your brain as an object. The configural processor is what allows people to see the face as a whole and not just its individual parts."

This test is about identifying emotions. I want to think I nail every one of the answers, but I actually don't have a clue.

Next is a series of upside-down faces. I'm supposed to match them to the right-side-up faces, but I can't. I know I can't.

The more defeated I feel, though, the more energized Dr. Klein appears. She leans over the laptop. "Humans who have no problem recognizing faces are very bad at identifying upside-down ones because once you turn that image upside down, you can no longer use the configural processing strategy to recognize that face. So you start using a feature-by-feature strategy instead, which is how we identify objects. It's comparable to how you are with regular faces because the human processor only works with upright images. Unlike monkeys, who are adept at recognizing other monkeys, no matter the orientation."

The thing I take from this is *Even monkeys recognize each other.*

"Now we're going to test your ability with object recognition. This way, we can know it's strictly a face recognition problem and that it doesn't extend to objects."

I sit there matching houses, cars, guns, landscapes, animals, and suddenly I'm thinking, *What if I get these mixed up too, all these things I've never had trouble identifying? What if I only thought I recognized a cat, a dog, a house, a car, but I find out I don't know them any better than faces?* I sit back for a minute and close my eyes, mostly because I want to get away—from this computer, this lab, this campus, my own head.

Dr. Klein says, "I want you to remember that everyone gets some right and some wrong. It's how the test was designed."

Which doesn't make me feel any better. But I open my eyes. I go on.

I feel even worse with the next one, the Bald Women test, which is photo after photo of regular, non-celebrity females with the hair and ears missing once again. I'm supposed to hit a button if I see one that looks different, but they all look the same to me so I don't even bother trying—I just hit Same over and over.

The last test reminds me of an eye exam. I lean on the chin rest and press my forehead against this contraption that looks like a mask. Dr. Klein wants me to study the computer screen, where there's a small camera pointed at my pupils. This, according to her, will record my method of processing a face.

"Normal perceivers go for the internal features of the face and use a triangular sequence that moves between the eyes, the nose, and the mouth. Prosopagnosics, on the other hand, start with the external features, such as the ears and the hair. They usually avoid the eye region."

This sounds about right. And then I wonder what Libby is doing and where she is.

LIBBY

I'm standing in the Department of Brain Sciences, Cognitive Neurology, at Indiana University, Bloomington, where there are answers all around me. I was young when my mom died and when my dad and I talked to the doctors about testing. I let my dad decide whether I should do it or not. But I'm here now, and I can ask to talk to one of these white-coated doctors or scientists. *My mom died of a cerebral hemorrhage, and I need to know if I'm going to die that way too.*

I'm pacing up and down the hall. If I'm tested, they'll either find out I have aneurysms in my brain or I don't. They will either be able to pin them off and try to control them or not.

But here's the thing—even if there aren't any aneurysms in there, these facts won't change: I will still be someone who watches; I will still be someone who is prepared and on the lookout, because at any moment the earth could stop spinning. I've lived through the worst thing that can ever happen to me, and I know firsthand what the world can do.

A man in a white coat passes by and nods at me. I nod back.

I think, *He could have answers.*

I watch him walk away.

I think, *If my mom was here, what would she say?*

My phone buzzes and I almost don't check it, but it could be Jack.

It's a text from Jayvee.

Libby + absent from school = questioning Atticus? I had one other thought. I realized that as bad as it is not to know, the not knowing is something too. You can still do something with that.

And then she adds:

As much as a person can while a person's still in high school in Indiana.

I wait for Dr. Klein to run the results. I tell myself it's okay. It's no big deal. *I mean, it's not as if you don't already know that you suck at recognizing people. But listen, you do all right. You get by. You're good at figuring out identifiers, and you've done it all on your own without any guidance or help.*

I am giving myself the pep talk of my life when Dr. Klein returns. She sits down across from me and says, "You're definitely prosopagnosic. Prosopagnosia is on a continuum. You can be mildly bad or you can be profoundly face-blind. You are profoundly face-blind. In fact, you're one of the most severe cases I've ever seen."

So it's official.

I expect to feel worse or maybe even better now that it's confirmed.

"What happens now? Is there a cure?"

I haven't come across one in any of my research, but that doesn't mean Dr. Amber Klein, brain specialist, won't know of one.

Her smile is upside down and apologetic. "We're certainly making great strides in our research, but no. There's no cure. We're experimenting with ways to teach people how to better manage their face blindness. We've been doing some repetitive training with faces. Research subjects will train for an hour a week. There are ten levels of difficulty. A teenage boy, a little younger than you, has been working with us for five months, and his eye movement strategies have become more normal . . ."

"Is he recognizing faces?"

"No, but we're hoping increased training will begin to help him in his everyday life."

She's starting to lose me, and she can tell this. She turns around to reach for something, and when she turns back, it's as if she's a whole new person. The slate's been wiped clean, so to speak.

The thing she reached for is a model of the human brain. She points to it as she talks. "Toward the back of your brain, over your right ear—just here—there is a specific area that's responsible for identifying faces—"

"Fusiform gyrus twelve." I reach up and run my fingers across the scar again, over my right ear.

"We could do an MRI, and this would provide us with more information. Many prosopagnosics also have trouble recognizing cars and places. They often have topographical agnosia, which means they lose their way easily and don't recognize their houses or places of work. They can have trouble with their hearing. We think prosopagnosia is the key to discovering how the brain processes objects in general. For so long, we've thought of the brain as one entity, but we're learning now about all these separate machines, if you will, that are a part of its makeup, and the fact that these machines don't interact with each other, that they aren't even aware of each other."

"Basically the face-processing area of my brain is either missing, defective, or unplugged? But if I do the MRI, there's still no cure."

"Yes."

There's nothing more she can do for me and I know that and she knows that.

She says, "I suggest telling people, at least your family. Let them know you have this. It will make things easier on you in the long run."

I pick up the phone and text Libby.

I'm done.

And I am.

"One more thing, Jack. Most developmental prosopagnosics don't expect anything from the face in the way that those with acquired prosopagnosia do. Just as a person born without sight has only ever known *not* seeing, those who are born with this don't feel that lack in the same way. But for those who have acquired it, it's not out of the ordinary for them to keep trying to use the face as the key to recognition. That's the instinct."

For some reason this is like a kick in the chest. *I did this to myself. If I hadn't climbed onto the roof that day . . . if I hadn't tried to show off . . . if I hadn't fallen . . . I wouldn't be sitting here talking to a brain specialist.* I should be heartbroken for six-year-old me lying on the front lawn, my world changed forever. But instead I just want to get out of here.

"Thanks, Dr. Klein. I should get home."

She shakes my hand, thanks me for my time, apologizes that she couldn't do more, as if it's her fault. I want to tell her not to be sorry, that she's not the one who pushed me off the roof way back when, but instead I say, "Good luck with the research."

"Jack?"

I turn back. I see a woman there with glasses and sharp cheekbones and hair swept up off her neck. She says, "One person in every fifty is face-blind. It might help for you to remember that. You're definitely not alone."

LIBBY

On the drive back to Amos, I ask him questions about the test, and he answers them in this very short *yes, no, yes, no* kind of way. Then we're quiet. He is far away, and I know what that feels like, to want to close yourself up. So I don't force him to talk anymore. We just ride.

We ride for ten miles without saying a word. The silence covers us like a blanket. I'm staring out past the road into the great beyond, but after a while the blanket of silence starts to feel smothering, like it's cutting off my circulation.

I almost tell him I was *this close* to getting tested too, but what comes out of my mouth is "I want to be a dancer. Not just a Damsel, but a professional dancer."

To his credit, he doesn't go veering off the road. He echoes, "A dancer." And he's still far away. But I can hear him tune in a bit.

"When I was little—not just young, but literally little—I took ballet. And I was great at it. I have this picture of me in a black leotard, standing in the most perfect fifth position you've ever seen. It was taken the night of our recital, my first ever, and I was glorious. Afterward my teacher told me, 'You will never be a dancer. I can continue teaching you but it will only be a waste of your parents' money. Your bones are too big. You don't have the body for it. The sooner you learn this, the better.'"

"Wow. What a bastard."

"It crushed me. For a long time I didn't dance, no matter what my mom said. She offered to find me a different teacher, but something was ruined. I let that woman ruin it for me." I stare at his profile, fixed on the highway. "But she can't stop me from dancing. No one's going to tell me not to dance anymore. No one should tell you what you can or can't do either. Including you."

We're riding in silence again, but everything is lighter and cleaner. The mood has lifted and he's back.

"My dad is having an affair."

"How do you know?"

"I just know. It's Mrs. Chapman. At school."

"As in Mrs. Chapman, chemistry teacher?"

"The very one."

"Really?" Except for being young, there's nothing about Mrs. Chapman that screams *Take me for your mistress.* "*And* you have to see her at school."

"Yeah."

"I mean, you have to run into her at school."

"Yeah."

"What a bastard."

"I'm sorry that people give you shit about your weight. I'm sorry for anything I did to make it worse for you."

"I'm sorry you have to date Caroline Lushamp."

He laughs, and suddenly the car is warm and crackling with electricity.

"I'm not dating her anymore." These five words surround us, taking over the air, until he says, "I'm sorry my friends can be assholes."

"I'm sorry you can't recognize the people you know. Maybe if you could, you'd pick better friends."

He laughs again, but not as hard.

"Look at it this way—everyone you meet, everyone you know, if they get on your nerves or piss you off, it's okay. The next day they'll just be new people. Different people."

"I guess." He's not laughing now.

We come up on a road sign: AMOS . . . 5 MILES.

He says, "We could keep driving."

"Into the sunset?"

"Why not?"

And suddenly it's like I'm watching us from the sky—two outlaws, Jack Masselin and Libby Strout, sitting together in the front seat of a badass mo-fo of an old car, his leg inches from hers, his hands on the wheel, breathing the same air, thinking the same thoughts, sharing things with each other that they don't share with anyone else.

His eyes are on mine again, and he says, "As someone recently diagnosed with prosopagnosia, I'm told that I don't process faces like normal people. For instance, I avoid the eyes. But I don't seem to have any trouble looking into yours. In fact, I like looking into them. A lot."

Our eyes lock.

As in *they lock*.

As in I can't imagine ever looking away.

"The road," I say, but you can barely hear it.

I think about making a move on her. It would be so easy—pull the car over, lean in, touch her cheek, lean in a little more (close enough so she can feel my breath), catch her eye, look right into her, maybe brush her hair off her face. All the things I've learned to do in order to be the Guy Girls Want.

Her head is turned away so that I can only see her hair. When she speaks again, her voice sounds a little throaty, a little full, and there's something else in it.

The something else is:

She might like you back.

Which means you might like her.

Because to like someone back *indicates reciprocating something that was already in existence.*

As in you liked her first.

As in I like Libby Strout.

Oh shit, do I?

And because I'm thinking about cancer and this old guy in San Francisco with face blindness and Dr. Amber Klein and aneurysms and how, when you get down to it, so much of life is out of our control, I decide to take control of something.

I reach over and take her hand. It's soft and warm and fits exactly in mine, and to be honest I'm not really expecting anything, but suddenly my entire body is wired, as if I've been plugged directly into the sun.

We stare down at our hands, as if we're seeing them for the first time.

Somehow, I remember I'm driving, so my eyes go back to the road, but I don't let go of her hand. I rub her skin with my thumb, and you can almost feel the electrostatic discharge, that flow of electricity between two electrically charged objects suddenly coming into contact. ESD, as it's called, can create amazing electric sparks, but it can also have harmful effects, like coal dust explosions or gas. Unlike with Caroline, who is mostly gas and coal dust, there aren't any harmful effects here.

Libby is solid. She is real. As long as I hold her hand, she won't vanish before my eyes.

LIBBY

He turns off the highway onto the Amos exit. We pass the Welcome Center and the Ford dealership and the mall and all the chain restaurants. We pass the old Victorians that line Main Street, and the little history museum, and the four blocks of downtown, and the courthouse. We pass the high school and the college and the mortuary, and then, finally, we pull into my neighborhood.

Do I like Jack Masselin? As in like *like him?*

At some point I'm going to have to get out of this car and move up the walk and open the door and go inside. I will have to shut that door—me on one side, him on the other—and he will move down the walk, away from this house, and climb back into his car and drive away. I will go to my room and lie on my bed and wonder if this really happened or if I made it up and how on earth I feel about it.

He rolls to a stop and turns off the car, and we're both staring at our hands again. I don't look up because if I look up, he might look up, and what if he kisses me?

My body might just explode into a million pieces of shimmering, glittering light.

I want her to look up. *Look up,* I think. *Look up. Look up.*

My phone buzzes, and we both jump. This is my alarm letting me know I only have thirty minutes before everyone gets home. *Shit.*

She doesn't even wait for me to turn it off, just drops my hand like a hot potato and goes leaping out of the car. It breaks the spell, and I sit there thinking, *What the fuck am I doing?*

I almost drive away, but instead I get out of the Land Rover, and she's already on her front step. For the first time this year, I can feel fall coming. There's a chill in the air that makes me think of bonfires, but my hand is still warm. I shove it into my pocket, and it burns right through my jeans to the skin.

She says, "Thanks for bringing me home." And I can hear it— she's nervous.

I look right into her eyes. "You are the most amazing person I've ever met. You're different. You're you. Always. Who else can say that except maybe Seth Powell, and he's an idiot. You, Libby Strout, are not an idiot."

She points at my chest. "You do like me."

"What?"

"Jack Masselin likes the fat girl, but you haven't fully accepted it yet."

Okay, I think. *Let's see where this goes.*

"I'm not saying you're right, but what if I did accept it?"

"I guess we'd have to do something about it, then." And she walks into her house and shuts the door.

LIBBY

I stand inside, heart skipping beats. I can hear him on the other side of the door. I can feel him there. I know the moment when he walks away, two minutes later, because the air around me goes back to being normal air, not dangerous, electric-storm air that might lightning-strike you at any moment. My heart is still skipping beats as he drives away.

I think about saying it as Mom passes the salad, as Dusty recites his lines from *Peter Pan,* as Dad passes the mac and cheese: *I have prosopagnosia. It's official. I was tested today by a brain specialist.*

No one knows I haven't been home all day except Marcus, who keeps saying things like "I called home today but nobody answered the phone. Were you asleep, Jack? You must have been sleeping, right? Otherwise you would have picked up." All these baiting comments, trying to trip me up. When Mom and Dad aren't looking, I give him the finger.

Dad catches me and says, "Hey. Not at the table."

I want to tell him not to talk to me. I want to say *You're the last person who should be reprimanding anyone.*

But I'm in this weirdly good mood, in spite of Dr. Amber Klein and in spite of my fucked-up brain. So I don't say a word to my dad or to Marcus, which is so much more than either of them deserves. I stay locked in my own head, reliving the ride there, the ride home, my hand intertwined with Libby's, the way she smiled at me, and the way she said, *I guess we'd have to do something about it, then.*

After dinner, I'm in the basement working on the Lego robot, trying to lose myself in the process of building something, but the only thing I'm building right now is the world's largest pile of discarded robot parts. The hardest stage of any project is coming up with it. Once I know what I want the thing to be, it's just a matter of collecting the pieces I need and putting them together in the right order. But right now I can't nail it down. I've got fifty different ideas for fifty different robots, but none of them are right or extraordinary enough.

I hear footsteps, and from the stairs a voice says, "Were you really sick today?"

Dusty.

"Not in a flu kind of way."

"Do you want to talk about it?"

"I'm good." He wanders over to me, sorting through the parts that are scattered across the worktable and the floor. I say, "Do you want to talk about anything? Are people still being shitty?"

"I'm good too. I'm Peter Pan."

And I get it. He wants to stay in this moment. The bad moments always have a way of coming around again, way too soon.

I go up to my room and climb out of my window, into the tree and onto the roof. I lie back and stare at the sky. I think about it being the same sky that I looked up at when I was six, before I fell, and about all that's happened in between then and now. It really shouldn't be the same sky, for all that's happened. It should look completely different.

Marcus was playing in the yard. I went up to the roof to get away from him and away from my mom, who was always telling me to watch him. It was harder to get up there than I expected. That surprised me. And it was dirtier—bird shit and twigs and an old softball that might have been there for the past twenty years. Our roof isn't flat—it has a slope—and I scooted to the edge of it, looking out over the street and the neighborhood. I held on with one hand, and Marcus looked up just then, and I let go because I wanted him to see that I was strong and fearless and bigger than he would ever be.

It takes less than a second to fall twelve feet, but it felt like it lasted forever. In that moment of falling, they say the memory goes wide open. You can see things you don't usually think of or see or remember. For me, it was my mother's face—specifically, it was her eyes. I can't remember what they looked like in that moment I saw them, but I remember that I saw them.

LIBBY

"Hello?"

"It's Jack. I was thinking about what you said."

"I say so many things. Can you narrow it down?"

"I was thinking about what you said about doing something to address this whole you-like-me-I-like-you situation."

"I never said I like you."

Silence.

"Jack?"

"What you've just heard is the sound of my heart dying a swift and sudden death."

"Hypothetically speaking, *if*—and I'm not saying I do—but *if* I was to like you, what would you want to do about it?"

"I would probably want to hold your hand."

"Probably?"

"Hypothetically, yes. I would definitely hypothetically want to hold your hand."

"Well then, I would probably hypothetically hold yours back."

"I would also hypothetically want to take you to a movie, even though I don't like movies as a rule because of the whole facial confusion situation."

"Which one?"

"Which movie?"

"I need to know if it's something I want to see."

"Won't it be enough just to be with me, holding hypothetical hands in the dark?"

"I'd at least like to know what kind of movie we'd be seeing."

"Uh. I think it would need to be a movie with some of everything. Comedy. Drama. Action. Mystery. Romance."

"That sounds like a really good movie."

"So would you hold my hand during it?"

"Probably."

"Okay. I'll take 'probably' for now. I'd also want to take you out to dinner, either before or after the movie, depending, and I would absolutely want to walk you to your door."

"What if I wanted to dance to my door instead?"

"Then I'm your man."

Are you? Is this what this means? My heart goes hopscotching out of the room and down the hall and out the door and into the street.

"But after I danced you to the door, I'd want to kiss you."

"You would?"

"I would."

And now my heart is nowhere on earth to be found. I can see it as it bypasses the moon and the stars and goes blasting into another galaxy.

"Hypothetically."

"Well then, I would let you kiss me."

"Hypothetically?"

"No. Definitely."

By the time we hang up two hours later, it's 1:46 a.m. I lie there for the rest of the night waiting for my heart to return to my chest.

THE NEXT EIGHT DAYS

JACK

At lunch on Monday, I sit across the table from Kam and Seth, who are elbow to elbow. I'm sketching design ideas for Dusty's robot, and I'm pretty much on fire for the first time, and I can *see* it, as in I finally know what I'm doing, and my blood is pumping and my heart is pumping like I've just run a marathon and sprinted all the way to the finish. Nothing, as in nothing, can stop the flow of these ideas, until Seth goes, "You know, Kam and me, we've got something that can help you out in your situation."

I look up, a little foggy, because my head is on the paper in front of me, not in the MVB cafeteria. Seth is grinning like a jackal, and whatever it is, I don't want to hear it.

But I say, wary as hell, "What situation is that?"

Seth elbows Kam hard, which makes Kam drop the three dozen french fries he was about to stuff down his throat. "Goddammit, Powell."

Seth keeps right on. "I did some research last night." He pulls a piece of paper out of his pocket.

"Jesus. Porn?" I should have known. I go back to sketching.

"Not porn. God." He actually has the nerve to sound offended, even though as far as I know Seth thinks the Internet was invented for two purposes: porn and poker. "Number one. They're easy to talk to."

"Who's easy to talk to?" I'm still making notes.

"Fat girls." My head snaps up so hard I probably give myself whiplash. He's trying to keep a straight face, but he can't help himself—he's snickering already.

"Two. 'Pretty women aren't always nice.'"

Kam goes, "That one's true."

I say, "What is it you're reading to me?"

"'Top Ten Reasons to Date a Fat Girl.' I found it online." He waves the paper, and then holds it up to his face again, reads something to himself, and starts howling. I make a grab for it, but he holds it out of reach, over his head. "Three . . ."

Kam rips the paper out of his hands and hands it to me. I crush it into a ball and get ready to launch it across the cafeteria into the trash, but I don't want anyone digging it out of there, so I stuff it into my back pocket instead. I lean over the table and whack Seth in the head.

He just keeps laughing. Kam says, "Moron." And crams the rest of the french fries into his mouth.

I know Seth thinks he's being funny, but my insides are burning, like I've inhaled an entire forest fire.

"Lay off her, man. I'm serious."

"Wow. Sure, sure, Mass. Whatever." He's wiping the tears away and trying to catch his breath. He sits quietly for a minute, and then, with one snicker, he launches into another laughing fit.

I try not to let it bother me. *Who cares what they think?* I tell myself it's not that she's fat. That's not what I'm worried about. I'm not worried at all. I just want them to leave me alone. Leave us alone. But part of me is going, *What if you're just shallow? What if that's your identifier?*

"You're a fucking idiot, Seth Powell." And I gather up my ideas and what's left of my lunch and walk away.

LIBBY

The Damsels Drill Team auditions sign-up sheet hangs on Heather Alpern's door. So far seven girls have signed up. I'm number eight. Jayvee hands me a pen, and I lean in and write my name. Behind me I hear, "Oh my God, you're trying out?"

Caroline Lushamp looks down at me with this weird pretend smile that makes her look like some sort of beauty queen serial killer.

I say, "Oh my God, how did you know?"

She blinks at me, blinks at my name on the sheet, blinks at Jayvee, blinks at me.

I say, "Just imagine it—we could be teammates." And then I squeeze her into the tightest hug. "See you at auditions!"

Jayvee can barely walk for laughing. She weaves like a drunk person through the halls. Finally, she straightens up and stops laughing long enough to say, "So what did you do about the Atticus situation? Test or no test?"

"No test. I decided he knew best after all."

"He usually does."

In driver's ed, we're assigned three to a car, and since the rest of the class is made up of sophomores, the lone juniors are lumped together: Bailey, Travis Kearns, and me.

I'm pretty sure Travis is stoned. He carries on a commentary in the backseat that goes something like: "Floor it, big girl . . . Go like the mother-effing wind . . . Open her up . . . Show this world what you can do . . . Take that beautiful big leg of yours and slam that gas pedal . . . Take us to the moon, sister . . . or at least to Indy . . . Take us to Indy . . . Take us to Indy . . . Indy . . . Indy . . . Indy . . ." (Several indecipherable words followed by mad laughter.)

Bailey is in the back next to him, and she's smashed up against the door, as far away from him as she can possibly get. But in true Bailey fashion, she's wearing a determined smile. Mr. Dominguez, in all his manliness, is in the passenger seat. I'm behind the wheel, and I can't help it—I'm *excited*. My hands are tingling and there is this crazy heat burning up from my feet, all the way up my legs, into my stomach, through my chest. I feel like I'm on fire, but in a way that lets me know I'm ALIVE.

You have to understand that for a long time there was a part of me that thought I would never drive or run or do any of the everyday things that people my age get to do. My world consisted of my bed and the sofa, and after a while, when I couldn't move easily from one to the other, I stayed in bed all day and night, reading, watching show after show, surfing around online, and, yes, eating. Sometimes I would hear Dean, Sam, and Castiel outside, and if I sat up enough, I could see out my window into the street and watch them play tennis or soccer or tag. I saw Dean and Sam leave for dances and dates (in my mind, they were dating me). I watched the youngest, Cas, climb one of the trees that hugged the house. I overheard phone conversations and make-out sessions and arguments. Sometimes I'd see Cas in my yard, looking up at my window, and I would sit very still, hoping he'd go away because it was one thing to spy and another to be spied on.

So now I'm driving, which is why I don't mind that Travis is nattering on or that Bailey is asking me about Jack and me and is there anything between us that means something and is there a *Jack and Libby* in any way, shape, or form that she should know about. Mr. Dominguez barks directions at me, and at some point yells at the two of them to shut up.

Even though this is my first time behind the wheel, I'm good at it. Like it's effortless. I feel AT HOME here. And at some point it hits me—*I'm driving*.

As in *I'm actually driving a car. Like a normal person. Like that person passing me on the other side of the road. Like the person in front of me. Like the person behind me. Like all these people walking down the street who probably have cars and licenses of their own. I AM DRIVING A CAR!*

This is one more thing I'll never get to share with my mom, and before I know it, I'm crying. I miss her, but *look at me behind the wheel, steering us down the street. Look at me waiting at this stoplight. Look at me making this turn.*

Mr. Dominguez says, "What the hell are you doing?"

Without taking my eyes from the road, I say, "I'm crying. And also driving. I'm crying *and* driving!" This makes me cry harder, and the tears are both happy and sad.

Bailey leans up and gives my shoulder a squeeze, and I can hear her sniffling. Dominguez goes, "Do we need to stop the car?"

"Never! I want to drive for days!" Suddenly I'm talking only in exclamation marks. And then I check my mirrors and, even though Dominguez hasn't told me to, I go beelining for the highway entrance because I can't hold myself back. I need to turn this car loose.

Travis yells, "Floor it!" And Bailey lets out a little squeal as she goes flying back against the seat.

I'm still crying, but now I'm also laughing because I'm free, and none of them can possibly understand. "You will never know what it's like to be trapped in your house like a veal," I say to Mr. Dominguez. "This is the best day of my life!" Even to me, my laughter sounds maniacal, but it doesn't feel that way. It feels big and sincere and endless, like I could laugh from now until the end of my life without interruption.

And as ridiculous as it sounds, I mean it. *This is the best day of my life.* I'm on the highway now and everything is whooshing by, but then I start whooshing along with it all, just like everyone else, like I actually belong out here in this world. Like I could drive all the way up into the clouds, propelled by happiness and freedom.

Someone turns on the music—"All Right Now" by Free. In the rearview mirror I can see Travis air-banging his head, and poor Bailey clutching at my seat, blond hair blowing everywhere. The song plays on and on as I practice passing in and out of lanes, long enough that eventually all of us, even Bailey, sing the chorus.

Two blocks from school, Mr. Dominguez makes us roll up the windows and sit up straight. But as I pull into the parking lot, we're all still singing.

JACK

After the Conversation Circle, Libby and I walk out of the gym together. We walk up the stairs and through the halls, side by side, and then we walk out to the parking lot. I want to hold her hand, but I don't, and my brain grabs onto this with both fists. *Why don't you hold her hand?* Keshawn, Natasha, and the rest of them are ahead of us, so it's just Libby and me.

I say, "I was wondering, hypothetically speaking, if you'd go out with me this weekend."

She either pretends to think about this or actually thinks about this.

"Take your time. You've got approximately two more minutes to respond."

"Until the offer expires?"

"Until I ask you again."

She gives me a smile that's all slinky and seductive. In this low voice, she goes, "I think, hypothetically, it sounds like fun."

LIBBY

Jack is five minutes early. His hair is as wildly gigantic as usual, but damp, as if he just stepped out of the shower, and I'm sitting next to him on the couch, and he smells like soap and so much *man*. I try not to stare at his hands, resting on his knees, at the way his skin looks even more gold against the dark blue of his jeans.

I've warned my dad that Jack is coming. That Jack is my friend. That Jack is taking me out for MY FIRST DATE EVER. *Yes, the same Jack you met in the principal's office.*

I hold my breath as we sit, the three of us (four, counting George, blinking at Jack from the back of my dad's chair), in an awkward triangle of So Many Things Not Being Said. My dad and Jack are making chitchat, and Jack does most of the talking. My dad watches him like he's trying to uncover his true intentions. He isn't necessarily being warm and friendly, but he's not being rude either, which is something to be grateful for.

But then Will Strout goes, "You can imagine how surprised I was when Libby told me she wanted to go out with you."

"I can."

"I know my daughter's amazing, but the question is if you do."

"I'm learning that."

"She seems to trust you, and she wants me to trust you too."

"I understand why you wouldn't. All I can do is try to prove myself to both of you, sir."

"Can you give me three good reasons I should let her leave the house with you tonight?"

"I acted like an asshole, but I'm not an asshole. I never meant to hurt your daughter. I would never purposely hurt your daughter."

Dad looks at me, and I try to give him a look that says *Please forgive him and let me go so that I don't die an old maid, and besides I really like him, even if you think it sounds crazy, and please, please trust me.*

He says to Jack, "So where are you planning on taking my daughter this evening?" He keeps saying *my daughter* like he's trying to drive the point home. *THIS IS MY CHILD, MY FLESH AND BLOOD. DO YOU KNOW HOW DEAD YOU WILL BE IF YOU DO ANYTHING TO MESS WITH MY ONLY KID?!*

"I thought we'd see a movie and get something to eat."

"You'll bring her home by eleven o'clock."

Me: "I'm a junior in high school."

Dad: "Yes, you are."

Me: "How about midnight?"

Dad: "How about ten thirty?"

Me (to Jack): "I need to be home by eleven."

Jack (laughing): "Not a problem. I promise to get her home by then, if not before."

Not too much before, I think.

My dad says to him, "When was the last time you had your car serviced?"

And now I can't tell if he's just messing with Jack or if he's being serious. I try to send him a telepathic message: *Please stop this. Please lighten up.* There's a good chance he's going to destroy my chances here before I can, and maybe Jack isn't my last opportunity to have a male nonrelation love me, but he's certainly my best opportunity right now, and besides, I actually like him.

I like Jack Masselin.

"August. I'm actually pretty handy, so I did it myself."

Dad studies him for what seems like the rest of my life. "You know, your father and I went to school together. We played on the football team in middle school and in high school."

And it's not exactly *I'm so thrilled you're taking my daughter out,* but it's something.

In the car I say, "I'm sorry about my dad."

"Are you kidding? He has every reason to kick my ass. If I was him, I'd never let me near you."

But all I hear is *I just want to be near you, Libby Strout. I want to kiss your lips right off your face.*

Jack says, "He's just protective, and he should be, especially after what I did to you. That's how I'd be if I ever had a daughter."

But what I hear is *I will always be protective of you. I will always look after you and our daughter, the one we're going to have together after we get married and I am loving you forever.*

I'm in the same car, only fifteen years in the future—somewhere far away from Amos. Jack Masselin is next to me like he is now, only our kids are in the backseat, or maybe just one kid—the daughter—my hand on his leg. I stare at his leg and then at his hands on the wheel. *I bet you'll be a wonderful father.*

I'm not sure where we're going, but we're headed to the east side of town, where the restaurants and the movie theater are. This is where my dad and I lived until they had to destroy our house to get me out.

As if he can read my mind, Jack says, "Didn't you use to live on this side of town?"

"Once upon a time. So where are we going?"

He grins at me, and I melt into the seat. My insides have gone warm and soft, and I lean into this feeling because it's not something I have all the time. *It's okay to be happy,* I hear Rachel say. *It's okay to let yourself enjoy the good times.*

Tonight could be the night. My Pauline Potter work-off-the-weight sex night. Jack Masselin, you just might be my first.

He says, "I was thinking we'd get something to eat and take it from there." But he might as well say *I'm taking you to the moon and back, and while we're up there, I'm going to collect the stars for you so that you can keep them.*

And suddenly I'm thinking about the daughter we're destined to have. *Beatrice,* I think. *We'll name her Beatrice.*

We drive past Olive Garden, Applebee's, and the Red Lobster that opened last month. I'm mentally ticking through all the restaurants in town—there aren't many—but we pass one after the other. I half expect him to just circle around and take me home, no food, no date. Or maybe drive across the Ohio line where no one will recognize him or me or us.

But then we're leaving Amos, and my heart deflates a little, which tells me I didn't actually expect him to do this, and now he's doing it—smuggling me over city lines like the daughter of some wealthy oil baron.

"Where are we going?" My voice sounds flat, as if it's underridden a semi about fifty times.

"Richmond."

"Richmond?" It comes out sounding like *ARE YOU F-ING KIDDING ME? RICHMOND?! WHY DON'T YOU JUST CHAIN A BOULDER TO MY LEG AND THROW ME IN THE RIVER?*

"Yes, Richmond. There's no way I'm taking you to one of the usual dumps in town. Not looking like that."

JACK

Clara's Pizza King is an institution. It's the best pizza for miles, and there's a red double-decker bus parked in the dining room. The place is crowded, but I've called ahead. We can sit in the bus or at a corner table upstairs that has a porch swing on one side. Libby chooses the porch swing.

We move through the tables, Libby in front of me, and I see people staring at her. This happens when I'm with Caroline—people look at her. But they look at Caroline because she's the kind of tall, sexy girl you look at.

As we walk, I can see where the path is too tight, where Libby will have to squeeze through. I offer to go first because that way I can choose which way to go so she doesn't have to worry about it. I'm clearing the way, and people are gawking, and it hits me that up until recently, I was one of them. Maybe not the snickering ones, but the ones sitting next to them. I don't know what to feel or do, so I stare back. *Do I know them or not know them?* I don't even care. They're watching her and me, and this table of boys starts saying shit. Does she hear them? I can't tell. Probably. I throw my head back—a move I like to think makes my hair instantly grow twenty times bigger, and me ten feet taller—and I give them the eye. They get quiet.

Upstairs, Libby takes a seat on the swing, and now I can sit on the other side of the table or I can sit next to her. I think, *Fuck 'em all,* these people who are staring. I say, "Is that space taken?" I nod down at the swing.

"You don't have to."

"What?"

"Sit by me."

"Move it, sister."

She shoves over, and we rock back and forth, like we're kicking back on our front porch on a summer afternoon. Each table has an actual phone—the old-fashioned kind with a cord—and after I call in our order, I take her hand.

I say, "My palms are sweaty."

"Why?"

"I'm nervous."

"Why?"

"Because I'm sitting next to you on this swing and you're beautiful."

She hesitates, like she's not sure whether to take the compliment. But then she says, "Thank you."

Being out in the world with her is different from being alone with her. For one, there are too many other people. For two, I'm on guard, ready to take on anyone who tries to get it started with her or me. For three, it's making me think about her weight in a way I haven't really, truly thought about until right this moment.

We're sitting there in silence, so I decide to tell her about Dr. Amber Klein and the tests and everything I haven't told her about my time as Jack Masselin, Lab Rat. Libby's not saying anything, but I can tell she's listening. Her head is cocked to one side, and I can see her eyes taking it all in.

Finally she goes, "How do you feel?"

"The same. Maybe a little worse. Maybe a little better."

"Are you going to tell your parents?"

"I don't think so. What's the point, right? I mean, there's nothing any of us can do, short of downloading facial recognition software directly into this brain of mine. Telling them won't magically create a cure. It'll just give them more shit to worry about."

"I'm sorry. I wanted there to be something they could do for you. Not because your brain isn't awesome the way it is, but because it would make you feel better."

Now it's my turn to not say anything. I sit looking at her until it's just us, Libby and me, no one else for miles. What I want to do more than anything is kiss her. I almost do, but then the waitress is standing there with our food.

As we eat, Libby is glancing around, and finally she looks at me and goes, "Richmond, huh?" And there's something in her tone that makes me set down my drink.

"I thought you'd like Clara's."

"I do like Clara's. It's just that I would have been okay, you know, going somewhere in Amos." And then she stares off toward the bus.

I say, "Listen, I may be keeping the face blindness a secret for now, but that doesn't mean I want everything in my life to be a secret. It doesn't mean I want to keep you a secret. I would never hide you away, if that's what you're thinking." As I say it, I ask myself, *Is that what I'm doing?*

She starts blinking at the table, at the menu, anywhere else but at me.

"Holy shit. That's what you were thinking. That I brought you out here so we wouldn't run into anyone."

"No."

"Good, because that would be crazy."

So why did you bring her here, asshole?

"I mean yes."

"Uh, because that wouldn't be crazy at all." Now her eyes find mine. "Okay," I say. "I get it. I'm king douchelord and you trust me but you don't. You don't know me well enough to know how deep the douchery goes."

The whole while I'm asking myself, *How deep* does *the douchery go? What if it goes deeper than you think?*

She says, "Maybe not." And I hate the careful, closed-off tone because it's like a fence between us.

"Listen. I brought you here because you're better than some shitty Amos chain restaurant. I brought you here because when I was six, I fell off the roof of our house, and my dad smuggled a Clara's pizza into the hospital, and those kinds of memories are pretty rare for me right now—the ones where my dad is this really great guy. I brought you here because this is the first place I wanted to go after I got out of the hospital and was well enough to sit up straight. I brought you here because it's one of the few places in a sixty-mile radius, if not the entire state of Indiana, that isn't boring or typical. Because *you're* not boring or typical."

And I realize *every word is true.*

I reach over the fence and take her hand. I kiss the knuckles, one by one. As I do I'm thinking, *How does this girl mean so much to me?*

"Libby Strout, you deserve to be seen."

"People can't help but see me." She says this to the tablecloth.

"That's not what I mean."

We sit there swinging, and now I'm kicking myself for bringing her here. I should have just gone to Red Lobster where we could have been stared at by everyone at school, including maybe Caroline, and where my idiot friends could have come over and hijacked our date with their stupidity.

I say, "Wait here," and then I'm up and out of the swing, down the stairs, and over to the jukebox, which hugs the wall behind the bus. This is the same jukebox my parents used to play when they were coming here on dates about sixty years ago. As I'm flipping through the musical choices, I'm thinking about how Libby Strout makes me want to drive thirty miles to the closest place that is almost good enough for her and run through crowded restaurants to find her the perfect song.

And then I see it. The Jackson 5. I choose the song I was look-ing for and also a couple of others—Sly and the Family Stone, Earth, Wind & Fire—so we can have a whole block of them. Then I go back to the table, which is the table in the upper northwest corner, the one with the girl in the purple dress.

She says, "You didn't have to do that. You don't have to do anything. I'm being dumb."

"You could never be dumb."

"I can be dumb."

She takes a bite of pizza. I take a bite of pizza. We eat in this weird silence.

And then suddenly the song is playing, as in *the* song. I wipe my mouth with the napkin and toss it aside. I'm on my feet, hand out.

Libby blinks up at me. "What?"

"Come on."

"Where?"

"Just come on."

And I lead her down the stairs to the center of Clara's, right to the one open spot, at the front of the restaurant, near the entrance to the dining room. Then I spin her into my arms, and we're danc-ing. *Oh so slowly.* "I'll Be There" is the obvious choice, but the one I chose is "Ben." If ever a song was written for Libby and me, it's this one. Two broken, lonely people who maybe aren't so broken or lonely anymore.

At first I'm aware of every eye in the room on us, but then all the faces fade away, and it's just Libby and me, my hands on her waist, all that *woman* in my arms. We're in perfect sync, moving together, making it up as we go.

LIBBY

I can feel the tears burning against the backs of my eyes. Every line is me, Libby Strout. It's us, but mostly me. And also Jack. *God.*

I could cry in the arms of Jack Masselin as an entire restaurant of strangers watches, or I could push the tears back and down until they're buried. I push them. And push them. I won't let them out. At some point, he leans in and, just like that, without a word, kisses my face, first one cheek and then the other. He kisses me where the tears would be if I'd let them fall, and it's the single loveliest thing anyone has ever done who wasn't my mom. Suddenly I'm filled with this safe, warm feeling that I haven't felt in a really long time. It's the feeling of *everything is going to be okay. You are going to be okay. You may already be okay. Let's us be okay together, just you and me.*

I suck in my breath and don't breathe again until the song is over. The jukebox goes jumping right into the next track, which is a fast one, thank goodness, and that's when Jack breaks out the moves.

He says, "Get a load of this, girl. *If you can handle it.*"

And he is grooving all over the place.

"Handle this!" And I'm dancing too, till we're dancing like lunatics, and I don't feel like crying anymore ever again.

He goes, "Do the Exploding Hair!"

And he shakes his head to the left, to the right, to the middle.

He has an unfair advantage because his hair is so much bigger, but I do my best to shake my hair all around.

I go, "Do the Lightning Strike!" And I jump and shake, jump and shake like I'm being electrified. He starts jumping and shaking too, and at some point, I look around and a handful of other people are on their feet and dancing at their tables.

Jack says, "It's a dance revolution!"

He takes my hand and twirls me round and round so that I'm spinning like a top and laughing. I think what an amazing world this would be if we all danced everywhere we went.

He walks me to the front door of my house, and when we get there I wait for him to kiss me good night, but instead he hugs me. This isn't a Fat Girl Rodeo hug. It's warm and enveloping in a good way, and I can smell the soap and outdoors on him, like he rolled in fresh grass. I want him to hold me forever, but then he pulls away and gazes down at me with half-closed eyes. "Good night, Libby."

And I say, "Good night, Jack." And I go inside and my dad is there, and I tell him about the dinner and then I go to my room and close the door and sit on the bed and think, *Why the hell didn't he want to kiss me?*

My phone buzzes. **Best date ever.**

Followed by: **I can't wait to do it again.**

Followed by: **This chick Mary Katherine really reminds you of us? From what I can tell, she's pretty much bats in the belfry.**

I write: **Yes, but in a kind of lovable way. She's got this big secret, and no one understands her. Does that help you make the connection?**

He writes back: **Oh I didn't say I don't see the connection, but tell me you don't think we're that crazy.**

Me: **I think we're even crazier.**

Jack: **I'll buy that.**

A few minutes later, he writes: **I can't stop reading. This may be the best birthday present I've ever gotten, next to the soldering iron they gave me when I turned nine.**

Me: **That's what I like about you. So manly, yet so cerebral.**

Jack: **Those are only two of the many, many things you like about me. And don't get me started on what I like about you. I'll never get this book read, and it's my life's mission to finish it tonight.**

He texts me off and on through the rest of the night, giving me a running commentary on what he's reading. Eventually, I fall back into the pillows, a big, loopy smile on my face. He may not have kissed me after our date, but it's almost definitely, undeniably, absolutely guaranteed that he will.

Monday morning, a tall girl with dark skin and a painted-on beauty mark finds me at my locker.

"Jack."

Caroline.

"Yes?"

Just in case it isn't her but some other tall girl with dark skin and a painted-on beauty mark by one eye.

"Did you have a good weekend?"

"Thanks for asking. Yes, I did."

"You know what people are saying, don't you?"

And here it comes.

"That I'm one badass dude?"

"About that girl. That Libby Strout. And you. They're saying you're *dating* her. That she's your new *girlfriend.* I was like, I know that can't be true, but they're like, no, it's true. He took her to Clara's."

"Who is 'they'?"

"It doesn't matter."

I can hear the hurt in her voice, buried underneath all the venom. I want to say *It's okay to be a person. We're all afraid. We all get hurt. It's okay to hurt. You'd be so much more likable if you just acted human.*

"We're not together anymore, Caroline, so, uh, not to be rude, but why do you care?"

"I think it's sweet that you want to be nice to her after what you did, but I'm just concerned about her. Girls like that, you can't mess around with them, Jack." She shakes her head. "You could end up breaking her heart."

"We haven't defined anything yet, but if you're asking me if I like hanging out with her? Absolutely. And do I think she's one cool chick? Yes. Do I think she's beautiful? Yeah, I do. I really do. I'm not messing around with her. I like her. Any other questions?"

She stands there, perfectly composed, perfectly Caroline, and says, "You know, you think you're all that, you pretend to be all that, but you're not."

"I know I'm not. Which is all the more reason I'm grateful she likes me anyway."

At home, I dig through the pile of clothes on my floor until I come up with the jeans I'm looking for. I pull the ball of wadded-up paper out of the back pocket. *Top 10 Reasons to Date a Fat Girl.*

I make myself reread it. It's like I need to prove to myself once and for all that she's fat and I don't care.

Every word of the article makes me sick. *How could I ever feel anything but lucky that this girl likes me?*

I go downstairs to the kitchen, walk directly to the stove, turn on one of the burners, and wave the paper over the gas flame till it catches fire. I hold the paper up and away from the stove and watch as the words burn away. And then I drop what's left of the paper into the sink, where it burns itself into a pile of ashes. I turn on the faucet and wash the remains down the drain, and for good measure, flick the switch to the garbage disposal and let it grind.

• • •

Back in my room, I call Libby. When she answers, I say, "I finished the book."

"And?"

"One, it was pretty damn terrifying. Two, Mary Katherine Blackwood was mad as a fucking hatter. Three, I see why you love it. Four, it might have reminded me of us just a little, although I'd like to argue that we're slightly more sane. And five, I think it would be pretty fucking awesome to live in a castle with you."

LIBBY

In my nightstand, underneath my headphones, my lip balm, and an assortment of bookmarks, I pull out a letter written on Christmas stationery.

> *These are for dancing alone onstage*
> *Or in your room*
> *Or anywhere your heart desires.*
> *They are for dancing in your dreams—*
> *dancing toward your future—*
> *dancing in love and creativity and joy—*
> *dancing because that is what you do.*
> *Because that's who you are, no matter what,*
> *inside and outside.*
> *You just*
> *keep*
> *on*
> *dancing.*

The shoes that came with this letter are in my closet. They're from the Christmas before my mom died. They will always be the last present I ever get from her, and I need to keep them safe forever, which is why I've never worn them.

But right now I'm sitting down and pulling apart the tissue

paper and taking the shoes out of their box and tying them on my feet. They are pink ballet toe shoes, and they are the loveliest thing I own. Even though she bought them too big, they're too small for me now and hard to walk in, but I shuffle over to my laptop and turn on some music. I'm going old-school with the Spice Girls, a band my mom secretly loved. The song is "Who Do You Think You Are," and it makes me think of my mom, of me, of where I might go one day, of what I might be.

My Damsels audition is Saturday. I know my routine by heart. I could do it in my sleep. But right now I do my own made-up dance that's kind of a ballet-hip-hop-electric-slide-shimmy-pop and I am amazing. I am the best dancer ever. I am a superstar. The shoes are magic. My feet are magic. I am magic.

SATURDAY

JACK

Marcus (tall, shaggy hair, pointy chin) stands over the kitchen sink, shoveling food into his face. I start to help myself to the coffee, and that's when I hear, "I said no."

A woman walks in followed by a man wearing an official Masselin's store shirt. His mouth is open in midsentence, but he closes it when he sees Marcus and me. By process of elimination, these are my parents.

Mom says to me, "Put the coffee down now." Then says to my dad, "We'll talk about it later," and it's clear they're in the middle of an argument. I reach for the largest mug we have and pour myself a cup of coffee.

Mom asks Dad just what does he want her to do, and she sounds like she's swallowing razor blades, like the guy at Sad Carnival, as we call it, the one out by Big Lots. I try not to eavesdrop, but I can feel my whole body go on alert, the way it always does when they argue.

Dad says to my mom, "Tonight."

"Not tonight."

Marcus and I look at each other. He mouths, "What now?"

Dad goes, "There's slow surgery and there's ripping off the Band-Aid, Sarah."

"I said not tonight." She fixes her eyes on me, and she is not happy. "I need you to pick up Dusty after you're done today."

"From where?"

"From Tams's house." Picking up Dusty or Marcus or anyone is normally the last thing I ever agree to. Try not being able to recognize anyone and then having to go find them. But this morning I'm not about to argue with my mom.

LIBBY

Even with half of the bleachers folded up, the new gym is an enormous place. You can barely see the ceiling from the floor, and the lights are blinding. From up above, I would look no larger than an ant.

And all at once, that's what I feel like—an ant.

My palms are sweating. My heart is clenching, but not unclenching. I can't catch my breath. I watch as it runs out of the gym as fast as it can, just like I want to do.

WHY IN THE HELL DID I VOLUNTEER TO DO THIS?

Heather Alpern and her three squad captains sit in chairs, legs crossed. The squad captains are all seniors, and they look identical, their hair slicked back into ponytails, faces shining. I find their sameness almost as terrifying as Ms. Alpern's catlike beauty. Most terrifying of all is Caroline Lushamp, captain of the squad captains, who locks her eyes on me like a squid. A few other Damsel wannabes are sprinkled along the bottom row of the bleachers, waiting their turns to try out.

Caroline says, "Are you ready?" in this super-friendly tone that is completely unnatural.

I can barely hear her because I am trapped in my mind and body, shivering and afraid. I suddenly feel like I have face blindness because no one looks familiar or nice, and my eyes are flying all over the gym, searching for help. They land on Bailey, Jayvee,

and Iris, at the very top of the bleachers. When they see me looking at them, they go blank, and maybe they can see my terror.
Which means everyone else can probably see it too. I tell myself
to move, to hide that terror and stuff it down and out of sight,
and then Jayvee waves her arms and yells, "Shine on, you crazy
diamond!"

You volunteered to do this because the dance is in you. And then
I think of something my mom used to say, about how as scary as it
is to go after dreams, it's even scarier not to.

"Are you ready?" Caroline doesn't sound as super-friendly this
time.

"Yes," I say. And then I shout, "Yes!"

For my audition song, I chose "Flashdance . . . What a Feeling" by Irene Cara, in honor of my mom, in honor of me. As I
wait for the music to begin, I tell myself, *Too many people in this
world think small is the best they can do. Not you, Libby Strout. You
weren't born for small! You don't know how to do small! Small is
not in you!*

And then the song takes off and so do I.

Shimmy shimmy kick kick. Shake boom boom.

It takes me about twenty seconds to forget about the staring
faces and all that shiny, pulled-back hair and which of the girls on
the bleachers may or may not be a better dancer than I am and the
fact that I'm twice as big as anyone in this room. After that first
thirty seconds, I disappear into the song. I become one with the
music, one with the dance.

*Kick. Bend. Twist. Flick flick. Shimmy. Shake shake shake.
Boom. Kick kick. Pop. Twist. Bend. Flick. Shimmy. Shake. Kick.
Boom boom boom.*

I'm carried away on the notes, across the gym, high up into
the rafters, out the doors, and through the school, all the way to

Principal Wasserman's office, until I'm outside in the sun, under the sky.

Twirl twirl twirl . . .

And then I'm in the sky. And now I *am* the sky! I sail over Amos, across Interstate 70, over into Ohio, and from there to New York and the Atlantic, and then to England, to France . . . I'm everywhere. I'm global. *I am universal.*

I end, out of breath, suddenly back in the gym. The girls on the bleachers are standing up and whistling. They clap and stamp their feet, and my friends are the wildest of all. Over by the entrance to the court, I see Jack Masselin, paint-spattered and beaming like the sun. He's slow-clapping, and then he taps his forehead in a salute before vanishing. He and the rest of my fellow delinquents are painting the bleachers today.

Heather Alpern says, "Libby, that was wonderful." And for the first time, I look directly at her.

Caroline goes, "How tall are you?"

And something in her loud, flat voice makes my stomach drop. The girls on the bleachers fall quiet and settle back into their seats.

"I'm five six."

"How much do you weigh?"

"One hundred twenty pounds."

Everyone stares.

"I'm sorry, did you mean my physical weight or my spiritual weight?"

The girls on the bleachers giggle. I am dripping, but I dab at my upper lip and the back of my neck as demurely as Queen Elizabeth.

"The weight that determines what size costume you would need."

I say, "Is there a weight limit for this squad?"

Caroline starts to speak, but Heather Alpern interrupts her. "Technically, there is not a limit. We don't discriminate against size." But they do. I can hear it in the careful way she's picking her words and I can see it in the tight corners of her smile.

"So why do you need to know my weight?"

Caroline sighs. Loudly. Like I'm as dumb as a rock. "For costume size." Then she smiles this slow movie-villain smile. "Would you be willing to lose weight if you were *wanted*?" The word echoes across the court. "You know. If you were to make the team?"

Ms. Alpern shoots her a look. "Caroline."

I say, "How much weight are we talking about?"

Caroline says, "A hundred pounds, probably more. Two hundred-fifty, maybe." Which is ridiculous, because that would mean I'd weigh about the same as my aunt Tillie's dog, Mango.

Like that, I'm a kid again in ballet class, and Caroline is my teacher, frowning at me in this same exact way, a way that tells me I don't belong here, even though I probably belong more than any of them because the dance is in me, and there's a lot more of me than there is of them, which means there is *a lot more dance in there*.

"Would you?"

"Caroline, enough."

"You want to know if I'd be willing to lose two hundred pounds so that I can dance in formation and carry flags *with you*?" I'm hot with anger, which doesn't help the dripping, but I make my voice quiet and controlled.

"Yes."

I fix my eyes on Ms. Heather Alpern, because she's supposed to be in charge here.

"Absolutely not."

I'm supposed to go back outside to the bleachers to serve my sentence and do my civic duty, but I can't. Instead I call Rachel and ask if she can take me home.

By the time we finish painting the locker rooms, it's almost 5 p.m. The sky is thick with gray and the air is heavy, the way it always feels before it rains.

Through the wide window of Tams's house, I can see a clump of kids, and I think, *Great.* This is why I don't volunteer to pick Dusty up, because this right here is the stuff of nightmares. I can't find him in a crowd, and my parents think Dusty's too young for a phone, so it's not like I can text him to say I'm coming, wait outside. The few times I do go get him, I usually wait in the car and blow the horn.

Because this apparently isn't a one-on-one Tams and Dusty playdate situation but the ten-year-old equivalent of Coachella, this is what I do now. The rain pelts the windshield like gunfire. The clump of kids doesn't move, so I honk again.

I wait a couple more minutes, and then I turn off the car and twist the rearview mirror so I can look at myself. The guy who stares back at me has seen better days. He's still got a split lip, and an eye that's fading from black and blue to violet, thanks to defending Jonny Rumsford. *Super.*

I search for anything I can use as coverage, for my face and from the monsoon. There's an old jacket, which must belong to

Marcus, wadded up on the floor below the backseat. I grab it and lunge out into the rain, jogging up the walk, jacket wrapped around my head. I can hear the mad chatter of a thousand high-pitched voices as I ring the doorbell. The door flies open, and I'm greeted by a blond woman with short-cropped hair. This, I think, is Tamara's mom. She invites me in, and I say through the jacket, "That's okay. I don't want to bring all this water in. If you could just send him out."

"Nonsense, Jack. Come on in." She holds the door open wider, and the wind is blowing rain onto her and onto the floor around her, so I step inside.

"It's really coming down," I say.

"You're telling me. They were supposed to be outside all day." She laughs, but it's laced with hysteria, and I can see how tired she is.

I'm hoping Dusty will yell hello or otherwise identify himself, but the kids all blink at me, and one of them says, "It's like God is peeing." And this must be some really clever ten-year-old joke, the kind you need to be ten to appreciate, because they all start laughing until they practically fall down.

The woman says to me, "Please take me with you."

I laugh as I stand there, trying to seem calm and casual and *Hey man, whatever.* Meanwhile, I'm trying to find Dusty in the bunch of kids, but they all look the same. Skinny, short, ears that stick out. All the kids are wearing party hats and only a handful of them are obviously white. I feel a distant flicker of panic in my chest.

The woman says, "Do you want to stay for a bit?"

"That's okay. Dusty and I have someplace to be." I put my hand on the doorknob as a way of saying *See?* I say to the room, "Anyone who answers to the name Dusty better join me now."

The kids stare at me. In that instant, the flicker of panic sparks into an inferno. If my brother is one of these staring, silent kids, he's not letting on.

I look at the group of them and say in their general direction, "Come on, man. We don't want you to be late."

When they don't budge, I zero in on the one who looks the most like my brother (ears that stick out, Adam's apple that sticks out, copper-brown hair) and go, "If you're worried about getting wet, I've got this jacket you can use." And then, because it's been a long day and I'm sick of being stared at, and because I'm telling myself *This is bullshit. How can you not recognize your own brother?* I do something I never do—I walk over, leaving big, dirty footprints on the carpet, and grab the kid's arm before he identifies himself. And drag him toward the door.

The boy I'm holding on to is fighting me, and it's then I look up and see this other kid walk into the room. He's got ears that stick out and an Adam's apple that sticks out and copper-brown hair, and he goes, "Jack?" And starts to cry.

The kid I've just, until this moment, been dragging away shouts, "Get off me!" Now the other party guests are buzzing, and one of the little girls is crying too. As I let him go, the kid practically spits at me. "Assface." And starts shaking.

The woman squats down in front of him. She says in this soothing voice, "It's okay, Jeremy. He was just joking around, but I think he realizes now that it wasn't funny." She shoots me a horrible look.

"Do you really think it's funny to come in here and scare people?" This is from a little girl with red hair who may or may not be Tams.

"No, I don't."

I wonder how many of them know me and how many of their

parents will hear about this. I feel like I'm going to be sick, and I almost walk out. *Let Dusty find his own way home. Let my mom come get him.* But it's as if the floor is holding me there. My feet are like anchors. They won't move. I just stand there, staring past the kids staring back at me, at the kid who walked in, the one who's still crying.

"I'm sorry." I say it directly to him a couple of times, but no one is listening. These kids could kill me if they wanted to. There are so many of them, and small though they be, fury is on their side.

An eternity later, the woman stands and says in this cold, cold voice, "*That* is your brother," like I'm the world's biggest child predator. She pushes Dusty toward me like she wants both of us gone, like Dusty, by association, is also guilty.

I'm not an assface, not in this way at least. I have a condition called prosopagnosia. It means I can't recognize faces, not even the faces of the people I love.

I add, "They grow so quickly at this age. Makes it hard to keep track of them."

And I grab the actual one-and-only Dusty and drag him outside. I throw the jacket at him, and he drapes it over his head, but it's clear he doesn't want to be near me, so he takes his sweet time coming down the walk. I'm soaked to the bone by now, but I hold the door open for him, and as he gets in he looks up at me with tears all over his face and says, "Why would you try to kidnap Jeremy Mervis?"

"I was only joking around."

He is studying me the way he does my parents these days, like he's not sure if he can trust me. "Fourth grade is hard enough without being known as the brother of a child stealer."

. . .

Rachel wants to know what happened. *This is a person who has seen you through your very worst. When you met her, you were taking up two hospital beds after being rescued from your HOUSE. She has been there for you and loved you through everything, just like a mom, only she isn't your mom.*

I tell her I don't want to talk about it, not now, and we ride in silence most of the way home.

In my room, I open my copy of *We Have Always Lived in the Castle.* Even though she's done a terrible, horrific thing, Mary Katherine doesn't feel anything—no pain or remorse or emotion. Not even when the villagers trespass across her property and chant songs about her.

> *Merricat, said Connie, would you like a cup of tea?*
> *Oh no, said Merricat, you'll poison me.*
> *Merricat, said Connie, would you like to go to sleep?*
> *Down in the boneyard ten feet deep!*

Merricat is happy enough in her house with her sister for company, but she still thinks about the villagers and wishes their tongues would burn right out of their skulls.

I remember being so full of pain and anger that I wished noth-ing but tongue-burning on everyone who hurt me, especially Moses Hunt. But here's the thing—Merricat poisoned her entire family. The only crime I committed was being fat.

"Why weren't you in the living room with the other kids?"

"I didn't feel like playing their games. I went out to the back porch to study my lines." The crying seems to have stopped, but he won't look at me directly.

"Did Tams and the others want you to play with them?"

He shrugs. "I don't think they missed me."

"But everything's cool with Tams, right?"

He takes a few seconds before each reply, and I can hear the hurt in his voice. The hurt I put there. "I guess."

I let him be, my mind racing, my heart still going *BAM BAM BAM*.

As we pull up in front of the house, Dusty says, "Jack?"

"Yeah." I want him to tell me he forgives me, that he loves me anyway.

"I really wish you hadn't tried to kidnap Jeremy."

"Me too."

"What if Tams's mom had called the police? What if they sent you to jail?" His voice shakes, and he looks like he's going to cry again.

"I'm not going to jail. I wouldn't have let them send me to jail. It was just a misunderstanding. That's all it was. I got confused."

He gets out of the car without a word, and as we go up the walk, I say, "Hey, little man, do you mind not mentioning what happened today to Mom and Dad?" The rain has let off, but I can still feel it in the air.

He hesitates, and I can tell he doesn't want to promise me anything. Ever. He tilts his face upward and latches his eyes onto mine. These are eyes that are shutting me out. They are looking at me but from very far away. Finally he says, "Okay."

After he goes inside, I sit down on the front step, damp as it is, because I'm not ready to go in yet. It's been a long day, and the evening is quiet and cool, like a hand against your forehead when you're running a fever. I stare out at the street and then up at the sky. My hands are still shaking. My heart is still pounding.

Today was really, really bad. Your brain is broken. It will never get better.

I can't tell you what Jeremy Mervis looks like. If he was to walk down the street right now, I wouldn't be able to recognize him. But I will never forget the look of terror in his eyes as I tried to drag him out of there. And I will never forget the look on my brother's face as he watched.

Today could have been worse.

I repeat it over and over even as I try to think of the five ways it could have been more horrible, but I can't because really what's worse than accidentally trying to kidnap some kid you don't know? My mind goes reeling back to Dusty. He's carrying around things that I can never know about, just like I am, just like we all are. I'm not sure what these things of his are, but I can guess. Dusty's sensitive, he's honest. He's a little eccentric. He's almost certainly gay, but I doubt even he knows it. Like Libby, he's not going to pretend to be someone he's not, and he's not afraid to be different. But other kids won't always like that.

I don't believe in God anymore, if I ever did, but out loud I say a kind of prayer. *Just keep him safe. Don't let anyone hurt him. And*

*while you're at it, look after Libby and old Jonny Rumsford too. And
my mom. And Marcus. And even Dad.*

I don't add myself to the list because that feels selfish. But
maybe I think it, just for a minute. *And me, I guess, even if I don't
deserve it. Maybe look out for me too.*

When I get inside, my mom is on the phone with Tams's mom,
and my dad is on the phone with the parents of Jeremy Mervis. So
much for secrets. Everyone is apparently very, very pissed.

My mom holds up a finger at me. "Jack Henry. Stay." She
points to the living room.

Ten minutes later.

Mom: "What is this about?"

Me: "Maybe I need glasses."

"I'm not just talking about the Jeremy Mervis kidnapping. I'm
talking about all of it, Jack. Getting in trouble at school. Fighting.
This isn't you."

Me: "I've just had a bad run, Mom. I'm the same lovable boy
you raised. Still your favorite child. Still me."

Mom: "I don't know what's happening with this family, but
this behavior ends now. If there's something going on, you need
to talk to us."

And here's my chance to spill it all out onto the floor, right next
to the stray piece of popcorn that's poking out from under the
couch and the PlayStation remote lying on the rug.

Mom: "Jack? Tell us what's going on."

But in that moment, I don't know what to say. Everything that's
wrong with me seems made up because it's not like I can point to

any of it and actually show them—my dad's secret affair, my secret brain disorder.

Me: "I'm sorry. I'll do better. That's the best I can do." I look at my dad. "That's the best any of us can do."

And maybe because he knows some of this might be his fault, my dad says, "I believe you, Jack, but this is pretty bad. You need to make amends with the families."

Mom: "We also want you seeing a counselor. Mr. Levine or one of the others. No going out for two weeks. School, work, home. That's it."

I want to say *Two weeks? Ground me for the rest of the year. Ground me from school while you're at it. Let me stay at home like Mary Katherine Blackwood, like Libby. It will make things so much easier.*

I feel all tied up. Hands, legs, feet. Every single part of me. Like they might as well stuff me in a box and leave me there.

I call the Mervises first. And then Tams's mom. In this dead voice, I apologize. I tell them I'm still reeling from my dad's cancer, from all the stuff happening at school. I say, "Please don't punish Dusty for my bad behavior. He's the best person I know."

As I hang up the phone, I add a postscript to my prayer. *Don't let anyone hurt him. Including me.*

LIBBY

I don't feel like dancing, but I get out the pink toe shoes and tie them on. I drop onto my bed and lean against the pillows and pull George onto my chest, inhaling a mouthful of musty fur. He starts kicking, so I let him go, and then he does something he's never done before—he sits beside me, petting me with his sharp, dirty little claws.

I cross my ankles so that I can see my toe shoes as I'm staring at the wall. For a minute, this feels like old times—lying in bed, locked away from everyone. I pretend I'm in my old house, across the street from Dean, Sam, and Castiel, my imaginary friends who were never actually my friends at all.

I'm Libby Strout, America's Fattest Teen, maybe the World's Saddest Teen, alone in her room with her cat while outside that room, the rest of the world goes on.

JACK

The night is cool and clear after the rain. I inch my way to the edge of the roof until I'm standing where I was standing before, twelve years ago, and I look out over the neighborhood and the house that used to belong to Libby Strout.

Maybe if I fell again, it would jar something back into place in my brain. I might see the world and the people in it in ways I don't now. I might conjure up a face from my memory or be able to think *Mom,* and instantly associate the word with a whole, added-up image of eyes, nose, mouth, the way everyone else does.

I stand there for a long time, trying to figure out a way to jump and bang my head in the same exact spot I hit it before. Maybe I should take a rock and hit myself with it instead. But what if I do more damage? What if I get complete and total amnesia?

I sit down and then I lie down, and the roof is damp from the rain. I let the water soak through my shirt as I gaze at the sky and all the stars that look just like all the other stars, and it might as well be a sky full of faces. I tell myself, *Libby is one of those stars.* I choose one and name it after her and keep my eyes on it as long as I can.

And then I blink.
Stay. Stay. Stay.
Don't go away.
But she's gone.

LIBBY

The phone rings, and it's Jack, the only person I want to talk to.

Something's wrong.

I can hear it in his voice.

At first, I can't understand what he's saying.

"I'm sorry," he says. He keeps repeating it, until I tell him to stop.

"Why are you sorry? What's going on?"

"I can't do this. I thought I could. I wanted to. But I can't. It's not fair to you."

"What's not—"

"You deserve to be seen, and I'll never be able to see you, not really. What happens if you lose weight? You'd need to stay large forever, and that's your identifier, but you're so much more than weight."

"What are you saying to me, Jack?"

Even though I know, and my stomach knows, and my bones know, and, most of all, my heart knows. All of me is sinking like a stone.

He says, "I can't be with you, Libby. We can't do this. I'm sorry."

And then he hangs up.

Just like that.

And I sink through the floor and into the yard and from there into the dark, deep core of the earth.

. . .

I think of Beatrice in her garden, and how she died for love. And then for some reason I think of another story my mom used to read me, "The Twelve Dancing Princesses." I walk to my bookshelf and search for it. I flip through until I find it—*Libby* in purple crayon. I wrote it very small, on the skirt of the youngest princess, Elise. She was my favorite, not just because she wins the prince, but because she has the loveliest heart. She is who I wanted to be.

I look at Elise's perfect hair and face and figure. Of course people love to watch her dance. Of course she marries the prince. I wonder what would have happened if Elise had looked like me.

JACK

Before I go to sleep, I write Libby this long apology text, but I end up deleting it because what's the point? It won't change the fact that there will always be this part of me that's searching for her, even if she's right there.

THE WEEK AFTER

LIBBY

Even though I don't expect to make the team, I still go around to Heather Alpern's office to see if she's posted the name of the newest Damsel.

And there's the paper on her door. And there's the single name listed on that paper: *Jesselle Villegas*. I tell myself, *You shouldn't be surprised. You shouldn't be disappointed. What did you think would happen when you talked back to Caroline?* But I am surprised. I am disappointed.

I tell myself, *You didn't really want to make the Damsels anyway. Not like that. Not having to dance in formation and carry flags and take orders from Caroline Lushamp.* But my heart feels like a deflated balloon.

Bailey and Travis and I wait outside for Mr. Dominguez to pull the car around. Travis's eyes are closed, and he looks like he's sleeping standing up.

Bailey says, "I heard about Jesselle."

"It's okay. I'm okay." Just to drive the point home of how COMPLETELY OKAY I am, I wave my hand at the air, so carefree, like I'm smacking away a mosquito.

She says, "It's that horrible Caroline."

"This will just free me up to pursue other things." *Like dancing*

by myself in my room and creating voodoo dolls with Caroline Lu-
shamp's face.

As I fish through my backpack for a lip gloss, Bailey is listing all
the other non-dancing, non-voodoo-doll-making activities I could
start doing. My hand closes around something. An envelope. I
yank it out and turn away to read it, even though I can guess what
it says.

You aren't wanted. (I told you so.)

I look up, expecting Caroline to be there watching me. Instead,
Bailey is reading over my shoulder.

"Who's that from?"

"No one." I shove the letter back into my backpack.

I told you so.

Does she mean *See there? Jack doesn't love you.* Or does
she mean *Why did you ever think YOU could audition for the Dam-*
sels?

"Libbs, who wrote that?"

"Don't worry about it."

"But—"

"Please, Bailey. I'm fine."

"I guess you're fine about Jack too, then."

"I don't want to talk about Jack."

Her mouth snaps shut. Then she says, "You can't always be
fine. No one's always fine. And I know you're used to being on
your own, and I know I should have been a better friend so that
you didn't have to get used to being on your own, but I'm here
now, and I wish you'd talk to me."

• • •

In the car, I ask Mr. Dominguez to, for God's sake, play some music, only I don't actually mention God because this will only set Bailey off and I already feel bad enough for barking at her. The first song Mr. Dominguez chooses is, of course, ancient 1970s rock. "Love Hurts," and if you don't know it, DON'T EVER LISTEN TO IT, ESPECIALLY IF YOUR HEART IS BROKEN. Immediately I get this lump in my throat, the kind that makes it impossible to swallow or even breathe.

One minute into the song, tears are rolling down my face, but Mr. Dominguez doesn't bat an eye.

I see Jack in the main hallway of school. He's flanked by Seth Powell and Dave Kaminski, who looks right at me, almost through me, while Jack saunters past like I'm invisible.

And maybe I am.

Like everyone else in his life.

Just one more person he can't see.

JACK

Conversation Circle is canceled today because Mr. Levine has some sort of staff meeting, and honestly I'm glad. I don't want to face Libby because I'm a miserable coward, and this is what miserable cowards do—we avoid facing things. I walk out of school with Kam, who's going, "What are you up to tonight? I hear Kendra's having some people over."

I can picture tonight like it's already happened—Kendra's enormous house, filled with yapping dogs no higher than your ankle, Caroline and the rest of them bitching about one thing and another, everyone drinking till they're stupid(er).

"Man, I'm still grounded." *Not that I would go if I could.*

He starts telling me a story about Seth, but I'm only half listening because a car comes pulling up and I watch as this girl who can only be Libby climbs in. The car rolls away, and I'm thinking, *Look up, look up.* But she doesn't even glance in my direction.

I find Mom-with-Hair-Down in the kitchen, standing in front of the window, drinking one of Dusty's juice boxes. She looks distracted and far away. I walk in coughing so I can give her fair warning.

She smiles, but it lands somewhere over my left shoulder. "What's up?"

"Just thirsty." I grab a juice box and lean against the counter. "Do you remember when I was playing Little League?"

"Sure."

"You would tell me who all of the players were before practice because I could never keep them straight."

"You were always getting them mixed up."

"It was pretty cool of you to do that."

"That's what we do." She says it so matter-of-factly that I love her more for it. She smiles into the distance, into the past, and laughs. "You were full of swagger, even then. I'm not sure where that came from. You didn't get it from us."

"I totally got it from you."

She smiles. Sighs. "So what's really up?"

"Are you and Dad getting divorced?"

"What? Why would you say that?"

This is my strong, no-bullshit mother, but there's something scared hidden deep in her voice, like I may know something she doesn't. It's like a knife through the gut, and I wish I'd never heard it, because there's no way I'm going to forget the sound of it, not if I live to be a hundred.

"You guys just don't seem like you lately."

"Things have been a little strained." She is wary. It's in her face and in her voice. It's in the way she crosses her arms over her chest. "But you're the child and I'm the parent, no matter how tall you get or how large you grow that Afro, which means I don't want you to worry."

Her smile is the punctuation, the thing that tells me we're done here. There's something in its protectiveness that brings on this wave of déjà vu, and suddenly I'm six years old and lying in the hospital. My mom is holding my hand. She's talking to my dad, and they're happy and relieved because I'm going to be okay and he doesn't have cancer yet and he hasn't even met Monica Chapman. Mom glances at me and then back at my dad, and her face seems different every time. *Is this when it started?* But her smile is the same.

And now, standing in our kitchen, I'm thinking about Dr. Oliver Sacks, who believed that the recognition of faces doesn't depend solely on the fusiform gyrus twelve, but on the ability to summon up the memories, experiences, and feelings associated with them. Basically, being able to identify the face of someone you know comes with a lot of meaning. It also gives them meaning—the people you know and love.

My mom already means a lot to me—she's *my mom,* after all—but would she mean even more if I could identify her face?

I say to her, "Just promise me you won't be one of those couples that stays together for the children. That only screws people up, including the children." I toss the juice box. Take a breath. Say the thing I probably shouldn't. "You deserve better."

The first attempts at facial recognition technology were made in the 1960s. Every face has distinct landmarks—about eighty of them—and the technology works by measuring these. Width of the nose, distance between the eyes, length of the jaw. All these things are added together to create a sort of faceprint.

Okay, so that particular kind of technology is beyond me, but what I can do is this: I stay up for hours connecting the wires that make up the robot's brain. This is a delicate job, like surgery. You can have the grandest design in the whole fucking world, but the thing every single book or video or website will tell you is that you need a complete circuit, perfectly wired, in order for the motors to work. If a single wire is disconnected, the motors won't spin and your robot won't function.

I can't do anything about my own brain, but I can make sure *the red wire goes here, the black wire goes there, must get the wiring right, must make the motor spin.* I'm going to fill this robot's mind with fully working fusiform gyrus twelves. He won't just have one; he'll have a hundred.

LIBBY

Before dinner, I tell my dad I'm going over to our neighborhood Walgreens to buy some "girl things." Ten minutes later, I'm walking up and down the aisles, fluorescent lights blinding me, filling a basket with junk food. Everything I used to eat—cookies, chips, soda. People are staring at me, and I know how I look: the fat girl getting ready to binge. I don't care. I suddenly want everything. There's not enough food on these shelves, not even with Halloween around the corner. I'm grabbing bags of candy, and the basket is full, so I march to the front of the store and find a cart, and I throw the basket in there and go back up and down the same aisles, filling it with all the food I missed.

I'm standing by the cereal, reaching for a box of Honey Nut Cheerios, when I feel my chest clenching but not unclenching. It clenches tighter and tighter, like someone has wrapped a corset around it. My palms are wet. My head is compressing, growing and shrinking at the same time. I can hear my breathing, and it's so amplified that, to my own ears, I sound like Darth Vader. A woman at the end of the aisle is frozen as she watches me. She looks scared. A boy comes over, wearing a Walgreens uniform, and he's maybe sixteen years old. He goes, "Are you okay? Miss?"

My breathing is getting louder, and I cover my ears to block it out. And that's when the ceiling starts to spin and the air disappears and my lungs stop working and I can't breathe at all. I drop everything and run away from the cart and all that food until I'm out the door. I stand in the parking lot, bent over at the waist, breathing in the fresh night air, and then I lie flat on the ground, as if this will open my lungs wider and make them work again, only the breath won't come. And then I close my eyes, and everything goes black.

This is the way it happened three years ago. My lungs stopped work-ing, and all the air everywhere, in my house, in the world, disap-peared, leaving me on my back, unable to talk or move. There was only panic.

I open my eyes, and instead of the dingy metal ceiling of a truck, I see the sky.

Get up, Libby.

I push myself to sitting and wait as the world rights itself. I look around slowly so that things don't tilt or spin. Inside Walgreens, I can see the sixteen-year-old boy with a phone to his ear and some-one on his way out the door to help the girl lying in the parking lot.

On your feet.

I pull myself to standing, and as I do, this feeling comes over me. It's this kind of quiet, peaceful feeling, and that's her, that's my mom. I want it to last, to keep her with me.

Live live live live . . .

And then I breathe.

I breathe.

At home, I stand in front of my mirror, wearing the bright purple bikini I bought myself when I first lost the weight. The tags are still attached because I've never actually worn it, but now I rip them off and let them fall onto the carpet. I look at myself.

In the glass, George watches me with the same expression he

always wears, and I think, *If only people were more like him.* He looks at me the way he does when I'm fully clothed, with makeup or without, laughing or crying. He is *unwavering,* which may be the thing I love most about him.

Still in my bikini, I sit down on my bed and open my laptop. I stare at the screen for approximately ten seconds, and then the words just pour right out of me.

THE NEXT DAY

LIBBY

It's the first day of swimming, which means for the entire hour of gym class I'll be fulfilling one of my worst nightmares: parading around in front of my classmates, wearing the world's smallest, most unflattering piece of clothing.

I'm in the locker room with thirty other girls, and this is exactly how the nightmare always begins. Everyone who isn't Caroline Lushamp or Bailey Bishop stares into their lockers, as if this will somehow hide them from sight. Even Kendra Wu is cheating by sitting down on the bench, talking a mile a minute like she's the most confident thing in the world, when she's draping a towel around her lap. She ties this around her as she stands, and I know this move because I've done it a hundred times.

I want to shout *We still see you, Kendra! You can't hide from the eyes of your peers! But who cares? You look great! We all look great! Our bodies are wondrous, miraculous things, and we shouldn't ever feel ashamed of them!*

Bailey is talking to me about a lifeguard named Brandon Something, who was her first real-life crush (not to be confused with her first crush of all, *Winnie-the-Pooh*'s Christopher Robin). She leans against the locker and waves her hands, like she always does when she talks, and of course she looks like she just stepped off the pages of *Seventeen,* even in the ugly, shapeless blob that is our regulation black one-piece.

I'm the heaviest girl here by a mile, and everyone keeps glancing at me to see when I'm going to take it all off, probably because it will make them feel better about their own bodies. I move as if I'm in slow motion, determined to run out the bell. I nudge off one shoe and then the other and place them—one and then the other—neatly, gingerly in my locker, as if they're made of the finest glass. I remove my bracelet and take the greatest, tenderest care to tuck it into my bag where it will be safe. I do everything but write it a poem, that is how long I'm taking to ensure its comfort. I reach into my pocket and pull out a hair tie and then, as if we have hours to get ready, I pull my hair back and smooth it into place, every last strand, just like I'm a squad captain for the Damsels.

Caroline walks by and says in my direction, "You can't delay the inevitable." But even Miss High and Mighty can't get to me today.

Finally, it's just Bailey and me and a girl named Margaret Harrison, who is chattering into her phone. Our teacher, Ms. Reilly, comes whisking through and, with barely a glance at any of us, goes, "Margaret, phone! Bailey, pool! Libby, swimsuit!" She would be an amazing drill sergeant.

Bailey waves. "See you out there, Libbs!" And goes bounding off, hair swinging, long legs high-stepping. It is a wonder I like her.

Now it's just Margaret and me. She's still blabbing away, but I really need her to disappear, so I start singing to myself. Loudly. I rearrange my shoes. I check on my bracelet. She continues blabbing, but now she's watching me. We could be here for days.

Finally, I'm like, *Screw it.* I pull off my top. Hang it up in the locker. Pull off my jeans. Hang them on the other hook. I grab my towel, slam the locker door closed. I throw the towel over my shoulder. I meet Margaret's eyes, and they are wide. The phone is still to her ear, but she has finally, finally stopped talking. I put one hand on my hip, the other behind my head. I do a little pose, and her face breaks into a smile.

She says into the phone, "Yeah, I'm still here." And gives me a thumbs-up.

I stroll into the MVB Aquatic Center.

Everyone stops.

Just. Stops.

From across the pool, Ms. Reilly shouts, "What is that supposed to be, Strout?"

I holler back, "A purple bikini."

And then I strike the same pose, one hand on my hip, one hand behind my head.

Ms. Reilly is padding toward me, her feet going *slap slap slap* on the wet cement. "What is that on your stomach?"

And she must be nearsighted, because I wrote it in giant letters across the widest swath of skin I own.

"'I am wanted,'" I say. "But don't worry about it washing off in the water. I used a permanent marker." And then I walk over to the deep end, drop my towel, and execute an Olympic-worthy dive that would impress even the most unimpressible judge.

My mom learned to swim the year she turned forty, the year before she died. She and I took lessons at the municipal pool near the park, and together we learned to tread water, breathe, do the back float, do the breaststroke, dive. To me, swimming was as natural as walking or sleeping. I felt at home in the water. My mom was more nervous, something she blamed on her age. "You just need to trust the power of the water," I told her. "Our bodies are designed to float, no matter what. The water will hold you up."

I haven't done much swimming in the years since. But it's

amazing how something like that comes back to you. As I cut through the water now, I forget where I am. It's me and the water. And my mom, just out of reach. I close my eyes, and I can see her in the lane next to mine.

I come up for air and open my eyes, and I'm back in the high school swim center, surrounded by gawking, laughing girls. This jars me for a second, but only a second. It is my job in life, apparently, to teach gawking, laughing girls lessons about kindness. If you had told me when I was seven or eight that this was something I'd be taking on, that I would never get a break from it no matter how good I felt about myself, I would have said *Thank you, but if it's all the same I'll take another job, please. What else do you have for me?*

I know what you're thinking—if you hate it so much and it's such a burden, just lose the weight, and then that job will go away. But I'm comfortable where I am. I may lose more weight. I may not. But why should what I weigh affect other people? I mean, unless I'm sitting on them, who cares?

I find the ladder and climb out. I brush the hair off my face and check my stomach. The writing is still there.

I pick up my towel and walk past them all into the locker room, where I dry off and pull on my shoes, which I chose especially for today. On one side, I've decorated them with this line from *A Separate Peace:* **Everyone has a moment in history which belongs particularly to him.**

This is mine.

JACK

I make my way through the crowd, pretending to be on my phone. I'm planning to avoid the main hall, even though it will mean going upstairs and around and down again to get to my next class. The closest stairs are in what we call the Four Corners, which is where the main hall branches off in four different directions, and if I'm wily enough, I can duck up these to the second floor. Otherwise, I'll have to trek all the way to the front hall and take the stairs there. I don't want to run into anyone.

I hear my name, but I concentrate on the back of every head in front of me. The hall is jammed with people, and we're barely moving. Someone is shouting my name over and over, and then this tall girl with dark skin and a painted-on beauty mark by her eye yanks at my arm and goes, "Didn't you hear me?"

"Caroline?"

"I said your girlfriend's up there. She's the reason we can't get through."

LIBBY

I stand in the middle of the main hallway. The only thing I'm wearing other than my shoes is my bikini. My suit and hair are still
damp, and I'm shivering a little but I'm telling myself, *This is your
moment in history. This belongs to you.*

Five. Four. Three . . .

Iris appears, out of breath. I say, "Did you bring them?"

"Right here." She holds up a stack of papers.

"You may want to get out of here."

She shakes her head. "I'm staying."

The bell rings and I jump. There's still time. I could run like the
Flash and maybe only be seen by a couple of people.

But I keep standing there.

As doors are being thrown open. As the entire student population of MVB High School starts flooding the hall. As everyone is
staring. As phones are held up. As—I'm sure of it—four hundred
pictures are being taken. As my chest is clenching. As my head
feels as if it's being filled with cotton. As my breathing grows rag-
gedy and uneven. As my palms go clammy.

I stand there.

JACK

I try to push my way through, but as I'm getting closer to the main hall, things slow down even more, and soon I'm trapped in a crowd, shuffling along, pressed into the girl in front of me and the guy behind me and the girl to my left and the guy to my right. Caroline is somewhere nearby, but I've lost her.

LIBBY

Iris and I are handing out sheets of paper, one for everybody, and they are going fast. My classmates are snatching them up and walking off, reading them while others aim their phones at me and take pictures. I try to pose for as many as I can, because if I'm going out on the Internet, dammit, I want to give them the best possible me.

Seth Powell and his giant Mohawk appear in front of me, and Jack Masselin is just behind him. Seth goes, "What's this all about? Is it spirit day?" He laughs so hard he shakes.

Jack is not laughing. He says, "What are you doing?"

"I'm reminding people of some basic truths."

Moses Hunt and his crew loom forward, and I give them a copy to share, even though they probably can't read. I say to Moses, "I hope you learn something, although I doubt you will."

He reaches for me like he's going to hug me, and Jack goes, "Hey!"

"Fuck you, Masshole. What's your problem?"

Seth goes, "His problem is that's his girlfriend." And laughs/shakes likes a tambourine.

I say to Jack, "Thanks anyway, but I don't need you to protect me."

And he says, "You need to put some clothes on."

• • •

Behind her desk, Principal Wasserman shakes her head. "I'm at a loss, Libby. Help me understand this." She holds up a copy of the thing I wrote. My Treatise for the World. "Someone's been harassing you? Sending you letters? Why didn't you come to me?"

"I don't know who sent them, and even if I did, I wouldn't rat them out, no matter how awful they are. But I felt like I needed to say something." I'm dressed now, but I'm still shivering. For one thing, my hair is damp. For another, I'm pissed. With a single comment, Jack Masselin has taken away some of the glory of my moment: *You need to put some clothes on.*

Principal Wasserman reads my treatise again and then sets it down in front of her. She folds her hands on top of it and looks at me, and I can see the anger in her eyes, but I know it's not directed at me. "I'm sorry," she says. "Truly."

My eyes are suddenly stinging, which takes me by surprise. I stare at my hands, willing myself not to cry. *No need to cry. You rocked it. You made your point. Maybe you even helped someone else today who needed to hear what you had to say.*

"We're done here."

I look up. "Really?"

"Just let this be the last time you take matters into your own hands, and let this be the last time I see you in here. Unless you get more letters. In that case, I want you to come here directly, without trying to address it on your own. And if you do find out who's sending them, I want to know that too."

YOU ARE WANTED

by Libby Strout

* * *

"You aren't wanted."

Someone wrote this to me recently in an anonymous letter. I wonder who out there feels like this is an okay thing to say to another person. I mean really. Think about it.

"You aren't wanted."

It's pretty much the most despicable thing you could tell somebody.

What they probably mean to say is "You are fat, and this disgusts me." So why not say that?

You don't know if I'm wanted or not.

But guess what? I am.

Believe it or not, I actually have a family who loves me and I also have friends. I've even made out with boys. The reason I haven't had sex is because I'm not ready yet. Not because no one wants me. The thing is, as hateful and small as you are, Person Who Wrote That Letter, I'm pretty damn delightful. I've got a good personality and a great brain and I'm strong and I can run. I'm resilient. I'm mighty. I'm going to do something with my life because I believe in myself. I may not know what that something is yet, but that's only because I am limitless. Can you say the same?

Life is too short to judge others. It is not our job to tell someone what they feel or who they are. Why not spend some time on yourself instead? I don't know you, but I can guarantee you have some issues you can work on. And maybe you've got a fit body and a perfect face, but I'll wager you've got insecurities too, ones that would keep you from stripping down to a purple bikini and modeling it in front of everyone.

As for the rest of you, remember this: YOU ARE WANTED. Big, small, tall, short, pretty, plain, friendly, shy. Don't let anyone tell you otherwise, not even yourself.

Especially not yourself.

JACK

I stand on the main floor of Masselin's, wishing baseball season lasted year-round, that I didn't have to wait till spring, and that we were all required to play. If I'm designing the world, every person in it is wearing a uniform, and this is how we find each other.

If this was how the world worked, I would recognize Monica Chapman, also standing on the main floor of Masselin's. I would know instantly that the woman my dad is talking to is her. I wouldn't have to wonder if she's been there other times before today, right in front of my eyes.

Instead, I interrupt the two of them, standing too close near a *Star Wars* display, where anyone, including my mom, could walk in and see them. They break apart, and then I read my dad's name tag, and the guilty look on his face.

She says, "Hi, Jack."

Maybe it's her, maybe it isn't, but I don't wait to find out. I look at my dad. I say, "You son of a bitch." And walk out.

At home, I swipe everything off the basement shelves and onto the floor. I throw stuff into the trash. I go wild, like a kid having a tantrum, crushing parts under my shoes, slamming things against the plywood table, breaking tools and all this shit I've spent so much time designing and building.

I go wilder, finally hitting a wall until my hand is bleeding. The pain of it feels good, and I like that contact of fist and bone. I hit it again and again. It's a way to feel something without standing behind this invisible electric fence that divides me from everyone else.

Half an hour later, I'm cleaning up the mess, all cool and collected, when a man skulks in wearing my dad's name tag.

He takes in the chaos around us and then looks me in the eye. "I'm ending it. With her."

"None of my business, man."

"I just wanted to tell you."

"Why now? What made you come to this life-altering decision?"

"That," he says, nodding at me. "That anger right there. I'd rather you didn't hate me."

"Don't put this on me."

"It's not on you. It's on me. I was given this second chance, not just beating cancer, but a second chance with your mom and a second chance to figure out what I want to do in life."

"I thought you loved the store."

"I love what it means, and I love the history. I loved going there as a kid. But that doesn't mean it's the thing I wanted to do with my life. I had plans."

This throws me because it's the first time I've ever thought about my dad doing anything else or having other options.

"I wanted to be an architect. Or an engineer."

And this throws me again because maybe we're more alike than I thought, and I'm not sure how I feel about this. *The only thing I do know, thanks to you and Monica Chapman, is the kind of person I don't want to be.*

"It's funny, right? That even though we're basically alone in here"—he thumps his chest—"it's easy to lose track of yourself."

I want to say *I know. I get it. It's easy to give everyone what they want. What's expected. The problem with doing this is you lose sight of where you truly begin and where the fake you, the one who tries to be everything to everyone, ends.*

He smiles this sad smile. "I've been shitty."

"So I guess Dusty got to you too."

"I guess so."

Marcus and his girlfriend, Melinda, are in our family room, hunched over his phone, whispering their heads off. Marcus looks up and says to me, "Have you seen this?" He holds out the phone.

I go over, take the phone from him, and there is Libby Strout, wearing nothing but her electric-purple bikini, basically telling the world to fuck off. I was there. I've already seen it. But now I'm looking at the way the light catches her hair and at the handful of freckles that dot across her arms and chest, like beauty marks that aren't painted on.

Then I make the mistake of reading the comments. Some of them are nasty. But some of them are really nice. I don't take a count, but I'm relieved to see the nice ones seem to outnumber the nasty ones. I give the phone back to my brother, and he barely notices because he and Melinda have started arguing.

She goes, "I'm serious. It's not funny, Cuss." This is what she calls him. "I feel sorry for her."

I say, "Why do you feel sorry for her, Da?" As in *Duh.* This is what I like to call her.

She blinks her big, dumb eyes at me. "I mean, it can't be easy being her."

"Why?" I shouldn't mess with her, the way I do with Seth, but I can't help it.

"Well. I mean. You know." She holds up the phone and points at the screen.

"She seems like she's doing all right to me."

Libby's "You Are Wanted" paper is upstairs on my desk. Ever since I read it, I've been trying to ignore the voice that's saying *This is your fault. If you hadn't grabbed her, she wouldn't be a target, and if she wasn't a target, she wouldn't have felt like she had to prove herself to the entire school.*

LIBBY

Martin Van Buren High is actually really beautiful, which is weird when you stop to think of how many people over the past ninety-some years of its lifetime have spent so much time dreading being here. We have a real, honest-to-God art gallery in our school, our gym seats ten thousand people, and Civic Auditorium, attached to the athletic center, is the town's venue for concerts and shows. There's a salad bar and a pizza bar and a sandwich bar in the cafeteria, and there's even a small convenience store by the nurse's office. But it might as well be Petak Island Prison, in the middle of a lake in the deepest, most remote part of Russia, where prisoners spend twenty-two hours a day in their cells and only get visitors twice a year. This is what it can feel like to be here.

Today is no exception. Everyone—and I mean *everyone*—knows my name now, and all of them can picture me in a bathing suit. Even the people who weren't actually there. The YouTube video is called *Fat Girl Fights Back: Libby Strout, formerly America's Fattest Teen, tells classmates "You Are Wanted."* It was posted last night and already has 262,356 views.

Imagine it.

I can tell you from experience that it is really weird and really unsettling. That guy over there with the *Game of Thrones* notebook. That girl and her friends with their band instruments. The cheerleaders. The *basketball team*. And oh right, the teachers.

I did not think this through.

It may be my imagination, but every pair of eyes lands on me as I walk through the halls. I walk and breathe, walk and breathe. I start to strut a little. I try adding in a sashay. I remember how it felt dancing in my room to the Spice Girls, and I tell myself, *That is who you really are. Some kind of superstar, just like in the song.*

I only get one moo. Everyone else just stares.

In the hallway, Mr. Levine says, "Everything okay, Libby?"

Which tells me, whether he's seen it or not, he must know about *Fat Girl Fights Back.*

"Just because I see you in our Conversation Circles doesn't mean you can't talk to me. It is kind of what I do, you know."

"I know. Thanks, Mr. Levine. Everything's great. Really." I'm not sure he believes me, but I hurry off before he can ask me anything else.

I eat lunch in the art room with Bailey, Jayvee, and Iris because right now it's more peaceful (i.e., less traumatic) than the cafeteria. They start talking, as they always do, about what they'll do beyond school, when MVB is over and we're free. Bailey is planning to be an artist and also a doctor, and Jayvee is going to be a writer.

At some point, Iris looks at me and says, "I wish I was like them. I wish I knew what I was going to do."

"You could be a singer. If I had a voice like yours, Iris Engelbrecht, I would sing all day just to hear myself."

Her ears turn bright pink. She takes a sip of her Diet Coke. "That's not a career, that's a hobby." She's quoting someone, maybe her mom.

"Tell that to Taylor Swift." I scroll through my phone, choose a song, and hit Play. They all go quiet as I start dancing. I say, "I'm going to be a dancer. Maybe I'll even be a Rockette." I kick my leg. I kick it as high as the sky.

Jayvee starts clapping and whistling.

"I'm starting my own dance club. I'll take everyone who can't be a Damsel or anyone who doesn't want to be a Damsel. We won't dance in formation and we won't dance with flags. We'll just get out there and do whatever we want, but we'll do it together."

"I want to be in your dance club!" Bailey is up and shaking it, hair flying.

"Me too." Jayvee climbs onto a desk, all jazz hands and waving arms. She tips an imaginary top hat and smiles the biggest, scariest stage smile anyone has ever seen.

Iris sets down her Diet Coke. She dabs at her mouth with her napkin. And then she starts to sing along, drowning out the Spice Girls with that big, gorgeous voice of hers. She shimmies a little in her seat, shoulders moving to the left, shoulders moving to the right. I grab a paintbrush and hand it to her, and like that, it's not a paintbrush, it's a microphone, and we're not in a high school art room; we're onstage, all of us, together, doing our own thing.

Until Mr. Grazer, art teacher, walks in and shouts, "What is going on in here?"

Bailey pipes up. "We're just expressing our art, Mr. G."

"Well, express it a little more quietly, Bailey."

JACK

A ring of chairs is arranged in the middle of the basketball court. It appears that in today's Conversation Circle—our very last one—we will be sitting in an actual circle.

I almost turn around and walk out, but it's the final day, after all, so I make myself take a seat, say hey to the collective group, and wait for Mr. Levine to join us. I stretch my legs in front of me, cross them at the ankle, tip my head back, close my eyes. Everyone will think I'm hung over or tired or just bored out of my mind, but actually my heart is beating a little too fast, a little too loud.

Whatever this circle is about can't be good.

I listen as everyone settles in, as their voices rise and fall. I hear Libby say something as she takes a seat, and then I hear the squeak of sneakers on the scuffed-up floor, and this is Mr. Levine.

He says, "You're probably wondering why, in this Conversation Circle of ours, we're sitting in a circle."

I open my eyes, sit up a little, try to look interested and like this doesn't scare the shit out of me. I glance over at Libby. I want to say *I'm sorry. I miss you.* But she's watching Mr. Levine, who's cradling a basketball.

"Today we're going to take turns saying five positive things about each person here. So if I'm starting, I'll say five great things about, let's say, Maddy." He tosses the ball to Maddy. "You're kind, punctual, polite, get along well with others, and you're a lot more confident than you were when we first started this Circle. Then Maddy says five great things about me."

Maddy goes, "You wear cool bow ties, you look like Doctor Who, you're pretty chill for a teacher, you don't lecture us too much, and you keep it interesting." She throws the ball back to Mr. Levine.

"Excellent, Maddy, and thank you. So next I would throw the ball to Jack or Andy or Natasha or Travis or Libby or Keshawn, until I've said something about everyone. We'll go round and round till everyone has taken a turn. Questions?"

Keshawn goes, "Like, anything, as long as it's good?"

"Let's say anything with a PG-13 rating." They all laugh except Keshawn, who looks disappointed.

So now we're all glancing around at each other, studying each other, no doubt trying to think of five nice things to say. I'm studying them too, but in a different way. After all this time, I can pick out Keshawn in this group, and Natasha must be the girl with long brown hair with her hand on his leg—at least I hope so, for Keshawn's sake. I know Libby because she's the largest of the girls, and I know Maddy, thanks to Mr. Levine. But as usual I'm having trouble with Andy and Travis. They're the same height, same build, and both have scraggly hair that falls in their eyes. You can tell some people by mannerisms, like the way they brush the hair off their face, but these guys just blink on through it.

I tell myself I'll be okay as long as Levine chooses someone else to go first. So now I try to think of what to say about these people. Keshawn and Natasha were caught having sex in one of the bathrooms, which is by far the best reason any of us have for being here, but I can't exactly mention this as one of my positive things. Maddy is here for stealing makeup out of random lockers. Andy destroyed school property (by pissing on it), and Travis, on a dare, lit up a joint *during class*. So yeah. The only person I can think of nice things to say about is Libby. And instead of thinking of five good things to say about her, I can think of a hundred.

Levine says, "Jack, why don't you start us off?"

Crap.

I flash him a grin. "Ladies first. Chivalry and all that."

"While I'm sure the ladies appreciate the gesture, I'm betting they won't mind in this case." He sits back in his chair, folds his arms across his chest, and waits.

For whatever reason, I look right at Libby. *Don't abandon me, Libby Strout, not when I need you most.* She frowns, and for a minute I expect her to tell me off or flip me off or maybe just get up and walk out. But she must see my panic because she goes, "I'm sorry, Mr. Levine, but before I forget—Travis, do we have a test tomorrow in driver's ed?" She's looking at the guy across from her, the one in the black long-sleeved jersey.

"What? Fuck, do we?" He blinks at her through his hair, his mouth popped open in an O, and suddenly I feel like laughing.

"I thought Dominguez said . . . Or maybe that was another class . . . Oh wait, wait. I'm thinking of history."

Mr. Levine is looking at her like he knows she's up to something, but all he says is "Go ahead, Jack."

Keshawn's a good basketball player. Natasha is a positive person who's always smiling. Maddy seems very smart. Andy helped take us to state last year in football. Travis has a great collection of vintage T-shirts. That kind of thing.

Here is what they say about me: Jack's good-looking. Jack's got it all together. Jack drives a cool car. Jack lives in a nice house. Jack's got a great smile. Jack's got great hair. Jack's smart. Jack's funny. Jack's a good baseball player. Jack will probably get into any college he applies to.

I know they mean well, but I'm left feeling deflated. Maybe they're all feeling like this too, but I want to go *You don't know me. If that's all you think I am, you don't have a clue.*

But whose fault is that?

I turn to Libby. "You're kind. Probably the kindest person I know. You're also forgiving, at least a little, but I'm hoping a lot, and in my book that's a superpower." Her eyes are on mine, and there's a lot going on there. "You're smart as hell, and you don't take people's crap, least of all mine. You are who you are. You know who that is, and you aren't afraid of it, and how many of us can say that." She's not smiling, but it's not about what her mouth is doing. It's about her eyes. "You're strong too. It's not just a matter of being able to knock down a guy with a single shot to the jaw." (Everyone laughs, except her.) "I'm talking about inner strength. Like, if I would draw that inner strength it might look a lot like a triangle made of carbyne. That's the world's strongest structure and the world's strongest material. You also make things better for people around you . . ."

I'm about to go on, but Mr. Levine says, "That's actually more than five. I want you to keep going, but I'd like to get through everyone today. Good work, though, Jack. Way to kick this off."

Libby is still looking at me, and her eyes are as open as the sky.

And then there's this *moment.*

It's almost like I see her. Not just the amber-colored eyes or the freckles on her cheeks, but really see her.

"Jack? It's Libby's turn."

I rub the back of my neck, where the hairs are prickling.

"Yeah. Sure." I throw the ball to her.

She stares at the ball for a moment, rolling it around in her hands, delicately, carefully, like she's holding the entire world.

Then she turns those eyes on me, and they're hard to read. She opens her mouth, closes it. Opens it again. It turns out she doesn't have five things to say about me. She has only one. "You're actually not a bad guy, Jack Masselin. But I'm not sure you know it yet."

LIBBY

I walk as fast as I can out of the gym without actually breaking into a run. But Jack falls in step beside me, Afro billowing and blowing like it comes with its own wind effects.

He says, "Thanks for what you said in there."

"It was nothing."

"Not to me. By the way, what you did yesterday? You're my hero."

"You told me to put clothes on."

"Because Moses Hunt was getting a little too close, and who knows what he might have done. I didn't want anyone grabbing you."

"Oh, the irony." And then, because for some reason I can't help myself, I tell him, "I've apparently gone viral."

"I know. I saw. Listen, some girl will see that video and you're going to give her the courage to buy her own purple bikini. You're going to make a difference. Just watch. Girls everywhere, of all sizes, are going to want one. Clothing manufacturers across the globe will be working overtime to produce enough purple swimsuits to satisfy the demand. Girls will stop asking *Do these jeans make my butt look big?* They won't care if it looks big or small. They'll wear what they want to wear and fucking own it."

He smiles, and there's something in it that makes me want to smile, but I don't because this is the boy who broke my heart.

He says, "It may not look like it, but you're actually smiling."

I can't wait for Christmas, so I carry Dusty's robot down the hall to his room and knock on the door. He yells, "Come in."

I push open the door, but I don't go in because he's still not really talking to me. Instead I set the robot on the floor and send it inside. I've named it the Shitkicker. It's a superhero.

The robot goes zooming into Dusty's room, where it says, "Hello, Dusty. I'm fighting shittiness everywhere! The Shitkicker is here to kick your ass!"

Dusty goes, "*My* ass?" And then starts laughing.

It's the best sound in the world. I poke my head into the room, and my little brother is rolling across his bed, and then he's up and on his feet and examining the robot from every angle.

He sees me and frowns. I hit the remote, and the Shitkicker says, "It's you and me against the world, Dusty."

My brother stares at the robot and shakes his head. "It's almost like it recognized me. How did you do that?"

The truth is the Shitkicker can't recognize Dusty any more than I can, but I programmed it so that Dusty is the only one it calls by name. To the Shitkicker, everyone is Dusty.

"Magic," I say. "So that he can always find you."

I push a button on the remote, and the Shitkicker says, "Don't be shitty!" And then I hit another button, and the robot is kicking its legs, only it's not really kicking anything—it's dancing. The

Jackson 5 come cranking out of a speaker in old Shitkicker's chest, and now Dusty is dancing along with it.

I hand my brother the remote and then I'm dancing too, and a couple of minutes later Dusty goes, "Is he carrying a *purse*?!" And of course he is, because the Shitkicker knows only the cool kids use them. And Dusty's howling over this, and now the three of us are dancing in sync, and as good as Dusty and I are, there's no doubt about it—the Shitkicker is definitely the man.

Top 2 Things I Miss About Libby
by Jack Masselin

• • •

1. The way I feel when I'm with her. Like I just swallowed the sun and it's shooting out of every pore.
2. Everything.

FOUR DAYS LATER

JACK

I'm due at Kam's house around nine. Caroline will be there. Everyone will be there. I don't want to see everyone—or anyone, actually—but this is the way it has to be. I'm Jack Masselin, after all. I've got a reputation to uphold.

I take a shower, pull on my clothes, shake out my hair. I grab the car keys, and I'm almost out of there when my dad (thick eyebrows, pale skin, Masselin's shirt) comes chasing after me.

"Hey, Jack, can we talk to you a minute?"

I think of every excuse—I've got a date and I'm already running late (true), I think the car's on fire (hopefully not true), I don't want to talk to you (true true true). "Sure thing, Daddy-o. What's up? But make it quick. The ladies don't like to be kept waiting." I almost add, *As you know.*

"This is serious, buddy."

Marcus, Dusty, and I sit on the couch side by side. Mom is opposite us on the ottoman that's the size of a small boat. She leans forward, hands on her knees as if she might leap up at any minute.

Dad clears his throat. "Your mom and I love each other very much. And we love you. The three of you are our life, and we'd never do anything to hurt you." He goes on like this for a while, all about how much he loves us and how he's lucky to have such a great, supportive family, how we were all there for him when he was sick, and he can never tell us what that means to him.

Meanwhile, Marcus, Dusty, and I are all looking at Mom because she's the one who tells it like it is. But she doesn't say anything. She doesn't even look at us. She's staring at some point just past our father, who is still talking.

Finally, Dusty raises his hand and goes, "Are you getting divorced?"

Dad's face crumples, and I can't look. Now no one's saying anything, and finally, in this very quiet voice, Mom says, "Your father and I think it's best to separate for a little while. We need to work on some things in our marriage, but those issues have nothing to do with you."

The conversation doesn't end there. Dusty has questions, and Marcus wants to know what this means for us, like, where will we live and can we still go to college?

Meanwhile, I'm here on the outside—always on the outside, even as the world crumbles around me—face pressed to the glass that divides us, looking in.

LIBBY

We're on our way to pick up Iris, and Jayvee is driving because she's the only one with a license. Bailey and I sit in back. Bailey says, "Dave Kaminski's having a party. I promised I'd stop by, just for a minute."

Jayvee catches my eye in the mirror. "Libbs? It's kind of up to you."

Bailey says, "Jack won't be there."

I say, "How do you know?"

"He doesn't really go to parties."

We roll up in front of Iris's house, but Iris is nowhere to be seen. Jayvee shoots her a text, and we sit there. When she still doesn't appear, Jayvee swears under her breath. "I'll be back." She leaves the engine running and goes marching up the walk.

"Libbs?" Bailey is peering at me, eyebrows raised like banners, mouth in a half-smile, eyes wide and shining.

"Okay."

Because I mean, why not? What do I have to lose?

And then, because I don't have anything to lose, I say, "Why didn't you stick up for me when I was bullied? Back in fifth grade. When Moses Hunt started banning me from the playground. Why didn't you do something or at least come talk to me? I stood there every day, too terrified to set one foot on the playground, and you never once came over to talk to me."

I say it matter-of-factly. I'm not emotional. I'm not upset. I just genuinely want to know. At first, I'm not sure she hears me. But then her eyebrows sink back into place and her half-smile disappears and her eyes go cloudy.

"I don't know, Libbs. I think I told myself we were friends, but not best friends, and that you seemed like you were okay. You're still like that. You get letters from some horrible person, and you brush it off. Jack tells you he can't go out with you anymore, and you're 'fine.'"

"But it was a big deal back then, and it was kind of obvious, but no one did anything."

"And I felt awful because I didn't, and then one day you were gone. You didn't come back."

"Is that why you're so nice to me now?"

"It's why I came up and said hi to you on the first day of school, but it's not why I'm nice to you. I'm nice because I like you. I'm just really, really, really sorry I wasn't a good friend then."

And it doesn't change anything, but it's enough.

"I could have been a better friend too. I could have talked to you. I could have told you how I was feeling." And then she hugs me, and I inhale her hair, which tastes like rainbows and peach pie, exactly how you think Bailey Bishop's hair would taste.

When we walk into Dave Kaminski's, the first person I see is Mick from Copenhagen. He's in the living room, dancing in this circle of girls, and his black hair is shining blue-black like crow feathers. Next to me, Jayvee goes, "*Hello,* Mick from Copenhagen," in this throaty voice, and then pretends to faint into Iris's arms.

I follow Bailey through the crowd, and Dave Kaminski's house doesn't look like a house but some sort of fraternity. It is literally crammed with so many people, we can barely move. The music is loud, and people are doing their best to dance, but it's more like jumping straight up and down in place.

My first high school party.

The music is good, and so I'm shaking my hips a little as I walk, and when I accidentally bump some guy, he yells, "Watch it!"

I tell my hips to be still and behave themselves, and finally we break through into the dining room, where Dave Kaminski is playing poker with a group of guys and a couple of girls. Bailey goes up to Dave and says something in his ear, and suddenly he's grabbing her until she's sitting on his lap, and she's laughing and play-hitting him, and then she hugs him and comes back over to us. "Dave's really glad we're here."

I say, "Apparently."

And then Dave Kaminski catches my eye and gives me this nod, and there's something in it that feels almost like an apology.

JACK

Caroline (dark skin, smells like cinnamon, beauty mark by her eye) and I are in Kam's sister's room. Literally every inch of wall is covered in posters of Boy Parade, so it's a little like sitting in the middle of a very small arena full of twenty-year-old guys. Their faces are everywhere, and their eyes are glued to us. They are smiling these unnaturally white smiles that glow in the dark.

She thinks I've brought her in here to make out. But instead I'm trying to see once and for all if I can trick sweet Caroline into coming out and having a real conversation with me. Because I miss Libby. Because I miss talking to someone the way I can talk to her.

After all this time, Caroline and I have our routine memorized. Until recently, I try to get in her pants, and she takes off her clothes because I'm not allowed to in case I mess up her hair. What comes next is we will almost have sex, and I'll hold her for a little while, and then I'll lie there wondering *When when when?*

Usually my heart's not in it, only my body, and my mind cooperates by going blank. But tonight my mind is in charge. Like Mr. Levine, it wants to know why. *Why are you doing this? Why are you even sitting here with this girl? Why do you keep ending up with this person? Why don't you just stop, Jack? Why don't you just live your life and be yourself?*

Which is why I go, "What's the best thing that's ever happened to you?"

She blinks at me. "I'm supposed to say 'Jack Masselin,' right?"

"Only if it's true, baby. Come on, I want to know. In the whole history of your life, what's the best thing that's ever happened to you?"

"I don't know, maybe when Chloe was born." Chloe is her little sister.

"What's the worst thing that ever happened?"

"When my cat Damon got hit by a car."

The worst thing that ever happened to me was fucking up my relationship with Libby Strout, but I say, "There's got to be something else."

"Why?"

"Because you used to be different. Shy. Quiet. Dorky."

"God, don't remind me."

"Okay, so what's one thing people don't know about you?"

She frowns down at the bed. "I hate the color brown. I don't like turtles. And I got my wisdom teeth out when I was fourteen."

Boring, boring, and boring. I almost say *I have a neurological glitch in my brain that keeps me from recognizing faces. Boom! Muahahahahahahaha.*

But instead I ask another question and another, and the whole time she answers in this flat, dull voice and picks at the comforter. As she talks, I'm barely listening to her answers. Instead I'm thinking, *All this time, I thought she was a security blanket, but there's no security here. How can there be when she doesn't see me any more than I see her? I might as well be alone.* And, of course, I am alone.

And then suddenly she lifts her shirt over her hair and drops it onto the floor. She readjusts her bra strap and leans back seductively. She bites her bottom lip, which is also part of the routine. A couple of years ago, the bottom lip thing slayed me.

I'm about to say something along the lines of *Please put your shirt back on* when this shift happens, before my eyes, and Caroline grows paler and fuller until she's no longer sitting there. It's Libby Strout, leaning back on one arm, plucking at the strap of her electric-purple bikini. But she's talking and telling me things and laughing and asking me questions, and I'm talking, and then she's sitting up and leaning in, and we're both just talking until she says, "Um. Hello!" And snaps her fingers in my face.

And it's Caroline again.

I stare at her, hoping she'll morph back into Libby, and she goes, "What is your problem? Why are you being so weird?" And she's got this sexy bra and this sexy body, and there isn't a single guy at MVB High, even the ones who are afraid of her, who wouldn't want to be me right now. I lay my hand on her leg and it's smooth and feels like satin, and all I can think is:

I don't love Caroline. I don't even like Caroline.

I force myself to think of things I like about this Caroline right now, the only one who's here.

She smells good. Her teeth are very . . . um . . . even. Her eyes are okay. Her mouth is nice.

I mean, I guess. But the shit she says? Not so nice. Libby has interesting things to say that aren't cruel or selfish.

I say to my brain, *Why are you doing this? Why can't you stop thinking about Libby? Why are you fucking with me?*

And as I'm sitting here having this in-depth conversation with my brain, Caroline goes, "I'm think I'm ready."

"For what?"

"It."

I'm trying to look into her eyes, but the room is dark except for the light that slips in under the door and her phone, which goes bright every other minute from all the texts coming in.

"*It.* Sex, Jack. I'm ready to have sex. With you." And then here comes the attitude: "*Unless you don't want to.*"

I've only been wanting to since birth, but inexplicably I hear myself say, "Why now?"

"What?"

"Why are you suddenly ready now? After all this time? What changed?"

Apparently my mouth has a mind of its own because it won't stop talking. My manlier parts are going, STOP TALKING, YOU IDIOT! SHUT THE FUCK UP! But my mouth isn't listening. Why isn't it listening?

"Are you gonna *argue* with me about this?"

"Is this really where you want to do it for the first time? I mean, look around you." I point to the walls of posters. I dislodge a stuffed animal from under my back and wave it in her face. "You wouldn't really want to do it in front of this little guy, would you?"

"Are you freaking kidding me?" And she shoves me so hard I go flying off the bed.

LIBBY

Mick from Copenhagen and I are dancing, his hair flashing blue-black, blue-black, and his smile flashing white, white, white. We are making up dances as we go—actually, I'm making them up and he's trying to follow along. "I call this the Wind Machine!" And then I act like I'm pushing through a windstorm. "I call this Shoes on Fire!" And then I'm jumping around like my shoes are on fire and I don't want to touch the ground.

When a slow song comes on, he holds out his hand and I take it. Dancing with him is different from dancing with Jack. For one thing, Mick is about fifteen feet tall, so my face is pressed into his chest. For another, he kind of just sways back and forth and shuffles his feet.

Stop thinking about Jack Masselin. Jack, who doesn't want you, at least not enough to give it a chance. Focus on Mick from Copenhagen and his shiny teeth and his giant hands.

When Mick says, "Come with me," I go with him. As Bailey watches, mouth open, I follow him up the stairs into what must be Dave Kaminski's bedroom. Mick turns on the desk light and sits down on the bed. I stand in the doorway staring at him. He smiles and I smile, and then he says, loud enough so I can hear him all the way over here, "I was wondering if I could kiss you. I've wanted to kiss you from the moment I saw you."

And even though he's not Jack Masselin, or maybe because he's not Jack Masselin, I walk across the room and sit down next to him, and suddenly we're kissing.

My neck is twisted, and I want to move it, but I don't want to move it because it's Mick from Copenhagen, and now I'm getting a cramp in it, so I shift just slightly, and now I'm getting a cramp in my calf. It is *the worst pain of my life,* but here is a gorgeous boy kissing my face off, so I soldier on.

In spite of the fact that my body is seizing up everywhere and I'm in excruciating pain, he's a good kisser. I'm guessing he's had a lot of practice, because it feels like he's showing off a little, doing all these intricate circle dances with his tongue. He's working it like a ringmaster, and don't get me wrong, there's nothing bad about it. This is probably the way they kiss in Copenhagen. He's probably been kissing people like this since he was two.

Then the kiss is over and we pull apart, and I feel this weird urge to applaud because it seems like he expects it. He says, "Wow."

"Yeah," I breathe. "Wow." Because what else am I supposed to say? *Next time, don't try so hard.* And *Excuse me while I walk off this cramp.*

"Have you ever been to Scandinavia?"

"No." I haven't been anywhere except Ohio. I wonder then if he knows I've spent part of my life locked inside my house.

"You should go sometime."

But what I hear is *Maybe I'll take you there. Maybe we'll go back and I'll show you where I'm from and you can meet my relatives and I will love you forever.*

And even though I don't want to meet his relatives and I don't want him to love me forever, I kiss him again. Because while I'm kissing him, there is no America's Fattest Teen, at least not for tonight. No cranes or hospitals. No dead mother. No Moses Hunt. Most important of all, no Jack Masselin. There is just me. And this boy. And a kiss.

JACK

I've never seen Caroline cry before, so for a minute I sit there, completely stupid, trying to figure out what to do. She is hiccupping and wheezing, like she's trying to catch her breath. I start petting her like she's a dog, and she shrugs me off.

"Why don't you want me?" She sounds small, like she's folded herself in half and then another half and then another. "What is it about me?" And now I go even more stupid because here is a side of Caroline I never knew existed. *Is it possible she's as insecure as the rest of us?*

I say, "You're beautiful. You're Caroline Amelia Lushamp." But this isn't what she's asking me. *Tell her you want her.* But I can't because I don't, not like that. I start to scramble. I give it my all. I tell her over and over again who she is and how beautiful she is, even as she's pulling on her clothes, even as she's grabbing her phone. Even as she says, "I can't do this anymore," and throws the door open, letting the light in. I'm temporarily blinded, and by the time I can see again, she's gone.

LIBBY

We kiss for what feels like hours.

We kiss even when someone stumbles into the room and blinds us with the overhead lights and then stumbles out again.

We kiss until he has many, many hands and a tongue in my ear, and I think, *I don't want to be Pauline Potter. I don't want him to be my first. I don't want him to be my anything.*

So I pull away and say, "I'm sorry, Mick, from Copenhagen. I'm not Pauline Potter."

And he sits back and says, "Who?"

"Never mind. I think I need a drink. I'm sorry, but I don't want to make out anymore."

And I kind of expect him to be devastated, but he just shrugs and smiles at me. "Okay."

He helps me up, and we walk out as I smooth my hair and shirt. I walk behind him, and even though I don't want to make out with him, Mick from Copenhagen is so cute I can't help thinking, *Girl, you ARE wanted.* And it feels pretty damn good.

JACK

I find Kam in the kitchen, knocking back shots. His white hair is plastered to his head and he's got one arm thrown around a girl who may be Kendra Wu (small, Asian, long black hair in a braid). I say, "What are we drinking?" The Girl Who May Be Kendra hands me something brown that doesn't look like beer.

I throw it down my throat. My esophagus burns like I just inhaled gasoline. I say, "Another."

And then they're all handing me shots.

Kam empties his own glass and slams it onto the counter. He pumps both fists into the air and howls.

A while later, I work my way through the party, searching for a black Mohawk because I am too fucked up to drive home, and suddenly I want to go home. I want to go home right now. I find the Mohawk attached to someone who is probably Seth outside by the pool. At this point, I don't bother lurking, trying to make sure it's him. I walk right up to the Someone Who Is Probably Seth and say, "I need a ride home."

He's like, "Sure, sure, Mass. Just wait till we finish." And he holds up a joint, takes a drag, and then starts laughing for no good reason.

I grab the joint out of his hand and take a drag, because maybe this is the secret of life right here. Maybe this will give me answers. Instead, I end up coughing like an old man for a good five minutes. Someone hands me a drink to wash it down, and then the pool tilts and the ground tilts and suddenly the sky is where the ground should be, and a boy with a Mohawk is leaning over me going, "Are you okay, man?"

I close my eyes because no, I'm not. I want to keep them closed and go to sleep here in the sky where the ground should be, but the world tilts worse with them closed. I open them again, and somehow I get on my feet. My only hope is that maybe Bailey Bishop is here, because she won't be drinking. But she doesn't always come to parties, and besides I'll never find her in this crowd of blond girls. I go back inside, and it seems like the house is even more packed with people, like the student bodies of three more high schools arrived while I was out by the pool.

I don't know anyone.

I shove my way through the kitchen, the dining room, the living room. People are hollering at me, and one girl makes a grab for me, holding on to my arm like it's a life raft. She smells like Caroline, but she isn't Caroline—she's skinny and white and has curly hair the color of margarine. She goes, "Oh my God, Jack Masselin!" And plants a kiss right on my mouth.

She tastes like cigarettes, and I push her away. "Masshole." She turns and dances with the people standing next to her.

I'm breaking every rule I've ever created for this exact kind of situation—I don't smile or nod or say "Hey, what's up." I don't flirt with every girl. I make eye contact, as if suddenly I'll be able to recognize who everyone is. (I don't.) I stare at one guy so long, he goes, "What the fuck are you looking at?" But I don't care. I'm amped as all hell because it feels like I'm doing something dangerous, *like any second they might figure me out.*

The room I'm in now has tripled in size and the walls are miles away. It is just people from here to the moon, and I will never make it through all of them. I feel like a rock star, complete strangers yanking at my shirt, at my arms, at me. I push through harder because the door must be there somewhere, and what I need right now is air. My lungs are filling with the fumes of smoke and booze and my ears are filling with the *boom boom boom* of the music and my brain is filling with all this information that I can't process.

I could drive myself home. Except that I'm wasted and I can't won't shouldn't will not drive.

I say to someone, "Where's the door?"

"What?" He's shouting.

"Where's the door?" I'm shouting too.

"Through there, man." He nods his head.

As I'm turning, a girl stumbles into me, and I nearly lose my balance. She clutches my arm, and she's laughing and laughing. "Sorry!" She grabs hold of my hand and starts spinning to the music. I let her go.

The air in here is so tight and close that the oxygen may be disappearing. There's not enough air left, and I picture us all laid out like cult followers after a mass suicide. I need to get to a window or a door, but I'm being swallowed by this room and these people and this music. *How are they not panicking?* Everyone seems happy, like they're having the time of their lives. *How are they not worried about the lack of air in here?*

I don't remember Kam's house being this big or complicated, but it feels massive. I say to the guy next to me, "Hey, how do you get out of here?"

"What?"

"Where's the door?"

"I just fucking told you where the door is."

It's like the worst déjà vu, and what if I'm trapped in here forever, trying to find a way out, destined to relive the same conversations and the same interactions over and over again?

In that moment, I want to give up and let the crowd carry me away until we're all moving as one colossal body with hundreds of arms and legs and mouths and eyes. The weight of it will suffocate me or flatten me until I'm as thin as a paper doll, and then maybe they'll carry me outside, where I can float off on the breeze or drift under a bush and lie in peace forever.

I close my eyes, and when I open them again I see it, just beyond the crowd—the front door. I'm shoving my way there when I run into Caroline. I mean, it's her. Same black shirt, same pants. She turns, and I don't see the beauty mark, but I tell myself it must have rubbed off when she pulled her shirt back on or maybe when she was dancing. Before she can say anything, I grab her and kiss her.

She can drive me home. She will get me out of here and I'll apologize and she can be the forgiver, and all will be fine.

It's a long kiss, one of my best, and even as I'm kissing her, I know something's wrong. But I keep right on doing it, and when I finally push away, I say, "That's how much I missed you."

LIBBY

"Is that Jack?" Iris points across the room.

The four of us turn like one person, just in time to see Jack Masselin grab some girl and start kissing her.

One by one, my friends look at me, and I realize that my hand is on my mouth. I am touching the lips that Mick from Copenhagen recently kissed, and all I can think is that Jack is free to kiss anyone and everyone he wants, but I don't have to stand here and watch it.

I push my way toward the back door, away from Jack and the girl. I can hear Bailey calling my name, but I don't stop. I can't stop. I also can't breathe.

Outside, I step into the cool night air and push my way past everyone gathered there until I'm around the corner and the night is suddenly quiet, and I'm alone. I lean against the house and fill my lungs.

JACK

Caroline has the weirdest look on her face as she gazes up at me, and then suddenly there are two of them. Two Carolines, side by side. Matching black shirts, matching pants, only this other one has a beauty mark by her eye.

The song ends, and there's this brief moment of quiet. The one with the beauty mark goes, "You're such a bastard." And then the music starts back up, but by now everybody is looking at us.

She starts to cry again, hiccupping and wheezing, and I know in my bones that *this* is Caroline, not the other one, the one without the beauty mark, the one who stands there with her eyes shining and her mouth all twisted up in a pretend frown. You can tell that whoever this is—the cousin, most likely—she's enjoying the hell out of this. I want to say to her *She's your family. Have a little compassion.* But that would be ridiculous coming from me, wouldn't it?

So I do the only thing I can do. I walk over, shut off the music, and say to the entire room, "I have a rare neurological disorder called prosopagnosia, which means I can't recognize faces. I can *see* your face, but as soon as I look away from it, I forget it. If I'm trying to think of what you look like, I can't conjure an image, and the next time I see you it'll be like I've never seen you before."

The room has gone dead quiet. I try to find Caroline in the crowd, to read her expression. I try to find anyone I know, but every single person here is a stranger. Together they're like a wall of stones, an embarrassment of pandas, one bleeding into the other. My heart is drumming away, and the sound of it fills my ears. I realize I'm shaking, so I jam my hands into my pockets, where no one will see. *Say something. Anyone.*

And then someone yells, "Fuck off, Mass, what the hell." And people are laughing and falling all over themselves, and the music starts blasting again, and a girl comes up to me and slaps me across the face, but I have no idea who she is. They think it's a joke. They think I'm a joke. And I can see them starting to turn on me.

The only movies I've ever really enjoyed watching are the old black-and-white horror flicks. I may have trouble telling the people apart, but I can recognize the Wolf Man, King Kong, Dracula, the Thing from Outer Space. Right now, I'm looking at a gang of villagers—faces identical—armed with clubs and torches, ready to chase Frankenstein's monster off a cliff. Only I'm the monster.

I push my way through them because there's nothing else to do. They crane around to stare at me as I carve a path to the front door, and someone trips me and somebody else goes, "Look at me, I can't see faces," and he's walking like a mummy, arms out in front of him, bumping into walls and people. I throw myself at the door, wrench it open, and as I'm trying to move around the mountain of a guy standing on the front step, I'm suddenly hit with the force of a small meteor right between the shoulder blades, and I go flying. I land in the yard, on my knee, and it takes me a minute to shake off the surprise and the pain. A hand is extended and I take it without thinking. It pulls me to my feet, and it's then I see that the hand belongs to the same mountain of a guy.

He goes, "Hey, Mass. You look like shit. Must be a bad night. It's about to get worse."

And then he takes a swing. His fists are coming at me too fast to duck, too fast to move. Over and over his fists make contact with bone, or maybe he's not the only one swinging. At some point, I hear myself say, "More weight."

And then the world goes black.

I'm rounding the corner of the house, into the front yard, when I see Moses Hunt punch Jack Masselin in the back. In slow motion, Jack falls, and as he hits the earth, I swear I can hear the impact. Now Moses Hunt is punching him in the face, and one of the other Hunt brothers, Malcolm maybe, is kicking him in the ribs.

I don't even think. I must let out some sort of scream, because I can feel my own eardrums shatter and I see the faces of Moses and Malcolm and Reed Young and their friends turn and stare at me, mouths agape, as I go flying through the air.

I sock Moses right in the nose, and it sends him staggering backward. Then I shove everyone off Jack, and I'm not even thinking. I'm suddenly filled with all this superstrength, and I'm single-handedly fighting them all until Dave Kaminski and Seth Powell and Keshawn Price are there beside me, scaring the bad guys away.

I watch as the Hunts run off down the street, tails between their legs, and as Dave bends over Jack, trying to shake him back to consciousness.

JACK

The first face I see is Libby's. For a minute, I don't know where I am. I think maybe it's a dream and that I've conjured her. I reach up and cover her face with my hand. She bats it away.

"He's awake."

But I have to touch her again to make sure she's real. I tweak the end of her nose.

"Please stop doing that. I'm real, Jack."

A guy with white, white hair appears beside her. "They were going to kill you, Mass."

"I'm okay." And now I'm feeling my chest, searching for my heartbeat, making sure it's still ticking. Once I can feel it battering away in there, I say again, "I'm okay."

A boy with a Mohawk pops up over Kam's shoulder. "Dude, she totally saved your ass." And then he starts laughing like a fool.

Libby says, "I'm going to drive you home."

"You don't have a license."

"Seriously?"

"What? I can drive." Even though I know I can't won't shouldn't will not do so.

"YOU'VE BEEN DRINKING. Where's your car?"

"Just down the street to the right. About three houses away."

She brushes past so now she's walking ahead of me, leading me away from the party, and I catch a whiff of something—sunshine.

LIBBY

At first we don't talk. It's as if the car is being powered by our minds, and the harder we concentrate, the faster we'll get there. He is staring out the window, not doing anything except sitting, but I'm completely and fully aware of him. The way one hand rests on the seat, the other on the window. The way every now and then the streetlights catch the gold flecks in his dark hair. The way his legs are longer than mine, and the way he sits, like he's perfectly at ease no matter where he is.

He must feel me thinking about him, because he says, "It feels good just to sit here. With one purpose. Knowing where we're headed. Knowing what we'll do when we get there. Cut and dried. Black and white."

"I guess it does." And I know what he means.

He looks at me. "Do you know who Herschel Walker is?"

"Football player?"

He whistles, then goes, "Ow." He cradles his jaw.

"When you're housebound, you watch a lot of TV." Even things you're not interested in, like ESPN documentaries and home improvement shows.

"Well, as you clearly already know, he was one of the most powerful running backs in football history, right? But when he was young, I guess he was afraid of the dark—like, terrified of the dark. And he was overweight and he stuttered, and all the other kids gave him hell for it. So what he does is he creates this Incredible Hulk inside him, someone who could stand up to people and never give up."

I decide I like Herschel Walker, and that in many ways, I *am* Herschel Walker.

"He'd read aloud every day, and by doing that, he taught himself not to stutter. In middle school, he started working out hard, and by high school he was a beast. He graduated valedictorian and won the Heisman Trophy, three years into his college career at UGA. When he retired from the pros, he started noticing this shift in his behavior, and that's when he found out he's got this thing called DID, dissociative identity disorder. Multiple personalities." He gestures like Mr. Dominguez in driver's ed. "You want to get in your left lane."

I change lanes and stop at the light.

"At the next light, you're going to turn left onto Hillcrest."

I see the map in my mind—my old neighborhood. I learned every street in it the year I got my first bike. I would take off and ride all over, my mom running alongside me, laughing, saying, "Libby, you're too fast." Even though I wasn't. But I remember the way she made me feel—like I could go anywhere and do anything.

Jack says, "So after all those years of pushing himself and not giving up, it's like the pressure did Herschel in. When he was asked about the DID, he compared it to hats—you know how we wear hats for all different situations? One for family. One for school. One for work. But with DID, it's like the hats get mixed up. So you're wearing the football hat at home, the family hat at work . . ."

"Too many hats." I think, *I know what this is like.*

"After a while, it gets hard to keep them straight."

And I wonder if we're still talking about Herschel Walker or if we're now talking about Jack.

He says, "I think we're more like Herschel Walker than Mary Katherine Blackwood. I actually don't think we're like her at all."

I can feel him looking at me, but I keep my eyes on the road.

He says, "Thank you for helping me tonight."

"I prefer to think of it as saving."

"Fine. Thank you for *saving* me." And now I can't help but look at him. And he smiles. It is slow at first, creeping across his face like a sunrise until suddenly it shines like the hottest point of the day. I sit on one hand so that I don't cover my eyes, which is what I want to do.

I smile at him.

And our eyes lock.

Neither of us breaks away, and I actually don't want to, even when I remind myself I'm driving, *Hello.*

I drag my eyes away and stare out the windshield, but everything is a blur. I can feel him looking at me.

You need to calm down, girl. Calm. Yourself. Down.

We hit a pothole, and the Land Rover sounds as if it's going to bottom out.

Jack says, "Christ, this car is shit."

We turn onto my old street, Capri Lane. I haven't been back here since that day they carried me away to the hospital. Jack is talking, but I'm not listening because everything is coming back to me. My mom. Being trapped in there. The feeling of not being able to breathe, of thinking this was it, of thinking I was dying. Of being rescued.

When I woke up in the hospital, everything was white. Blue, gray, black, white, like they were the only colors in the world. "You had an anxiety attack," my dad said. "You're going to be okay, but we need to make sure it doesn't happen again."

We're getting closer to my house, and I can see it coming toward me, only it's nothing like it used to be because, of course, they had to tear my house down, didn't they? Even though it was the last place I saw my mom alive. Even though memories of her were in every wall and floor.

I expect to drive right by it, but Jack says, "Pull over here." At first, I wonder if he's playing some sort of messed-up joke. But no, he's waving at the two-story house across the street and saying, "Let's see if my brother's in there. If he is, he can drive you home." He gets out of the Land Rover and starts up the walk.

I don't move.

Then—somehow—I open the door. I set one foot on the ground. I pull myself out. I set the other foot on the ground. I stand there.

I say, "That's your house?"

He turns. "Come on already." And then he looks past me at where I used to live, and his face goes blank, almost like he's seeing a ghost.

"How long have you lived there?" It's all I can do to get the words out.

He doesn't answer. He looks like he's having a stroke.

"Jack? How long have you lived there? In that house?"

Silence.

"Answer me."

"All my life."

And the world

just

stops.

"Can you tell me what happened, Libbs? Can you tell me what has you so panicked?"

"All of it." That was my answer, even though I knew my dad was expecting something more specific. *"Everything. It was you. Me. Aneurysms. Death. Cancer. Murder. Crime. Mean people. Rotten people. Two-faced people. Bullies. Natural disasters. The world has me panicked. The world did this. Especially the way it gives you people to love and then takes them away."* But the answer was actually simple. I had decided to be afraid.

I don't know how long it takes me to speak. Finally I say, "I used to live there." I point at the new house, shiny and big and perfectly intact, that sits on top of the grave that is my old one. The new house is nothing like the one that was there before it.

"I know."

"How do you know?" And by now, I'm waiting for it. I just want to hear him say it.

"Because I was there the day they cut you out."

JACK

Marcus is driving, and I'm in back. My brother is in a mood about having to leave the house, and now he's shooting me death looks via the rearview mirror. He won't even turn on the radio, this is how bad it is. The three of us are driving in silence except for Libby going "Turn here" and "Make a right there." Her voice sounds frostbitten. Now that I'm doing nothing but sitting, my head has gone heavy from the booze.

It's warm in the car and quiet. So quiet. I must blur off for a bit because my phone buzzes and I jump. I dig it out of my pocket and there's a text from Kam.

You ok, man?

I text back: **Fine.**

Seth said something about you going blind?

I stare at the screen, at the back of Libby's head. I click my phone off, then click it on again. I write:

I'm face-blind. Prosopagnosia. It's a thing. Just diagnosed.

When he doesn't write back, I shove the phone into my pocket.

I get this urge to shout into the silence, but I don't. In a few minutes my phone buzzes again. I don't bother to look at it.

We eventually get to her neighborhood, and Marcus slows the car to a crawl, inching along, peering out the window. Part of me hopes we'll never find her house so that I can make this right, and another part of me is just done. Done with her. Done with everything.

Inevitably, we're there, and I'm struck all over again by how her house looks exactly like all the other ones. If I was designing a home for Libby Strout, it would be exceptional. It would be one of a kind. It would be bright red with a tin roof, at least two stories, possibly more, a state-of-the-art weather station, and lots of turrets. Also a tower, but not one to lock her in. It would be a place where she could sit and look out over and beyond the town, as far as the horizon, maybe even past it.

Marcus says, "We're here."

Libby tells him thank you and practically hurls herself out of the car. I always forget how fast she is. She's at her front door by the time I manage to get myself up the walk.

She whips around to face me. "What? What is it, Jack? What? What?"

"I'm sorry I didn't say anything. But I didn't want to embarrass you any more than I already had."

"You could have mentioned it."

"I could have mentioned it. If it helps, I'll write you a letter of apology." I give her a hopeful smile, but she waves her hand at me like she's erasing it.

"No. Keep that to yourself, do you understand me, Jack Masselin? Put that smile away. That doesn't work on me. You're so worried that you can't ever be close to anyone, but it's not the face blindness that's to blame; it's you. All the smiling and the faking and pretending to be what you think people want you to be. That's what keeps you isolated. That's what screws you up. You need to try being a real person."

I drop the smile.

"Next to my mom dying, being cut out of my house was the worst moment of my life. Do you know I got hate mail? Everyone had something to say about what happened, about how fat I was, about my dad. They wanted to make sure I knew just how disgusted they were and how disgusting I was. They sent them to the hospital and they sent them here. They found my email and sent them directly. I mean, who does that? Who sees a story like that on the news and says, *I'm going to write her a letter and give her a piece of my mind. I wonder if I should mail it to the hospital or just hand-deliver it.* Did you and your brothers have a good laugh over it?"

Her eyes are blazing. She is daring me to say *Yes, that's exactly how it was, my brothers and I split a rib over it. We love to watch people almost die.*

Instead I say, "I'm sorry."

In that moment, I want to write not just one apology letter but hundreds, one for every horrible person who ever did or said anything mean to her.

"There's no way anyone would have done that if they knew you. And just so you know, not everyone was wishing you harm. We were rooting for you. I was rooting for you."

"What did you say?"

"I was rooting for you."

Something passes across her face, and I can see it—she knows I'm the one who sent her the book.

My dad is sitting in front of the computer. The minute he hears me come in, he's up and pointing at the clock on the wall. "What happened?"

I tell him because I'm too tired to pretend everything's fine. Honestly, he does need to worry about me. I can't protect him forever. So I tell him everything, starting with Mick from Copenhagen and the fight and Moses Hunt and taking Jack home and realizing he was there the day they knocked down our house, and finding out that all this time he was Dean of Dean, Sam, and Castiel. And then I tell him the other things I stopped telling him a while ago—about the letters and the Damsels and the purple bikini. I'm weary and angry and sad and heartbroken and empty, and more than anything, I want to go to sleep. But my dad is all I have.

He is pacing as I talk, and as soon as I stop, he stops. He says, "I need to know that you're okay. I need to know if I should go over to the Hunts' and punch that kid myself."

He is angry at the world outside this house, and that makes me love him even more.

"I'm good, Dad."

"You'd tell me." It's a question. "You will tell me."

"I will. Always. From now on." And then I say, "I'm sorry. For everything I put you through."

I can tell he knows I'm talking about *everything,* not just tonight.

"I'm sorry too, Libbs."

And it hits me square in the face. All the grief my dad has taken and swallowed and carried—not just the loss of my mom, but the loss of compassion from the people who blamed him for what happened to me. If he got mad, I never saw it. He just carries on, making sure I eat healthy, trying to keep me safe and feeling loved.

And then, maybe to prove there are no secrets between us, he tells me about the woman he's been seeing off and on for a while. Her name is Kerry and she teaches math at one of the middle schools. She's his age, married once, no kids. He didn't want to tell me because he's not sure where this will lead or what their relationship means, and he wants to be careful with me, with her. But I think really he just didn't want me to feel bad about being the only one in the world who hadn't moved on.

I say this to him now, and he takes my hand. "It's not moving on, Libbs. It's moving differently. That's all it is. Different life. Different world. Different rules. We don't ever leave that old world behind. We just create a new one."

It's after 1 a.m. when Marcus and I get home. I stand in front of the open fridge for at least five minutes, maybe more, willing something good to materialize—a pizza, a whole chicken, a giant steak, or a rack of ribs. When it doesn't, I grab a soda and some kind of guacamole/spinach/cheese dip, scrounge up some chips from the pantry, and sit down in the dark kitchen to eat myself a feast.

I'm halfway into the chips when my phone lights up across the room, where I left it. I get up, in case it's Libby, even though I know it won't be. It's Kam. He says:

> **Shit. This prosopagnosia is one trippy mo-fo. But hey man, we've all got something. We're all weird and damaged in our own way. You're not the only one.**

I read it three times because, honestly, I'm stunned. Maybe Dave Kaminski will actually turn into one of the good guys before adulthood.

Another text comes in.

> **Douche.**

I text back.

> **Dick.**

And then I leave everything and walk up the stairs to my parents' room. I bang on the door. I just bang the hell out of it till another door opens and this skinny kid with big ears goes, "Jack?"

"Sorry to wake you, buddy. Can you get Marcus?"

"Sure."

The door to my parents' room opens, and the woman who answers looks half-asleep. Her hair is sticking up, and she's got one eye closed. "Jack?" At the sight of me, both eyes open wide, and she's reaching out toward my face, my chest. "Oh my God, what happened to you?" And I remember, *Oh yeah, the Hunt brothers kicked the shit out of me.*

"It's nothing. I'm fine. Listen, I need to talk to you and Dad." I look past her, but the room is empty. Behind me, there's the sound of a door opening, and the man who must be my father appears from the guest room.

The five of us sit on my parents' bed, just like it's Christmas Eve and we're kids again. Marcus hasn't said a word. He just stares at me from under all that hair.

I say to them, "It's a rare neurological disorder."

Mom is googling as I talk.

Dad: "Are you having vision problems or headaches?"

Dusty: "Maybe it's a concussion."

"It's not a vision problem, and it's not a concussion."

Dad: "I get confused sometimes too. I forget names all the time. All these years at the store, I still can't remember people."

"It's not the same. There's a specific part of our brain called the fusiform gyrus twelve that identifies and recognizes faces. For some reason, mine is missing or doesn't work."

Dusty wants to know where it is, and I show him, and then

Mom finds a diagram of the brain. They all lean in, even Marcus, and Mom reads, " 'People with prosopagnosia have great difficulty recognizing faces, and may fail to recognize people that they have met many times and know well—even family.' " She glances up at me like *Is this true?* and I nod. " 'Prosopagnosia is caused by a problem with processing visual information in the brain, which can be present at birth or develop later due to brain injury.' "

Marcus says, "Like when you fell off the roof."

I tell them I was tested, and they have a million questions. I answer them as best I can, and at some point my mom says, "I want you to remember that you can't feel responsible for everything. We're your parents, and we will figure *us* out. All you need to do, any of you"—she looks at my brothers—"is be a kid for now and let us be there for you."

"All of us?" Dusty says. "Even those of us without neurological disorders?"

"All of you."

LIBBY

I've always thought you should be able to freeze time. This way you could hit the Pause button at a really good point in your life so that nothing changes. Think about it. Loved ones don't die. You don't age. You go to bed and wake up the next morning to find everything just as you left it. No surprises.

If I could freeze time, this is the moment I would choose, falling asleep on my dad's shoulder, George on my lap, like I'm eight years old again.

This is what I know about loss:

- It doesn't get better. You just get (somewhat) used to it.
- You never stop missing the people who go away.
- For something that isn't there anymore, it weighs a ton.

By the time I started eating—really eating—the loss was already so big it felt like I was carrying around the world. So carrying around the weight wasn't any heavier. It was trying to carry around both that got to be too much. Which is why sometimes you have to set some of it down. You can't carry all of it forever.

JACK

It's almost dawn by the time I get to bed. I lie on top of the blanket, wide awake, shoes on, clothes on, staring at the ceiling. I feel full, and also empty, but not in a bad way. Maybe empty's not the right word. I feel light.

I may love Libby Strout.

Not just like *like her.*

Love.

As in I love her.

I love her rollicking, throaty laugh that makes her sound as if she's got a cold. I love the way she struts like she's on a catwalk. I love the hugeness of her, and I don't mean her actual physical weight.

And then I start thinking about her eyes. If you asked me to tell you what Caroline's eyes look like, I couldn't tell you. Even though I can describe them when I'm looking directly into them, I can't describe them when she's not in front of me.

But I can tell you what Libby's eyes look like.

They are like lying in the grass under the sky on a summer day. You're blinded by the sun, but you can feel the ground beneath you, so as much as you think you could go flying off, you know you won't. You're warmed from the inside and from the outside, and you can still feel that warmth on your skin when you walk away.

I can tell you other things too.

1. She has a constellation of freckles on her face that remind me of Pegasus (left cheek) and Cygnus (right cheek).
2. Her eyelashes are as long as my arm, and when she's flirting, she does this deliberate, slow blink that knocks me off my feet.
3. Also there's her smile. Let me tell you, it's amazing, like it comes from the deepest part of her, a part made of blue skies and sunshine.

And then I'm like, *Wait a damn minute.*

I sit up. Rub my head. Maybe it's the booze, but . . .

When did I start being able to remember her face?

And suddenly I'm having this total *Sixth Sense* experience as my mind scrolls back over the weeks I've known her. I run through every single time I've seen her, every instance I've been able to pick her out of a crowd or find her out of context. I test myself.

Picture her eyebrows.

Slightly arched, as if she's always amused.

Picture her nose.

The way it wrinkles when she laughs.

Picture her mouth.

Not just the red of her lips, but the way the corners turn up, as if she's smiling even when she isn't.

Picture all the pieces together.

The way her cheekbones curve out and her chin curves in, almost like a heart. The fierceness and softness and glow of her that make her look so ALIVE.

All this time, I thought it was her weight that made me see her.

But it's not her weight at all.

It's her.

LIBBY

I'm up early, even though it's Sunday. I leave my dad a note and then I'm out of the house, bundled in a jacket and scarf. After a block, my hands are freezing, and I jam them deep into my coat pockets. I'm meeting Rachel in the park because I have something to tell her. *I know why I punched Jack Masselin.*

There's a chill in the air that feels like winter, or at least the start of it. This is my least-favorite time of year because everything dies or goes to sleep, and there's too much death and stillness, and the sky turns gray for so long, you think it will never be blue again. Right now the sky can't quite make up its mind. It's blue in patches, gray in patches, with spots of white, like a faded quilt.

Rachel has brought us hot cider from the coffee shop by her house. We sit looking at the golf course, blowing on our drinks to cool them down. I tell her a little about Mick from Copenhagen and Moses Hunt and taking Jack home.

"Jack as in Jack?"

"Jack as in Jack."

Before she can ask me about him, I tell her about the dance team I'm starting with Bailey, Jayvee, and Iris. "The best thing is, anyone can join. No weight restrictions or height restrictions or age restrictions or sex restrictions. No restrictions at all. If you can dance, even a little, you're in. And we dance for the joy of dancing, whenever and wherever we want."

"Can I join?"

"Of course."

"Will there be twirling?"

"Of course!"

"And costumes?"

"Yes, but each one will be different."

She tells me about her new girlfriend, Elena, a graphic designer she met at Winkler's Bakery. She says they have a lot of silly things in common but also real things, important things, like they were the same age when they came out to family and friends. She blows on her drink, takes a sip. She eyes me over the cup. "You know, that's what you've been doing in a way—coming out. Coming out of your room. Coming out of your house. Coming out of your shell."

"I guess I have." I think about Jack, as alone in himself as I was in my room for all those years.

As if she reads my mind she says, "So why did you do it? Why did you hit him?"

"Because after all I've been through, I felt like he was trying to single-handedly pick me up and stuff me back into that house and lock me in. Like he was telling me I was right to be panicked and I was right to be afraid."

"No one can lock you back in, Libby. You choose whether you let them."

"I know that now, like really know that. I thought I knew that then, but I didn't."

"So are you still friends?"

"He lied to me."

"Or he might have been trying to protect you. I'm not defending him, but he probably thought he was doing the right thing."

"Maybe." And then I tell her about the letters.

She sets down her drink. "When was the last time you got one?"

"It's been a while. Since before I wore the purple bikini."

"Did you find out who was writing them?"

"No, but I'm pretty sure I know. And I feel sorry for her because this person will never come out. She keeps who she really is locked away where no one can find her, where she can't even find her."

Rachel picks up her drink again. "To Libby Strout, the biggest person I know, and I don't mean on the outside."

We tap our recycled cups.

"And to Rachel Mendes, for loving me even though you don't have to."

I almost say *And for saving my life* because for some reason I'm thinking of myself at eleven and then at thirteen. That girl feels like a different girl, someone from a lifetime ago, not anyone who has anything to do with the me I am now. Except that I know I wouldn't be me without her. I wouldn't be Libby Strout, high school junior, with my very own group of friends. I wouldn't have danced or twirled or tried out for the Damsels. I wouldn't have stood up for myself or worn my purple bikini. I wouldn't have gone to Bloomington or Clara's with a boy I liked. *Really* liked. I wouldn't have had my heart broken because I would have been too afraid. And even though the ache of that heartbreak hurts like hell, it's so much better than feeling nothing.

Another thing I wouldn't be doing: sitting on this bench, the cold biting my cheeks and nose, drinking hot cider with a good friend. And even though I didn't know this exact moment existed, I wanted to be out here in the world to see it.

• • •

After Rachel leaves, I leave my copy—*the* copy—of *We Have Always Lived in the Castle* on the bench with this note:

> **Dear friend,**
>   **You are not a freak. You are wanted. You are necessary. You are the only you there is. Don't be afraid to leave the castle. It's a great big world out there.**
>
> **Love, a fellow reader**

Her dad tells me she's at the park with a friend, and that's where I'm headed. My phone rings, and it's Kam, but I don't answer.

So what if it was Dr. Klein calling to say she was wrong, that there's a cure? What would I do? Would I alter my brain if it meant getting to recognize people the way everyone else does?

Would I?

I turn this over in my mind, trying to imagine it, trying to picture how it might change me.

I wouldn't be me anymore, would I? Because as long as I can remember, this is how I find people. I study them. I learn their details.

The thing is I don't know what it means to see the world like others do. Maybe I don't recognize myself in a mirror, and maybe I can't exactly tell you what I look like, but I don't think I'd know myself the way I do without prosopagnosia. The same goes for my parents and my brothers and my friends and Libby. I'm talking about all the details that make them *them*. They look at each other and see the same thing, but I have to work harder to see what's there behind the face. It's as if I take the person apart and then reconstruct them. I rebuild them the same way I built the Shitkicker for Dusty.

This is me.

Does it make me feel special? A little. I've had to work really fucking hard to learn everyone, and even if skin color and hair color help me find people, that's not who they are to me. It's not about that. It's about the important things, like the way their face lights up when they laugh, or the way they move as they're walking toward you, or the way their freckles create a map of the stars.

I'm on the edge of the park, bundled in my jacket, scarf pulled up over my chin, when a rust-colored Land Rover comes cruising along. It slams to a stop in the middle of the road, and, engine still running, Jack Masselin climbs out and *swaggers* over to me.

"What are you doing here?"

"Your dad said you were here. Jesus, it's cold. Are you really walking back to your house?"

"What. Are. You. Doing. Here?" I say it slower and louder.

"Look, I'm sorry I didn't tell you where I lived and that I saw you the day you were rescued. I should have told you, and you have every right to be pissed at me."

"Yeah, you should have."

"I know. I was wrong. But if it's okay with you, there's something else I need to say right now. We can go back to that later, and you can give me hell about it all you want."

"What, Jack?"

"You're the one I see."

"What?"

"You're the one I see, Libby Strout. You."

"What do you mean?"

"I see you. I remember you. I recognize you."

I wave at my body. "It's not like you have fat blindness."

"Christ almighty, woman. Work with me here."

"So what? You use identifiers to figure out who people are. The weight is mine."

"Your identifier is you. I remember your eyes. Your mouth. The freckles on both cheeks that look like constellations. I know your smiles, at least three of them, and at least eight of your expressions, including the ones you only do with your eyes. If I could draw, I would draw you, and I wouldn't need to look at you to do it. Because your face is stuck in my mind."

And then he closes his eyes and describes how I look in a way I've never heard before. As I'm hearing it, my heart is racing, and I know this is something I'll never forget, not even fifty years from now.

He opens his eyes and says, "I know the way you move. I know the way you look at me. I see you see me, and you're the only one who looks at me that way. Whether I'm with you or away from you, I don't have to think about it or put the puzzle pieces together. It's just you. That's what I know."

"That doesn't have to mean you love me. Just because you see me."

His eyebrows shoot up, and he's laughing. "Who said anything about love?"

I want more than anything to disappear into thin air.

"If, hypothetically, I did love you, though, it's not *because* I see you, and, *Oh well, at least I can see her, so I might as well love her.* I'm pretty sure I *see* you because I *love* you. And yeah, I guess I love you because I see you, as in *I see you, Libby,* as in all of you, as in every last amazing thing."

I wait for him to say *hypothetically* again, but he doesn't.

Instead he looks at me.

I look at him.

And we're having a moment.

It lasts for seconds, maybe minutes.

I pull the scarf up over my nose. I want to pull it over my whole head.

"Here."

He hands me something. I turn it over in my palm, and it's a magnet. OHIO WELCOMES YOU.

At first, I don't know why he's giving this to me. We've never been to Ohio together. I've only been to Ohio once.

Years ago.

With my parents.

Suddenly, I'm transported back to my house, back to the day my mom first stuck that on our fridge. *"We're going to fill this up with magnets of all the places we'll go," she said. "Ohio may not seem exotic, but one day, when this is covered, you'll look back on it and think,* That's the one that started it all.*"*

He says, "I never should have taken it."

"Taken it?"

"From your house. I went back that day, to see what I could learn about you. I had to tell the security guy to pay attention so you weren't looted."

"After you looted this."

"Yeah. And your book, the one I sent you."

"What made you keep the magnet?"

"It reminded me of you."

"Wow, you are sappy."

He laughs, rubs his jaw. "Apparently."

"That's okay." My voice is muffled by the scarf. I fold my hand around the magnet. It sounds silly, but I can't help thinking, *She held this. Part of her is still here.* "I'm glad you took it."

It's the one that started it all.

"Libby Strout." His mouth and eyes are serious. I don't think I've ever seen him so serious. "You are wanted."

And then he tugs the scarf away.

He takes my face in his hands, carefully, delicately, like it's a rare and precious jewel.

And he kisses me.

It's the greatest kiss of my life, which I realize isn't saying much. But it's one of those world-expanding kisses that I'd put against any other kiss that has happened and will ever happen to anyone anywhere. It's as if he's breathing for me, or maybe we're breathing for each other, and I'm merging into him and him into me, so that my limbs aren't limbs, and the bones melt away and then the muscle and the skin until all that's left is electricity. The hazy-gray, early-morning sky morphs into the night sky, and stars are everywhere, so close I feel I could really collect them and take them home, maybe wear them in my hair.

I don't know who pulls away first, maybe him, maybe me. But then we're standing with our foreheads touching, which I'm grateful for because there's this part of me that's inwardly shrieking, *Oh my God, it's Jack Masselin,* and I'm not awed, but I'm almost embarrassed because I know this boy in a way other people don't, and he knows me.

Eventually, our heads right themselves, our eyes move up and find each other, and I don't have to wonder what I look like to him, because I can see me there, in the reflection of his pupils, as if he really has stored me away and is carrying me around with him.

He says, "Huh." And breathes out like he's been holding it all this time.

"Yeah." I try to be funny, because this world is still new to me and I'm still finding my footing. I say, "I mean, it didn't exactly shake the earth." And my voice trembles, just a touch.

But the thing is it did. It really did. It shook the damn pants off it.

We are doing it. This is happening. We are meeting and changing the world, his world and mine.

My body is like a single nerve ending from head to toe. Everything feels alive and *more*. My heart is opening, like the heart of Rappaccini's daughter, Beatrice, when she meets young Giovanni after he wanders into her garden. As I stand there, I can almost feel it unfold, petal by petal, beat by beat.

JACK

I say, "I love you."

She says, "I love you too." And then she laughs. "It's kind of crazy. I mean *you*."

"I know. What the hell?"

She covers her mouth with one hand, but her eyes are shining. I'm thinking about a field of grass on a summer day. I'm thinking about the sun and being warmed from the inside and being warmed from the outside.

I take her hand under the gray-blue sky and I'm home.

ACKNOWLEDGMENTS

Holding Up the Universe comes from my heart, as well as from my own loss and fear and pain, and from real people who are dear to me. Those people—along with many others—help hold up my universe. I wouldn't have been able to write this book without them.

First and foremost, thank you to my readers around the world, who have become my family. (#ReadersAreLife) I love you epically and eternally.

Thank you to my incomparably brilliant, bright, bright place of an agent, Kerry Sparks, who is the savviest, wisest, most delightful human on the planet, and who is always, always looking out for me in every way. Thanks, too, to the entire team at Levine Greenberg Rostan Literary Agency. You have turned my world from black-and-white to Technicolor.

Thank you to my lovely-beyond-lovely editor, Allison Wortche, and every single one of her impeccable instincts. She doesn't wield a red pen, she wields a magic wand. And thank you to my fantastically superb UK editor, Ben Horslen, for all his genius.

Thank you to everyone at Knopf, Random House Children's Books, and Penguin UK for their kindness, support, and immense belief in me, and for being the very best there is. With endless thanks to Barbara Marcus, Jenny Brown, Melanie Nolan, Dominique Cimina, Jillian Vandall, Karen Greenberg, Kim Lauber, Laura Antonacci, Pam White, Jocelyn Lange, Zack O'Brien, Barbara Perris, Alison Impey, Stephanie Moss, Rosamund Hutchison, and Clare Kelly. And with thanks to David Drummond for the utterly spectacular cover.

Big thanks to my superstar assistant, Briana Bailey, for all she is and does, to the incredible Shelby Padgett (who is, I swear, part wizard), and to Lara Yacoubian, WBA forever. Also to Letty Lopez, and all the *Germ Magazine* editors, directors, writers, and contributors, with extra appreciation and hugs to Briana, Shelby, and Jordan Gripenwaldt. You make me lovely and you make me proud of all we—*you*—have done.

I did not have to be rescued from my house the way Libby was, but I have struggled with weight issues and anxiety over the years— particularly when I was Libby's age—and I know what it feels like to be bullied. In addition to my own experience, I drew on the experiences of family and friends, who also understand firsthand what Libby has gone through.

I am not personally face-blind, but I have family members who are. My teenage cousin has learned to recognize the people in his life, not by faces, but by the important things like "how nice they are and how many freckles they have." Thank you to him for helping me see as he sees.

And huge thanks to the remarkable—and prosopagnosic—Jacob Hodes, who gave the book a meticulous going-over. He offered me vital feedback on what worked and what didn't, as well as invaluable suggestions for how to make Jack's journey as real and authentic as possible.

Thank you to the Prosopagnosia Research Centers and Dr. Brad Duchaine, of the Department of Psychological and Brain Sciences at Dartmouth College, for his help and generosity. He, along with Dr. Irving Biederman, professor of neuroscience and psychology at the University of Southern California, patiently answered all my many questions.

I also want to acknowledge Chuck Close and Oliver Sacks, whose varied works have provided inspiration and information, and members of the Yahoo Face Blindness–Prosopagnosia group, who offered such fascinating, illuminating insight.

Thank you to Dr. William Rice III, of Wake Forest Baptist Medical Center, for his medical expertise, and my beloved cousin Learyn von Sprecken, engineering dynamo, who helped Jack and me with his mind-blowing projects.

Thanks also to:

My early readers, Louis Kapeleris, Angelo Surmelis, Garen Thomas,

Nic Stone, Becky Albertalli, and devoted *All the Bright Places* fan Margaret Harrison, whose blurb for *Holding Up the Universe* would read: "To be honest, after *All the Bright Places,* I was kind of waiting for someone to get hit by a truck or something on the last page. I'm glad no one got hit by a truck." And my fellow YA author, hero, and friend Kerry Kletter. Not only is she a terrific writer, she's a terrific editor. She arrived at one of the most pivotal moments in this book's life and stayed by my side through it, offering love and some much-needed hand-holding, as well as the smartest eleventh-hour edits an exhausted writer could ever hope for. I will always love you for what you gave to Jack, Libby, and me.

My other YA author friends for continued camaraderie and inspiration, and all of the booksellers and librarians and educators and bloggers I have met over the past two years. You are rock stars supreme, and I can never thank you enough for all you have done for me.

The Jackson 5 for keeping me company as I wrote, Sam and Dean and *Supernatural* for helping me escape at the end of a long day, and the prolific and talented Jack Robinson for writing what has become one of my favorite songs of all time—"I Love to Love"—and graciously allowing me to quote his lyrics.

My family and friends, near and far, especially my heart home, Louis, Angelo, Ed Baran, and my literary kitties—I wouldn't have made it through the past two years without you.

This book is for my funny, stoic, brilliant dad, who was always having to ask me to turn down my music (but who was the one responsible for building me the world's best—and biggest—stereo system).

And it is for my mother, who gave me dancing shoes and the words to accompany them. She taught me to walk in other people's skin, to know that I could be anything I wanted to be and do anything I wanted to do, and she never once made me forget that I am wanted. *Holding Up the Universe* is the first book I've written that she will never read, but *you* have read it, and that means more than I can say.

ABOUT THE AUTHOR

Jennifer Niven is the author of the *New York Times* and international bestseller *All the Bright Places*. She has also written four novels for adults, as well as three nonfiction books, and the screenplay for the movie version of *All the Bright Places*. Additionally, she is the founder of *Germ Magazine,* an online literary and lifestyle magazine for readers high school age and beyond. She grew up in Indiana and now lives in Los Angeles.

For more information, visit JenniferNiven.com or GermMagazine .com, or find her across the social media universe on Facebook, Twitter, Instagram, Tumblr, Pinterest, or Snapchat, happily interacting with readers.

**The story of a girl who learns to live
from a boy who wants to die . . .**

Jennifer Niven

ALL THE
BRIGHT PLACES

Theodore Finch wants to take his own life.
Violet Markey is devastated by her sister's death.
They meet on the ledge of the school bell tower,
and so their story begins.

Read on for an extract . . .

FINCH

I am awake again. Day 6.

Is today a good day to die?

This is something I ask myself in the morning when I wake up. In third period when I'm trying to keep my eyes open while Mr. Schroeder drones on and on. At the supper table as I'm passing the green beans. At night when I'm lying awake because my brain won't shut off due to all there is to think about.

Is today the day?

And if not today—when?

I am asking myself this now as I stand on a narrow ledge six stories above the ground. I'm so high up, I'm practically part of the sky. I look down at the pavement below, and the world tilts. I close my eyes, enjoying the way everything spins. Maybe this time I'll do it—let the air carry me away. It will be like floating in a pool, drifting off until there's nothing.

I don't remember climbing up here. In fact, I don't remember much of anything before Sunday, at least not anything so far this winter. This happens every time—the blanking out, the waking up. I'm like that old man with the beard, Rip Van Winkle. Now you see me, now you don't. You'd think I'd have gotten used to it, but this last time was the worst yet because I wasn't asleep for a couple days or a week or two—I was asleep for *the holidays,* meaning Thanksgiving, Christmas, and New Year's. I can't tell you what was different this time around, only that when I woke up, I felt deader than usual. Awake, yeah, but completely empty, like someone had been feasting on my blood. This is day six of being awake again, and my first week back at school since November 14.

I open my eyes, and the ground is still there, hard and permanent. I am in the bell tower of the high school, standing on a ledge about four inches wide. The tower is pretty small, with only a few feet of concrete floor space on all sides of the bell itself, and then this low stone railing, which I've climbed over to get here. Every now and then I knock one of my legs against it to remind myself it's there.

My arms are outstretched as if I'm conducting a sermon and this entire not-very-big, dull, dull town is my congregation. "Ladies and gentlemen," I shout, "I would like to welcome you to my death!" You might expect me to say "life," having just woken up and all, but it's only when I'm awake that I think about dying.

I am shouting in an old-school-preacher way, all jerking head and words that twitch at the ends, and I almost lose my balance. I hold on behind me, happy no one seems to have noticed, because, let's face it, it's hard to look fearless when you're clutching the railing like a chicken.

"I, Theodore Finch, being of unsound mind, do hereby bequeath all my earthly possessions to Charlie Donahue, Brenda Shank-Kravitz, and my sisters. Everyone else can go f--- themselves." In my house, my mom taught us early to spell that word (if we *must* use it) or, better yet, not spell it, and, sadly, this has stuck.

Even though the bell has rung, some of my classmates are still milling around on the ground. It's the first week of the second semester of senior year, and already they're acting as if they're almost done and out of here. One of them looks up in my direction, as if he heard me, but the others don't, either because they haven't spotted me or because they know I'm there and *Oh well, it's just Theodore Freak.*

Then his head turns away from me and he points at the sky. At first I think he's pointing at me, but it's at that moment I see her, the girl. She stands a few feet away on the other side of the tower, also out on the ledge, dark-blond hair waving in the breeze, the hem of her skirt blowing up like a parachute. Even though it's January in Indiana, she is shoeless in tights, a pair of boots in her hand, and staring either at her feet or at the ground—it's hard to tell. She seems frozen in place.

In my regular, nonpreacher voice I say, as calmly as possible, "Take it from me, the worst thing you can do is look down."

Very slowly, she turns her head toward me, and I know this girl, or at least I've seen her in the hallways. I can't resist:

"Come here often? Because this is kind of my spot and I don't remember seeing you here before."

She doesn't laugh or blink, just gazes out at me from behind these clunky glasses that almost cover her face. She tries to take a step back and her foot bumps the railing. She teeters a little, and before she can panic, I say, "I don't know what brings you up here, but to me the town looks prettier and the people look nicer and even the worst of them look almost kind. Except for Gabe Romero and Amanda Monk and that whole crowd you hang out with."

Her name is Violet Something. She is cheerleader popular—one of those girls you would never think of running into on a ledge six stories above the ground. Behind the ugly glasses she's pretty, almost like a china doll. Large eyes, sweet face shaped like a heart, a mouth that wants to curve into a perfect little smile. She's a girl who dates guys like Ryan Cross, baseball star, and sits with Amanda Monk and the other queen bees at lunch.

"But let's face it, we didn't come up here for the view. You're Violet, right?"

She blinks once, and I take this as a yes.

"Theodore Finch. I think we had pre-cal together last year."

She blinks again.

"I hate math, but that's not why I'm up here. No offense if that's why you are. You're probably better at math than I am, because pretty much everyone's better at math than I am, but it's okay, I'm fine with it. See, I excel at other, more important things—guitar, sex, and consistently disappointing my dad, to name a few. By the way, it's apparently true that you'll never use it in the real world. Math, I mean."

I keep talking, but I can tell I'm running out of steam. I need to take a piss, for one thing, and so my words aren't the only thing twitching. *(Note to self: Before attempting to take own life, remember to take a leak.)* And, two, it's starting to rain, which, in this temperature, will probably turn to sleet before it hits the ground.

"It's starting to rain," I say, as if she doesn't know this. "I guess there's an argument to be made that the rain will wash away the blood, leaving us a neater mess to clean up than otherwise. But it's the mess part that's got me thinking. I'm not a vain person, but I am human, and I don't know about you, but I don't want to look like I've been run through the wood chipper at my funeral."

She's shivering or shaking, I can't tell which, and so I slowly inch my way toward her, hoping I don't fall off before I get there, because the last thing I want to do is make a jackass out of myself in front of this girl. "I've made it clear I want cremation, but my mom doesn't believe in it." And my dad will do whatever she says so he won't upset her any more than he already has, and besides, *You're far too young to think about this, you know your Grandma Finch lived to be ninety-eight, we don't need to talk about that now, Theodore, don't upset your mother.*

"So it'll be an open coffin for me, which means if I jump, it ain't gonna be pretty. Besides, I kind of like my face intact like this, two eyes, one nose, one mouth, a full set of teeth, which, if I'm being honest, is one of my better features." I smile so she can see what I mean. Everything where it should be, on the outside at least.

When she doesn't say anything, I go on inching and talking. "Most of all, I feel bad for the undertaker. What a shitty job that must be anyway, but then to have to deal with an asshole like me?"

From down below, someone yells, "Violet? Is that Violet up there?"

"Oh God," she says, so low I barely hear it. "OhGodohGodohGod." The wind blows her skirt and hair, and it looks like she's going to fly away.

There is general buzzing from the ground, and I shout, "Don't try to save me! You'll only kill yourself!" Then I say, very low, just to her, "Here's what I think we should do." I'm about a foot away from her now. "I want you to throw your shoes toward the bell and then hold on to the rail, just grab right onto it, and once you've got it, lean against it and then lift your right foot up and over. Got that?"

She nods and almost loses her balance.

"Don't nod. And whatever you do, don't go the wrong way and step forward instead of back. I'll count you off. On three."

She throws her boots in the direction of the bell, and they fall with a *thud, thud* onto the concrete.

"One. Two. Three."

She grips the stone and kind of props herself against it and then lifts her leg up and over so that she's sitting on the railing. She stares down at the ground and I can see that she's frozen again, and so I say, "Good. Great. Just stop looking down."

She slowly looks at me and then reaches for the floor of the bell tower with her right foot, and once she's found it, I say, "Now get that left leg back over however you can. Don't let go of the wall." By now she's shaking so hard I can hear her teeth chatter, but I watch as her left foot joins her right, and she is safe.

So now it's just me out here. I gaze down at the ground one last time, past my size-thirteen feet that won't stop growing—today I'm wearing sneakers with fluorescent laces—past the open windows of the fourth floor, the third, the second, past Amanda Monk, who is cackling from the front steps and swishing her blond hair like a pony, books over her head, trying to flirt and protect herself from the rain at the same time.

I gaze past all of this at the ground itself, which is now slick and damp, and imagine myself lying there.

I could just step off. It would be over in seconds. No more "Theodore Freak." No more hurt. No more anything.

I try to get past the unexpected interruption of saving a life and return to the business at hand. For a minute, I can feel it: the sense of peace as my mind goes quiet, like I'm already dead. I am weightless and free. Nothing and no one to fear, not even myself.

Then a voice from behind me says, "I want you to hold on to the rail, and once you've got it, lean against it and lift your right foot up and over."

Like that, I can feel the moment passing, maybe already passed, and now it seems like a stupid idea, except for picturing the look on Amanda's face as I go sailing by her. I laugh at the thought. I laugh so hard I almost fall off, and this scares me—like, really scares me—and I catch myself and Violet catches me as Amanda looks up. "Weirdo!" someone shouts. Amanda's little group snickers. She cups her big mouth and aims it skyward. "You okay, V?"

Violet leans over the rail, still holding on to my legs. "I'm okay."

The door at the top of the tower stairs cracks open and my best friend, Charlie Donahue, appears. Charlie is black. Not CW black, but black-black. He also gets laid more than anyone else I know.

He says, "They're serving pizza today," as if I wasn't standing on a ledge six stories above the ground, my arms outstretched, a girl wrapped around my knees.

"Why don't you go ahead and get it over with, freak?" Gabe Romero, better known as Roamer, better known as Dumbass, yells from below. More laughter.

Because I've got a date with your mother later, I think but don't say because, let's face it, it's lame, and also he will come up here and beat my face in and then throw me off, and this defeats the point of just doing it myself.

Instead I shout, "Thanks for saving me, Violet. I don't know what I would've done if you hadn't come along. I guess I'd be dead right now."

The last face I see below belongs to my school counselor, Mr. Embry. As he glares up at me, I think, *Great. Just great.*

I let Violet help me over the wall and onto the concrete. From down below, there's a smattering of applause, not for me, but for Violet, the hero. Up close like this, I can see that her skin is smooth and clear except for two freckles on her right cheek, and her eyes are a gray-green that makes me think of fall. It's the eyes that get me. They are large and arresting, as if she sees everything. As warm as they are, they are busy, no-bullshit eyes, the kind that can look right into you, which I can tell even through the glasses. She's pretty and tall, but not too tall, with long, restless legs and curvy hips, which I like on a girl. Too many high school girls are built like boys.

"I was just sitting there," she says. "On the railing. I didn't come up here to—"

"Let me ask you something. Do you think there's such a thing as a perfect day?"

"What?"

"A perfect day. Start to finish. When nothing terrible or sad or ordinary happens. Do you think it's possible?"

"I don't know."

"Have you ever had one?"

"No."

"I've never had one either, but I'm looking for it."

She whispers, "Thank you, Theodore Finch." She reaches up and kisses me on the cheek, and I can smell her shampoo, which reminds me of flowers. She says into my ear, "If you ever tell anyone about this, I'll kill you." Carrying her boots, she hurries away and out of the rain, back through the door that leads to the flight of dark and rickety stairs that takes you down to one of the many too-bright and too-crowded school hallways.

Charlie watches her go and, as the door swings closed behind her, he turns back to me. "Man, why do you do that?"

"Because we all have to die someday. I just want to be prepared." This isn't the reason, of course, but it will be enough for him. The truth is, there are a lot of reasons, most of which change daily, like the thirteen fourth graders killed earlier this week when some SOB opened fire in their school gym, or the girl two years behind me who just died of cancer, or the man I saw outside the Mall Cinema kicking his dog, or my father.

Charlie may think it, but at least he doesn't say "Weirdo," which is why he's my best friend. Other than the fact that I appreciate this about him, we don't have much in common.

Technically, I'm on probation this year. This is due to a small matter involving a desk and a chalkboard. (For the record, replacing a chalkboard is more expensive than you might think.) It's also due to a guitar-smashing incident during assembly, an illegal use of fireworks, and maybe a fight or two. As a result, I've agreed involuntarily to the following: weekly counseling; maintaining a high B average; and participation in at least one extracurricular. I chose macramé because I'm the only guy with twenty semihot girls, which I thought was pretty good odds for me. I also have to behave myself, play well with others, refrain from throwing desks, as well as refrain from any "violent physical altercations." And I must always, always, whatever I do, hold my tongue, because not doing so, apparently, is how trouble starts. If I f--- anything up from here on out, it's expulsion for me.

Inside the counseling office, I check in with the secretary and take a seat in one of the hard wooden chairs until Mr. Embry is ready for me. If I know Embryo—as I call him to myself—like I know Embryo, he'll want to know just what the hell I was doing in the bell tower. If I'm lucky, we won't have time to cover much more than that.

In a few minutes he waves me in, a short, thick man built like a bull. As he shuts the door, he drops the smile. He sits down, hunches over his desk, and fixes his eyes on me like I'm a suspect he needs to crack. "What in the hell were you doing in the bell tower?"

The thing I like about Embryo is that not only is he predictable, he gets to the point. I've known him since sophomore year.

"I wanted to see the view."

"Were you planning to jump off?"

"Not on pizza day. Never on pizza day, which is one of the better days of the week." I should mention that I am a brilliant deflector. So brilliant that I could get a full scholarship to college and major in it, except why bother? I've already mastered the art.

I wait for him to ask about Violet, but instead he says, "I need to know if you were or are planning to harm yourself. I am goddamn serious. If Principal Wertz hears about this, you're gone before you can say 'suspended,' or worse. Not to mention if I don't pay attention and you decide to go back up there and jump off, I'm looking at a lawsuit, and on the salary they pay me, believe me when I say I do not have the money to be sued. This holds true whether you jump off the bell tower or the Purina Tower, whether it's school property or not."

I stroke my chin like I'm deep in thought. "The Purina Tower. Now there's an idea."

He doesn't budge except to squint at me. Like most people in the Midwest, Embryo doesn't believe in humor, especially when it pertains to sensitive subjects. "Not funny, Mr. Finch. This is not a joking matter."

"No, sir. Sorry."

"The thing suicides don't focus on is their wake. Not just your parents and siblings, but your friends, your girlfriends, your classmates, your teachers." I like the way he seems to think I have many, many people depending on me, including not just one but multiple girlfriends.

"I was just messing around. I agree it was probably not the best way to spend first period."

He picks up a file and thumps it down in front of him and starts flipping through it. I wait as he reads, and then he looks at me again. I wonder if he's counting the days till summer.

He stands, just like a cop on TV, and walks around his desk until he's looming over me. He leans against it, arms folded, and I look past him, searching for the hidden two-way mirror.

"Do I need to call your mother?"

"No. And again no." And again: *no no no.* "Look, it was a stupid thing to do. I just wanted to see what it felt like to stand there and look down. I would never jump from the bell tower."

"If it happens again, if you so much as *think* about it again, I call her. And you're going to do a drug test."

"I appreciate your concern, sir." I try to sound my most sincere, because the last thing I want is a bigger, brighter spotlight directed at me, following me throughout the halls of school, throughout the other parts of my life, such as they are. And the thing is, I actually like Embryo. "As for the whole drug thing, there's no need to waste precious time. Really. Unless cigarettes count. Drugs and me? Not a good mix. Believe me, I've tried." I fold my hands like a good boy. "As for the whole bell tower thing, even though it wasn't at all what you think, I can still promise that it won't happen again."

"That's right—it won't. I want you here twice a week instead of once. You come in Monday and Friday and talk to me, just so I can see how you're doing."

"I'm happy to, sir—I mean, I, like, really enjoy these conversations of ours—but I'm good."

"It's nonnegotiable. Now let's discuss the end of last semester. You missed four, almost five, weeks of school. Your mother says you were sick with the flu."

He's actually talking about my sister Kate, but he doesn't know that. She was the one who called the school while I was out, because Mom has enough to worry about.

"If that's what she says, who are we to argue?"

The fact is, I was sick, but not in an easily explained flu kind of way. It's my experience that people are a lot more sympathetic if they can *see* you hurting, and for the millionth time in my life I wish for measles or smallpox or some other recognizable disease just to make it simple for me and also for them. Anything would be better than the truth: *I shut down again. I went blank. One minute I was spinning, and the next minute my mind was dragging itself around in a circle, like an old, arthritic dog trying to lie down. And then I just turned off and went to sleep, but not sleep in the way you do every night. Think a long, dark sleep where you don't dream at all.*

Embryo once again narrows his eyes to a squint and stares at me hard, trying to induce a sweat. "And can we expect you to show up and stay out of trouble this semester?"

"Absolutely."

"And keep up with your classwork?"

"Yes, sir."

"I'll arrange the drug test with the nurse." He jabs the air with his finger, pointing at me. "Probation means 'period of testing somebody's suitability; period when student must improve.' Look it up if you don't believe me, and for Christ's sake, stay alive."

The thing I don't say is: I want to stay alive. The reason I don't say it is because, given that fat folder in front of him, he'd never believe it. And here's something else he'd never believe—I'm fighting to be here in this shitty, messed-up world. Standing on the ledge of the bell tower isn't about dying. It's about having control. It's about never going to sleep again.

Embryo stalks around his desk and gathers a stack of "Teens in Trouble" pamphlets. Then he tells me I'm not alone and I can always talk to him, his door is open, he's here, and he'll see me on Monday. I want to say no offense, but that's not much of a comfort. Instead, I thank him because of the dark circles under his eyes and the smoker's lines etched around his mouth. He'll probably light up a cigarette as soon as I go. I take a heaping pile of pamphlets and leave him to it. He never once mentioned Violet, and I'm relieved.

VIOLET

154 days till graduation

Friday morning. Office of Mrs. Marion Kresney, school counselor, who has small, kind eyes and a smile too big for her face. According to the certificate on the wall above her head, she's been at Bartlett High for fifteen years. This is our twelfth meeting.

My heart is still racing and my hands are still shaking from being up on that ledge. I have gone cold all over, and what I want is to lie down. I wait for Mrs. Kresney to say: *I know what you were doing first period, Violet Markey. Your parents are on their way. Doctors are standing by, ready to escort you to the nearest mental health facility.*

But we start as we always do.

"How are you, Violet?"

"I'm fine, and you?" I sit on my hands.

"I'm fine. Let's talk about you. I want to know how you're feeling."

"I'm good." Just because she hasn't brought it up does not mean she doesn't know. She almost never asks anything directly.

"How are you sleeping?"

The nightmares started a month after the accident. She asks about them every time I see her, because I made the mistake of mentioning them to my mom, who mentioned them to her. This is one of the main reasons why I'm here and why I've stopped telling my mom anything.

"I'm sleeping fine."

The thing about Mrs. Kresney is that she always, always smiles, no matter what. I like this about her.

"Any bad dreams?"

"No."

I used to write them down, but I don't anymore. I can remember every detail. Like this one I had four weeks ago where I was literally melting away. In the dream, my dad said, "You've come to the end, Violet. You've reached your limit. We all have them, and yours is now." *But I don't want it to be.* I watched as my feet turned into puddles and disappeared. Next were my hands. It didn't hurt, and I remember thinking: *I shouldn't mind this because there isn't any pain. It's just a slipping away.* But I did mind as, limb by limb, the rest of me went invisible before I woke up.

Mrs. Kresney shifts in her chair, her smile fixed on her face. I wonder if she smiles in her sleep.

"Let's talk about college."

This time last year, I would have loved to talk about college. Eleanor and I used to do this sometimes after Mom and Dad had gone to bed. We'd sit outside if it was warm enough, inside if it was too cold. We imagined the places we would go and the people we would meet, far away from Bartlett, Indiana, population 14,983, where we felt like aliens from some distant planet.

"You've applied to UCLA, Stanford, Berkeley, the University of Florida, the University of Buenos Aires, Northern Caribbean University, and the National University of Singapore. This is a very diverse list, but what happened to NYU?"

Since the summer before seventh grade, NYU's creative writing program has been my dream. This is thanks to visiting New York with my mother, who is a college professor and writer. She did her graduate work at NYU, and for three weeks the four of us stayed in the city and socialized with her former teachers and classmates—novelists, playwrights, screenwriters, poets. My plan was to apply for early admission in October. But then the accident happened and I changed my mind.

"I missed the application deadline." The deadline for regular admission was one week ago today. I filled everything out, even wrote my essay, but didn't send it in.

"Let's talk about the writing. Let's talk about the website."

She means EleanorandViolet.com. Eleanor and I started it after we moved to Indiana. We wanted to create an online magazine that offered two (very) different perspectives on fashion, beauty, boys, books, life. Last year, Eleanor's friend Gemma Sterling (star of the hit Web series *Rant*) mentioned us in an interview, and our following tripled. But I haven't touched the site since Eleanor died, because what would be the point? It was a site about sisters. Besides, in that instant we went plowing through the guardrail, my words died too.

"I don't want to talk about the website."

"I believe your mother is an author. She must be very helpful in giving advice."

"Jessamyn West said, 'Writing is so difficult that writers, having had their hell on earth, will escape all punishment here-after.'"

She lights up at this. "Do you feel you're being punished?" She is talking about the accident. Or maybe she is referring to being here in this office, this school, this town.

"No." *Do I feel I should be punished?* Yes. Why else would I have given myself bangs?

"Do you believe you're responsible for what happened?"

I tug on the bangs now. They are lopsided. "No."

She sits back. Her smile slips a fraction of an inch. We both know I'm lying. I wonder what she would say if I told her that an hour ago I was being talked off the ledge of the bell tower. By now, I'm pretty sure she doesn't know.

"Have you driven yet?"

"No."

"Have you allowed yourself to ride in the car with your parents?"

"No."

"But they want you to." This isn't a question. She says this like she's talked to one or both of them, which she probably has.

"I'm not ready." These are the three magic words. I've discovered they can get you out of almost anything.

She leans forward. "Have you thought about returning to
cheerleading?"

"No."

"Student council?"

"No."

"You still play flute in the orchestra?"

"I'm last chair." That's something that hasn't changed since
the accident. I was always last chair because I'm not very good
at flute.

She sits back again. For a moment I think she's given up.
Then she says, "I'm concerned about your progress, Violet.
Frankly, you should be further along than you are right
now. You can't avoid cars forever, especially now that we're in
winter. You can't keep standing still. You need to remember
that you're a survivor, and that means . . ."

I will never know what that means because as soon as I hear
the word "survivor," I get up and walk out.

On my way to fourth period. School hallway.

At least fifteen people—some I know, some I don't, some
who haven't talked to me in months—stop me on my way to
class to tell me how courageous I was to save Theodore Finch
from killing himself. One of the girls from the school paper
wants to do an interview.

Of all the people I could have "saved," Theodore Finch is

the worst possible choice because he's a Bartlett legend. I don't know him that well, but I know *of* him. Everyone knows *of* him. Some people hate him because they think he's weird and he gets into fights and gets kicked out of school and does what he wants. Some people worship him because he's weird and he gets into fights and gets kicked out of school and does what he wants. He plays guitar in five or six different bands, and last year he cut a record. But he's kind of . . . extreme. Like he came to school one day painted head-to-toe red, and it wasn't even Spirit Week. He told some people he was protesting racism and others he was protesting the consumption of meat. Junior year he wore a cape every day for an entire month, cracked a chalkboard in half with a desk, and stole all the dissecting frogs from the science wing and gave them a funeral before burying them in the baseball field. The great Anna Faris once said that the secret of surviving high school is to "lay low." Finch does the opposite of this.

I'm five minutes late to Russian literature, where Mrs. Mahone and her wig assign us a ten-page paper on *The Brothers Karamazov*. Groans follow from everyone but me, because no matter what Mrs. Kresney seems to think, I have Extenuating Circumstances.

I don't even listen as Mrs. Mahone goes over what she wants. Instead I pick at a thread on my skirt. I have a headache. Probably from the glasses. Eleanor's eyes were worse than mine. I take the glasses off and set them on the desk. They were stylish on her. They're ugly on me. Especially with the bangs. But maybe, if I wear the glasses long enough, I can be like her. I can

see what she saw. I can be both of us at once so no one will have
to miss her, most of all me.

The thing is, there are good days and bad days. I feel almost guilty saying they aren't all bad. Something catches me
off guard—a TV show, a funny one-liner from my dad, a comment in class—and I laugh like nothing ever happened. I feel
normal again, whatever that is. Some mornings I wake up and I
sing while I'm getting ready. Or maybe I turn up the music and
dance. On most days, I walk to school. Other days I take my
bike, and every now and then my mind tricks me into thinking
I'm just a regular girl out for a ride.

Emily Ward pokes me in the back and hands me a note.
Because Mrs. Mahone collects our phones at the start of every
class, it's the old-fashioned kind, written on notebook paper.

Is it true you saved Finch from killing himself? x Ryan. There is
only one Ryan in this room—some would argue there's only one
Ryan in the whole school, maybe even the world—and that's
Ryan Cross.

I look up and catch his eye, two rows over. He is too good-
looking. Broad shoulders, warm gold-brown hair, green eyes,
and enough freckles to make him seem approachable. Until
December, he was my boyfriend, but now we're taking a break.

I let the note sit on my desk for five minutes before answering it. Finally, I write: *I just happened to be there. x V.* Less than a
minute later, it's passed back to me, but this time I don't open it.
I think of how many girls would love to receive a note like this
from Ryan Cross. The Violet Markey of last spring would have
been one of them.

When the bell rings, I hang back. Ryan lingers for a minute, waiting to see what I do, but when I just sit there, he collects his phone and goes on.

Mrs. Mahone says, "Yes, Violet?"

Ten pages used to be no big deal. A teacher would ask for ten and I would write twenty. If they wanted twenty, I'd give them thirty. Writing was what I did best, better than being a daughter or girlfriend or sister. Writing was me. But now writing is one of the things I can't do.

I barely have to say anything, not even "I'm not ready." It's in the unwritten rulebook of life, under How to React When a Student Loses a Loved One and Is, Nine Months Later, Still Having a Very Hard Time.

Mrs. Mahone sighs and hands me my phone. "Give me a page or a paragraph, Violet. Just do your best." My Extenuating Circumstances save the day.

Outside the classroom, Ryan is waiting. I can see him trying to figure out the puzzle so he can put me back together again and turn me into the fun girlfriend he used to know. He says, "You look really pretty today." He is nice enough not to stare at my hair.

"Thanks."

Over Ryan's shoulder, I see Theodore Finch strutting by. He nods at me like he knows something I don't, and he keeps on going.

FINCH

Day 6 (still) of being awake

By lunch, it's all over school that Violet Markey saved Theodore Finch from jumping off the bell tower. On my way to U.S. Geography, I walk behind a group of girls in the hallway who are going on and on about it, no idea that I'm the one and only Theodore Finch.

They talk over each other in these high voices that always end in question marks, so that it sounds like *I heard he had a gun? I heard she had to wrestle it out of his hands? My cousin Stacey, who goes to New Castle, says she and a friend were in Chicago and he was playing this club and he totally hooked up with both of them? Well, my brother was there when he set off the firecrackers, and he said before the police took him away, he was all "Unless you want to reimburse me, I'll wait for the finale"?*

Apparently, I'm tragic and dangerous. *Oh yeah,* I think.

That's right. I am here and now and not just awake, but Awake,
and everyone can just deal with it because I am the second freakin'
coming. I lean in and say to them, "I heard he did it over a girl,"
and then I swagger all the way to class.

Inside the classroom, I take my seat, feeling infamous and
invincible and twitchy and strangely exhilarated, as if I just
escaped, well, death. I look around, but no one is paying any
attention to me or Mr. Black, our teacher, who is literally the
largest man I have ever seen. He has a red, red face that always
makes him look like he's on the verge of heatstroke or a heart
attack, and he wheezes when he talks.

The whole time I've been in Indiana, which is all my life—
the purgatory years, I call them—we've apparently lived just
eleven miles away from the highest point in the state. No one
ever told me, not my parents or my sisters or my teachers, until
now, right this minute, in the "Wander Indiana" section of
U.S. Geography—the one that was implemented by the school
board this year in an effort to "enlighten students as to the rich
history available in their own home state and inspire Hoosier
pride."

No joke.

Mr. Black settles into his chair and clears his throat. "What
better and more . . . appropriate way to start off . . . the semester than by beginning . . . with the highest point?" Because of
the wheezing, it's hard to tell if Mr. Black is all that impressed
by the information he's relaying. "Hoosier Hill is . . . 1,257
feet above sea level . . . and it's in the backyard . . . of a family
home. . . . In 2005, an Eagle . . . Scout from Kentucky . . . got

permission to . . . build a trail and picnic area . . . and put up a sign. . . ."

I raise my hand, which Mr. Black ignores.

As he talks, I leave my hand in the air and think, *What if I went there and stood on that point? Would things look different from 1,257 feet? It doesn't seem very high, but they're proud of it, and who am I to say 1,257 feet isn't something to be impressed by?*

Finally, he nods at me, his lips so tight, it looks like he's swallowed them. "Yes, Mr. Finch?" He sighs the sigh of a one-hundred-year-old man and gives me an apprehensive, distrustful look.

"I suggest a field trip. We need to see the wondrous sights of Indiana while we still can, because at least three of us in this room are going to graduate and leave our great state at the end of this year, and what will we have to show for it except a subpar public school education from one of the worst school systems in the nation? Besides, a place like this is going to be hard to take in unless we see it. Kind of like the Grand Canyon or Yosemite. You need to be there to really appreciate its splendor."

I'm only being about twenty percent sarcastic, but Mr. Black says, "Thank you, Mr. Finch," in a way that means the direct opposite of thank you. I start drawing hills on my notebook in tribute to our state's highest point, but they look more like formless lumps or airborne snakes—I can't decide.

"Theodore is correct that some . . . of you will leave . . . here at the end of . . . this school year to go . . . somewhere else.

You'll be departing our . . . great state, and before . . . you do, you should . . . see it. You should . . . wander. . . ."

A noise from across the room interrupts him. Someone has come in late and dropped a book and then, in picking up the book, has upset all her other books so that everything has gone tumbling. This is followed by laughter because we're in high school, which means we're predictable and almost anything is funny, especially if it's someone else's public humiliation. The girl who dropped everything is Violet Markey, the same Violet Markey from the bell tower. She turns beet red and I can tell she wants to die. Not in a jumping-from-a-great-height kind of way, but more along the lines of *Please, earth, swallow me whole.*

I know this feeling better than I know my mom or my sisters or Charlie Donahue. This feeling and I have been together all my life. Like the time I gave myself a concussion during kick-ball in front of Suze Haines; or the time I laughed so hard that something flew out of my nose and landed on Gabe Romero; or the entire eighth grade.

And so, because I'm used to it and because this Violet girl is about three dropped pencils away from crying, I knock one of my own books onto the floor. All eyes shift to me. I bend to pick it up and purposely send the others flying—boomeranging into walls, windows, heads—and just for good measure, I tilt my chair over so I go crashing. This is followed by snickers and applause and a "freak" or two, and Mr. Black wheezing, "If you're done . . . Theodore . . . I'd like to continue."

I right myself, right the chair, take a bow, collect my books, bow again, settle in, and smile at Violet, who is looking at me with what can only be described as surprise and relief and something else—worry, maybe. I'd like to think there's a little lust mixed in too, but that could be wishful thinking. The smile I give her is the best smile I have, the one that makes my mother forgive me for staying out too late or for just generally being weird. (Other times, I see my mom looking at me—when she looks at me at all—like she's thinking: *Where in the hell did you come from? You must get it from your father's side.*)

Violet smiles back. Immediately, I feel better, because she feels better and because of the way she smiles at me, as if I'm not something to be avoided. This makes twice in one day that I've saved her. *Tenderhearted Theodore,* my mother always says. *Too tenderhearted for his own good.* It's meant as a criticism and I take it as one.

Mr. Black fixes his eyes on Violet and then me. "As I was saying . . . your project for this . . . class is to report on . . . at least two, preferably three . . . wonders of Indiana." I want to ask, *Wonders or wanders?* But I'm busy watching Violet as she concentrates on the chalkboard, the corner of her mouth still turned up.

Mr. Black goes on about how he wants us to feel free to choose the places that strike our fancy, no matter how obscure or far away. Our mission is to go there and see each one, take pictures, shoot video, delve deep into their history, and tell him just what it is about these places that makes us proud to be a Hoosier. If it's possible to link them in some way, all the better. We have the rest of the semester to complete the project, and we need to take it seriously.

"You will work . . . in teams of . . . two. This will count . . . for thirty-five percent . . . of your final grade. . . ."

I raise my hand again. "Can we choose our partners?"

"Yes."

"I choose Violet Markey."

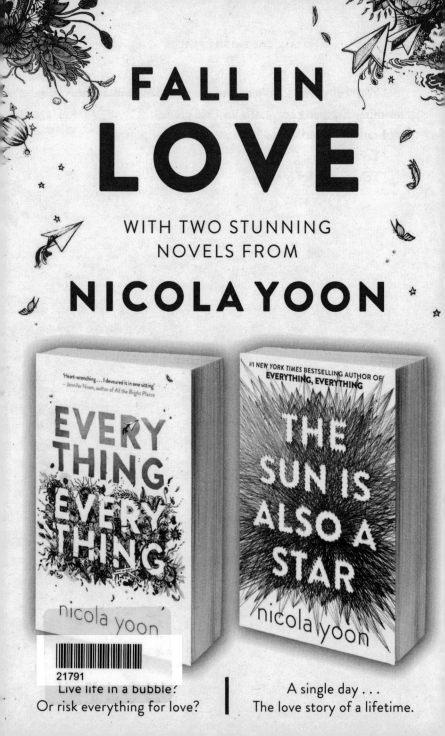